Penguin Books

The Survivor

Thomas Keneally was born in Australia in 1935 and educated in Sydney. He trained for several years for the Catholic priesthood but did not take Orders.

He began writing when a schoolteacher and his first novel, *A Place at Whitton*, was published in 1964. His work has been highly acclaimed and he has been showered with honours; he received the Miles Franklin Award for *Bring Larks and Heroes* (1967) and again for *Three Cheers for the Paraclete* (1968); the Royal Society of Literature Award for *The Chant of Jimmie Blacksmith* (1972) and the Booker Prize for *Schindler's Ark* (1982). In 1983 he received the Order of Australia for his services to literature. He is also a member of the Australia–China Council.

Thomas Keneally is married with two daughters and lives in Sydney.

Other fiction by Thomas Keneally

Thomas Keneally

The Survivor

Penguin Books

Penguin Books Ltd, Harmondsworth, Middlesex, England
Viking Penguin Inc., 40 West 23rd Street, New York, New York 10010, U.S.A.
Penguin Books Australia Ltd, Ringwood, Victoria, Australia
Penguin Books Canada Ltd, 2801 John Street, Markham, Ontario, Canada L3R 1B4
Penguin Books (N.Z.) Ltd, 182–190 Wairau Road, Auckland 10, New Zealand

First published in Australia by Angus and
Robertson Ltd 1969
Published in Great Britain by Penguin Books 1970
Reprinted 1985 (twice)

Printed and bound in Great Britain by
Cox & Wyman Ltd, Reading
Set in Linotype Baskerville

To W. H. CROOK

AUTHOR'S NOTE

Those familiar with Antarctic affairs will notice that liberties have been taken for the sake of this fiction. On the domestic scene, the Antarctic Division, even in the days when it was an agency of the Department of External Affairs, had no Sydney office. In a broader Antarctic context, one of Leeming's parties should have discovered the Usarp Mountains, which were not in fact located until 1960. Nothing would have been achieved by forestalling fictionally the United States traverse party that made the discovery.

The characters of Leeming and Ramsey are not based on those of any historic Antarctic journeyers. Similarly, no don, living or dead, has a counterpart among the provincial academics who appear in this book.

I must thank, however inadequately, Rear-Admiral J. L. Abbot, USN, commander of Operation Deep Freeze, whose generosity enabled me to see the Antarctic continent, and the Commonwealth Literary Fund, with whose help this book was written.

1

At the beginning of his sixty-third, decisive summer, Alec Ramsey drove down from his university town on the tableland to the wheat, sheep, and cattle towns on the inland plains. Beyond Milton, where he picked up Kable, the browned fields and retarded crops of wheat seemed omens, strangers to this rich plain, wandered in from a remoter west for one bad season. Kable, assistant director of Extension (as he was called) and Ramsey's lieutenant, was cheery. Ramsey had often heard that Kable coveted the post of director; and he would have given it up to Kable without much argument that summer. In the meantime, Kable directed the large Extension office the university kept in Milton, eighty miles from the campus itself. Kable's succulent bride, Valerie, saw to it that when she and her spouse were in Alec Ramsey's presence they maintained a sober tone of almost antiphonal, versicle-and-response naivety, luring others into forays of irony and self-betrayal. But away from Valerie, Kable could not manage to keep this front up. For instance, he asked with a directness Valerie would have found alien, "Alec, why didn't Morris Pelham do this trip?"

Alec told him that Pelham's wife was sick and that

Pelham was already up to the ears in planning the programme of summer schools. Did Kable think Pelham could do a better job where they were going? Kable chuckled.

They were going to a town called Pinalba to make arrangements for a visit there by a Duke of Edinburgh study group. Both of them knew how the self-made men of Pinalba felt civically proud for the honour but sensed in their bones that the project was somehow quaint, precious. Pinalba was a town for selling irrigation equipment in, for shipping beef from, for the playing of bowls and the having of florid alcoholic adventures in. It was hard to imagine that something as familiar and earthy as Pinalba could be an object of disciplined study. If their wives had been offered film contracts they would not have been more suspicious. The mayor, informed by trunkline call from Ramsey, had, in the second before shire pride suffused him, said, "You're not really bloody serious!"

Now Kable said he had a proposition to make to Ramsey, and put on a face of menial apology. He had conditionally agreed that Ramsey should speak to the Pinalba Rotarians that night.

"On what?" asked Ramsey, without needing to, since his rare and widely publicized lectures had given him a name in the north of the state as a professional survivor of what probably figured in the minds of the men of Pinalba as some damned expedition or other.

"The gentleman who arranges for guest speakers thought the Antarctic business . . . well, they'd be interested in that sort of thing. They're men of action and, at the moment, it's well worth our while to get them interested, if not enthralled."

They crossed a wooden bridge thirty miles from the town. The timbers rang against each other and Ramsey would have had to shout to be heard. Instead he frowned all the way across without glancing towards Kable. He hoped this would undermine the man, but knew that Kable was more likely to be despising him for his primness about Leeming than having any genuine second thoughts.

Clear of the bridge, Ramsey said, "When was that particular *conditional* arrangement made?"

"This morning, by telephone. I took the liberty ——"

"*Liberty* is the exact word for it."

"Now look, Alec, I can't speak to them. . . . I have already, four times in two years. But I made it clear, of course, the decision was yours. Just the same, since we depend on the population outside the university for the success of our work, I thought you would probably be willing."

Ramsey was angry enough to put forward an argument that Kable would have no trouble pre-judging and pre-condemning. "Your father wouldn't have made that presumption. Your father was very reticent about Leeming." Kable's father had been secretary to the 1924 expedition. Nor were Kable and Ramsey the only links within the university with that unaccountably forgotten journey, for Leeming's nephew worked in the physics department. Ramsey thought in vague terms of this fact as something perverse.

Kable said, "My father was reticent by nature. Besides, he died a long time ago. I was seventeen, I think." There were overtones to this, Ramsey was sure, overtones that meant, "My father died in 1932. Since then? The depression, the Spanish war, the rape of Central Europe, the decimation of Jews, the bomb, the ICBM, the computer, the Yangtze's annual flooding to the tune of two million deaths. Isn't it getting late in the century to go maidenly over the death of a polar death-seeker in the 1920s?"

About to lose his temper, Ramsey was sickened to sobriety by the vision of sharing two days' meals with Kable in Pinalba, of showing the university's flag with

3

him, jollying up the graziers and the mayor, the local radio station and the editor of the tri-weekly paper. For his sanity's sake, Ramsey needed Kable's good will—or what passed, between Kable and himself, for good will.

Kable had at least the grace to suppress immediately the overtones, the comment they implied. He went on in a begging-to-inform sort of way, "If the study-group programme is to be properly planned, Alec, we'll have to charm them into pledging facilities now—making their properties available for inspection and so on. What they do for the study group will be based on pledges they give us within the next few days, and the pledges will be based on how much good feeling we generate. I mean, look at it from their point of view. A person doesn't necessarily rush at the idea of having royalty and assorted other people tramping through the homestead garden asking about sheep dip."

Alec said, "I wish to God I knew something about Santa Gertrudis cattle."

Kable chose to laugh. "A safer topic for Pinalba," he agreed.

At the moment, ahead of their car, a farmer in an idling tractor talked with a farmer in an idling truck. Between them, they occupied without any self-consciousness half of the narrow highway, and Ramsey had to edge blindly round them on the wrong side of the tar. But before he had done even that, they focused his irritation at being expected to speak, after a mock-ritual dinner in a country pub, about the grotesqueries of the pure and dreadful continent. He saw them glance sideways as he honked them in passing, and chose to decide that they reacted to the university shield on the car door with a grain of off-hand awe and a ton of off-hand contempt, as if it were something as irrelevant as Kant's theory of knowledge that was passing them by on wheels. Bloody frontiersmen! Endowed by acci-

4

dents of history with six-cylinder cars, refrigerated beer, twenty-five-tine scarifiers, crop-dusting, a twice-daily flight to Sydney. Chagrined at them over Leeming, he envied them for exuding ownership as he had never been able to. Their sweat was proprietorial sweat, their laughter owned towns and pastures.

Then, swinging the car into a clear vista of bitumen and what were, after all, ailing paddocks, he corrected himself and almost confessed his narrowness with a laugh. But, by managing briefly to care that Kable would be likely to use it against him in other company, he checked the admission. "As old Alec will admit himself in his more clear-headed moments. . . ."

So Ramsey kept his balance until that evening, when the Rotarians gathered for dinner. Then he was immediately irked by the way Eric Kable introduced him to the burghers of Pinalba.

"This is Alec Ramsey, my boss from the university." (My world is not alien to yours of wool prices, departmental inspections, transport costs. I, too, strive on a level of reality. As witness, here is—not my director, not my departmental head—my *boss*!)

Yet Ramsey had ceased to worry about status and would not have resented the same quirk in Morris Pelham.

Everyone wore a round white badge three times the width of his lapel. The badges said such things as:

> J. M. P. Harcourt
> "Harker"
> Classification:
> Stud Beef Breeding.

When Ramsey and Kable first arrived, all these badges had been standing alphabetically in a rack on the wall, and M. T. Seagram ("Bantam", Harvesting Equipment) had

had charge of handing them to their proper owners: the Jims, Petes, Tossers, Midges, Lofties, and Skeeters who had found the promised land in Pinalba. Patient M. T. Seagram was hard put to it pressing a badge marked "Guest Speaker" on Alec, who tried to pocket it.

"It's all right. Don't be bashful, Alec—it is Alec, isn't it? Yeah, don't be bashful."

The headmaster of Pinalba's high school laughed and offered to pin the thing on.

"Is that straight?" Alec wanted to know, squinting down the line of his chest out of his salient eyes at the fatuous disc on his lapel. "Sure you wouldn't like me to tie a bow of blue ribbon around my balls?"

The headmaster hooted. M. T. Seagram said, "Only on ladies' nights."

They sang the hymn "By Rotary means, in Rotary ways, Help us, dear Lord, thy name to praise." Then those thin, embittered women who serve the meals in country hotels brought in the soup. The president rose and Brother Eric Kable was thanked for bringing along tonight's guest speaker, Mr Alec Ramsey of the university, who was going to speak about an expedition he'd been on to. . . . Where *was* it, Alec? Alec told him, with secret malice, "Oates Land." The man who arranged the speeches mumbled something which Alec hoped was a rebuke, but the invincible president merely blinked. "Yes, well I'm sure we're all looking forward to hearing about it later on in the evening," he said. Self-made, in making himself he had had no time to assimilate Antarctic geography and was now not ashamed for what was an honourable ignorance. Improperly, this was why, as he stood asking for volunteers to attend a field day in some distant town, Alec could easily have let himself rise up and strike the man.

The sergeant-at-arms forestalled him by standing and fining members for a range of esoteric offences. He was a

6

Texan, some Pinalba girl's dreamboat from a U.S. aircraft carrier, lost to Galveston, selling refrigerators on a plain beyond mountains in Australia. And rising during the second course of shreddy corned-beef and saying, "President Lance, I have it on good authority that Pete Hogben was seen carrying Nancy Spurling's parcels for her in the Pinalba Mall last Saturday. Now Nancy being a far from undelectable girl and Clive Spurling being away in Sydney, it seems to me that Pete may be hatching something contrary to the sanctity of the matrimonial state and a little fine might make him think about that seriously." And Pete rose calling some fellow Rotarian a bloody Judas and fumbling for twenty-cent pieces.

As everyone laughed through their pulpy mouthfuls, Ramsey went cold and was as homesick as a child for Ella and for his cool and different tableland.

"President Lance, I have it on similarly good authority that Russ Healey, when asked to navigate a carload of bowlers home from the Killarney open day, was so—shall we say?—inebriated that the vehicle finished in a ditch on a cotton farm that happened to belong to a fellow-country-man of mine. Just when the Prime Minister is busting a most venerable gut to further friendly relations with God's Own Country, Russ undoes it all by this act of drunken aggression."

Laughter, laughter. Well, hadn't some of them been ditched along with sodden Russ Healey?

"I'll tell you what," one of the survivors was saying above catcalls. "It could of been serious, but by Christ it was funny at the time. You know what the bastard said when we came to a stop? The car's on an angle of forty-five and the windshield's gone and he leans back and says, 'Well, that's about as far as we'll get tonight,' and he goes to sleep."

The demoniac Texan sat down for a moment to finish

his vegetables. M. T. Seagram leant over to Alec. "Where was it he said you'd been?"

"Well, that was where the base was really. Oates Land."

"Oh." M. T. Seagram took a guess. "Africa?"

"Antarctica."

"Antarctica?"

"Leeming's last expedition."

"Leeming? I've heard the name. . . ."

"You probably heard of him at school."

"Bantam" nudged the man at his side. "Bloody intelligentsia, me."

Stung to action by "Bantam's" pretensions, the sad and craggy ladies began to serve jam tart with custard. Alec sat nursing his jaw and inhaling deeply while his stomach yawned in panic at the thought of violent, anti-social, and unprofessional gestures. "I'll hit someone," he mourned to himself. "I'll hit that bloody 'Bantam', I'll strangle that ugly American in his own nasal twang." He felt sick, beyond work, febrile with hostility. It was the staple agony of his life that they were making mock of with their fines-box and mace. If it got beyond him he *would* hit somebody; so he promised himself, and cut the caterer's paste of tart and custard with a casual spoon. And by an action at the back of the throat halfway between a yawn and a retch, he reduced it to a swallowable state while reading the Rotary banners that covered the walls. Rotarie de Le Mans, Rotarie von Hagen, Rotary Club of Akron, Ohio, all served to underline the brotherhood of Clive Spurling, Pete Hogben, Russ Healey and his ditched brethren. In Le Mans, Hagen and Akron, and in Saskatoon, Tampico, Spanish Town, Torquay and Groningen, the fellowship of J. M. P. Harcourt and M. T. Seagram was fortnightly concelebrated and mystically fortified. And someone who should have known better rose to bawl, "President Bert or

8

Kurt, President Lance or Franz, I have it on good authority. . . ."

M. T. Seagram's neighbour spoke over the bent back of jam-tart-savouring M. T. Seagram.

"Hey, didn't Leeming die or something like that?"

"Something like that. Though tell me one damned thing that bears similarity to death."

"I beg your pardon?"

"That's how you can always tell an Australian. He uses *I beg your pardon* interrogatively."

By a hair's-breadth, M. T. Seagram's friend avoided begging it once more—just as interrogatively as last time. He was hurt, Ramsey couldn't help but see. He was right to be hurt. Any man who interrupted a club dinner by means of metaphysics and a touch of language-use was a bastard.

"Leeming died on a glacier in Antarctica," Ramsey called out in urgent politeness to the man two spaces away.

The Rotarian accepted this: his anger hadn't had time to set, and he realized or suspected that Ramsey was, this way or that, one of the bereaved.

"He has my respect, going to that place."

"He has mine too," Ramsey responded with a belliger-ency that luckily passed for intense reverence.

"I suppose you must ——"

But the sergeant-at-arms was up again, shooting the cuffs of his drip-dry, reaching for his box.

"President Lance, I have it on good authority that yester-day was Eric Kable's wedding anniversary. It seems he's been paying for his mistake for eighteen years now, and . . ."

Ramsey whispered to Seagram, "Excuse me," stood up urgently, rasping his chair and actually depressing Sea-gram's shoulders in his apparently bilious urgency, and signalling with his eyes for the man who had thought

9

Leeming had died or something to pull his chair in close to the board and make a passageway.

". . . that since Valerie Kable is such a lovely lady and since his possession is our loss. . . ," the sergeant-at-arms was braying.

Ramsey considered calling to him in mid-flight something such as, "Don't fool yourself, Davy Crockett. She'd take on anyone but the barber's cat. And ask Brother Eric if he isn't a queer?"

Behind him murmurs of awakening concern developed, so he took the stairs quickly. At the street door he failed by a fraction to have the courage of his anger, to turn into the saloon bar and later be found, quietly drinking there, by Kable and President Lance and the mace-rattling Texan who would no doubt try to fine him for sickening at dinner. He regretted that he was still too aware of his mission in the town to deliberately construct that insult, to make it clear that he favoured the drifting population of the bar against the communion of elders upstairs. Grudgingly, he turned into the street.

It was a night of dry warmth in Pinalba, whose townlights scarcely restrained the sharp stars. All sounds were distanced, as he wanted them to be after the rowdy brotherhood upstairs. There was a lonely argument, high, forlorn voices, progressing in the doorway of the coloured peoples' pub. The very way it came to the ear told you that you were in a flat town and a town that was at the hour of plate-scraping and tea-leaves.

Not his town. He fled it as far as the river, and was listening to a small weir functioning somewhere in the dark when Kable found him.

"Is there anything I can do, Alec?" Kable asked like someone lodging a complaint.

"They don't give a damn. . . ." But he knew he was making himself even more absurd by saying it. In fact, shrouded in the long dying fronds of a willow that infringed the foot-bridge, Alec heard but did not see Kable despairing of him in the dark.

"You make it sound as if he did it all for Pinalba Rotary and they—swine that they are—don't appreciate it."

"Don't you worry. I know he didn't necessarily do it for anybody. But what he went through is its own monument."

"*They* don't deny that. Besides, it's such an old, old monument."

"It doesn't deserve to round off an evening of Pete Someone making up to Clive Spurling's wife in the Pinalba Mall. It doesn't deserve to land in a ditch with Russ Healey."

"It could do a lot worse."

But he didn't listen to Kable; rather to water edging over the soft lip of the weir, renewing him. Not a basic renewal, of course, but an excellent *ad hoc* one.

Softly he quoted the president, mocking the man across the man's town. "An expedition to. . . . Where was the expedition to exactly, Alec?"

Kable, baffled but never berserk, gave three or four comforting pats to the bridge handrail. "My God, you know that fellow spent three years under the Japanese? He worked on the Burma railway. You had to see one friend die, Alec, and admittedly that friend was a man among men and it seems to have had an . . . irradicable effect on you. But that fellow watched dozens of friends die. The difference seems to me to be that he wouldn't . . . he wouldn't throw a tantrum if you didn't know the geographical details of what he went through."

Alec was not angry. He had taken a seat on the parapet and could read the fluorescent river-marker below. Three feet one inch, it said; and for the men still convened at the hotel thousands of dollars were involved in that river level, so low with the summer still to come. But they had the grace, the humility, to be gay after their fashion.

Alec said, "Perhaps he should throw a tantrum. Or more likely, he's made of solider materials than me. You can't make quantitative comparisons in these matters, Eric. In any case, it wasn't a tantrum. . . ." He paused to wish it merely were so. "I took exception, that's all. Holy Mother Texas is lucky not to be one cowboy short by now." Suddenly he was professional enough to want to make sure that Kable had excused him satisfactorily to his hosts. "You told them I had a ruptured ulcer, I hope? And there'll surely be no need to go back?"

"I told them this had been coming on on the way here."

"God bless you, Eric."

"I think you ought to go back, Alec."

"No. You can substitute for me." A last St Elmo's fire of rancour played across the surface of his tongue. "Or get Lance to tell you all about the Burma Road."

"You really are a deep-dyed bastard, aren't you, Alec?" Kable had never been so blunt before. Never mind; Valerie would moderate him when he went home.

In the meantime Ramsey chuckled for want of some more obvious gesture of despair. He said, "It would be something to think I was. I'm afraid I'm not consistent enough to fit the definition fully. But Leeming happens to be a fairly . . . personal subject to me. Could you possibly go back and give fuller apologies?" He added, "For your ailing boss?"

2

He met Morris Pelham, senior lecturer in his department, on the front steps of the Extension building. A scholarship to a good English school and Cambridge had put paid to the rawer notes of Pelham's Yorkshire accent, but the intonations placed him still, especially when he asked a question, as he did now.

"How did you get on with the heir-apparent?" By which Kable was meant.

Often Ramsey could bring himself to speak only in an oblique, eye-avoiding way to Pelham, for he knew the young man had taken up some of the work he himself had neglected over the past year when so much energy had gone into domestic anguish shared with Ella. He feared that Pelham had undertaken these matters out of loyalty, actual loyalty to him, Ramsey, and out of a dour passion to see things functioning properly. He feared, too, that Pelham was sometimes secretly bitter but never said a bitter word outside the dining-room of the Pelhams' weatherboard house in town.

Today, newly home from Pinalba, full of the yeast of homecoming, Ramsey felt able to answer Pelham's small, canny smile without flinching. They liked each other, and

13

Ramsey sometimes thought of generations of Pelham miners or farmers behind Morris, all of them by way of the opening pages of *The Rainbow* out of Ealing Studios, all of them careful with their laughter and their friendship, their weekly two ounces of special mixture and their nightly pint. That was how he knew he especially liked Pelham: he didn't bother dreaming up genealogies for his enemies.

"The heir-apparent?" he said. "Kable? I made him angry, Morris. I walked out of a maniac ritual called a Rotary Club dinner."

"In Milton?"

"In Pinalba."

"Well, at least it isn't his town."

"He seemed to think I'd ruined the chances of that Duke of Edinburgh lot."

"Oh, rubbish. They're all snobs, those boots-and-all boys from the bush. They'll turn out the best of everything for anything marked 'Dukie'. He knows that."

"But I wasn't very tactful to some of them. I started to talk like a character in a Sartre play. They were polite over our stay, but I got '*Mister* Ramsey' everywhere I went. The news got round, you see. That I was a smart bastard. Anyway, how's the poet?"

"Making a phone call upstairs. He had a very successful visit to the C. of E. girls' school this morning. . . ."

Ramsey half-listened, and breathed the seasonable sweet climate of this high town and university where, he liked to think, he had set like a jelly. It was a temperate place to work if you discounted the bitterness of the winters; and Extension faced a park full of thick British trees secreting deep cool beneath their heads of foliage. In Pinalba, he thought, they never saw shade so emphatic.

". . . abused him afterwards for using slang," Pelham was retailing. "Silly old cow."

"Who?"

"Miss Fowler, the English mistress."

"Abused the poet for using slang?"

" 'Abused' used in the local sense. Upbraided. As if those who give some increase to the language aren't entitled to use slang."

"What did he say to them?"

"Oh, something about Australians not caring about the arts as long as they got their weekly screw."

"Is that all?"

"Yes, but I think Miss Fowler thought he was using the word in the American sense. One of the junior mistresses told me later that she'd lent the old lady a Norman Mailer novel, you see, where 'screw' doesn't mean income, not by any means. Anyhow the girls thought he was marvellous. Not Mailer, of course. The poet."

Who, at that moment, appeared in the lobby. An inquisitive-seeming little man, no apparent extravagances in him, a widower in tweeds and a knitted tie for his course of four lectures in the university town. Forty-eight he might have been; visaged like a corner grocer, pert- and chatty-looking; probably secretly varicosed beneath the wide-cuffed trousers. Yes. But a genuine metaphysician, begetter of metrical fire, super-being.

He had flown up from Sydney while Ramsey was in Pinalba. Now, as he came down the steps, he seemed to Ramsey to frown slightly at finding an ancient university buff with Pelham, his guide. Ramsey felt his blood jolt with exhilaration. At sixty-two he could have faced kings and tycoons, dowager empresses and sirens without a change of pulse. But he still savoured the handclasps of literary figures, for he thought of them as special phenomena. He could not, and hoped he never would, accept them as mere physical dross—but only on condition that they had written something that struck his own literary chords. On that subjective level, this man was for Ramsey a greater than William Butler Yeats, whom Ramsey disrespected. So he was impatient for the man to reach them and half-expected to be able to read absolutes in that face which was, fifteen yards away, pedestrian.

Pelham introduced them.

The poet smiled in a way that was frankly self-congratulatory. "But I was hoping it was you, Mr Ramsey. Let me tell you, you are a hero of my retarded boyhood."

Ramsey smiled most unheroically, almost as if he was expecting a blow.

The poet explained, "I'm trying something to do with Leeming." He blushed a little, outlining his ambitions. "It's a sort of poetic symphonic suite that deals with the realities of the expedition, but in terms of the master themes of Leeming's personality in so far as an outsider like myself can know them. Do you want to hit me?"

"Why would I want to hit you?"

"Well, I am an intruder, and everything I've written so far is based on my own presuppositions, which, I hope, will probably be killed by any chats I have with you."

"No, no," Ramsey said quickly. "I'd trust your presuppositions over anything I could say." He grabbed for saner topics and apologized for the poor size of the lecture fee. Pelham then began to tell them with solemnity what he intended to urge the committee to do about improving the fee and paying the increase retrospectively to the poet.

The poet demurred. "It doesn't matter. I'm on holidays. *This* is my holiday, one of my little projects: meeting Mr Ramsey. And it's no use talking to poets about adequate pay. They've never seen it."

"In any case," said Pelham by way of compensating, "the vice-chancellor is having us all in for drinks after tonight's lecture. Alec, I didn't know if you'd be coming here this afternoon, so I had Barbara telephone Mrs Ramsey and she accepted in your name."

16

Alec smiled specifically at the poet. "That will be fun, won't it?"

"The vice-chancellor? He knows how to keep me in my place." The return smile was a little courageous, as if the vice-chancellor was well known but not well liked by the poet. "He worked on the Trust when he was in Canberra."

"And you worked with him?"

"*For* him."

"Of course." Inwardly, Alec was playing with the concept of the two hemispheres behind the man's tidy and customary face. One hemisphere: the public service; secretaryship of a national reserve trust concerned with ecology and the spawning of trout; a bungalow of brick in a utopian little city ringed by worn primeval hills. The second hemisphere: the freakish region of Xanadu, a little ravaged by the Calvinism of the public servant but municipally intact. A man close to the vision, this little man; an eighteen-carat bolt from the blue, ectopic as hell.

Ramsey said nothing about Xanadu as an unlikely sister town to Canberra, but promised they would meet again at the vice-chancellor's and went upstairs to attend to his mail.

Upstairs, dumpy loyal Barbara waited with her hips just as big as he remembered them. In these latter days of his failing efficiency, she was dowager-empress of Extension as Pelham was regent. He suspected she did not resent her function as Pelham resented his, but her motives were almost certainly not as pure as Pelham's and derived perhaps from denied motherhood. He had taken thought frequently enough on what would happen to Barbara when he retired and she was left high and dry in her late thirties with a director capable of doing his own work, requiring a mere secretary, not a chatelaine.

He strode into the office, attempting to convey that he was feeling more *au fait* with the demands of the department than he had been when he left things in minor turmoil two afternoons past. He told Barbara, "Just met the poet, but I didn't ask him how to fit the rhythm to the vision."

Barbara was down on her fat knees, ferreting in the bottom shelf of the steel cabinet; and Ramsey felt envious of her expertise, as if it were not his own office at all.

"Another lost opportunity," she said in friendly contempt.

"Yes," Ramsey told Professor Sanders that evening, "Chimpy and I played together in the 1922 team that beat Wales. Chimpy played like an immortal. And as Dylan Thomas would have said, 'there was lamentation in High Street but laughter rearing in the Foundry Hotel where Mews the Chimp gives birth in loud labour to wild suppositions and Ramsey the line-out specialist brings up his deep Welsh beer in the landlady's second-best aspidistra bought lovingly at auction in Pontypool.' "

They all laughed—Lady Mews, Professor Sanders, the Pelhams, Ella. They probably enjoyed a smoking-in-church feeling, the delicious minor blasphemy of hearing Sir Byron Mews, the vice-chancellor (still upstairs), called Chimpy in his own living-room.

It was rarely now that Ramsey's whimsy had any exercise; it had been provoked by the savour of Ella's welcome to him and the less important savour of the meal they had had together. He wished now that the Kables were not expected any second and that Chimpy would stay wherever he was; the company was very pleasant as it stood.

But talk decelerated then: the Pelhams still seemed shy and shyly torn between admiration of Sir Byron and Lady Mews's contemporary panelling and the lights of colleges blazing the academic year away in end-of-term parties farther down the hill. Professor Sanders, polite wencher that he was, sat turning his eyes with prim asexuality from face to face, although even Ramsey responded to sweet young Mrs Pelham whose sherry-glass seemed stuck in her hand like the candle of an unwilling pilgrim.

Lady Sadie said, "I don't know what could be keeping Byron."

If Pelham conjured up stoic generations of miners, Sadie's generations would have been (one would think) good horsewomen, brave girls at births and good-humouredly up to dealing with any horse-play behind the marquee. In fact she was a plumber's daughter and scholar-ship girl from Cricklewood. What had been her craggy loveliness, now verging on craggy venerability, condemned her to being suspected by middle-class girls such as Mrs Pelham. But Ramsey could sense a backwardness in accepting Lady Mews as a pleasant sixty-year-old not in Mrs Pelham but in Ella. There was that infinitesimal steeliness in Ella's manner that only he was accustomed to sensing. She was married to a man seventeen years senior to her, but the irony of this difference in age was not the same as that of old-man-young-wife jokes as much told and favoured by travelling salesmen. It was that she saw danger even in personable grandmothers. Part of her unalterable and Draconian view of love was that *she* would be wronged if anyone was. Yet Ramsey felt that apart from the child she had lost and the onset of obsessive periods in his own life, her anxiety had to do precisely with the fact of his age. An old man very nearly and every summer threatening him. While she might be able to deal with Lady Sadie's seasoned grace, she could do nothing when he left her bed for old bitch death.

Saving his dignity, she gave the seat beside her a little subliminal pat with the force of a loving request; that is, thought Ramsey, an edict.

Then, just as Mrs Pelham was daring to relinquish her glass for refilling, the Kables arrived. At their coming-in, Ella and Ramsey glanced at each other coyly, shamefaced at sensing that there was something to be learnt from them. This was that although Eric and Valerie did not nurture conjugal fidelity in the ferocious way Ella did, there was a fidelity in their public teamwork which the Ramseys could never hope to match. Their objectives were limited and sure. Eric wanted the directorship; to be a university baron instead of an outrider at Milton; to nudge (at least) the heart of university power and politics. Ramsey, irked to pithiness by the Kables, had once told Ella that Valerie K. wanted the directorship on the tableland for Eric because she preferred to be laid by scholars. None of this, though, detracted from the unison of their public bearing.

"Are you feeling better now, Alec?" she said. "Eric tells me you weren't yourself in Pinalba."

Ella frowned in an extreme way, instantly convinced that she had been denied news to which she had right.

"Maybe I was suffering from being too much myself," Ramsey told the Kables. "But I'm over it now. I believe we must congratulate you on an anniversary."

Valerie turned matriarchal and implied decades of domestic heroism. Her unlined face, a little sun-raw from all her "dashing down to the coast", gave the lie to this tiny spasm of histrionics.

"Eighteen years," she murmured, but lingeringly, weighing her sacrifices.

"An old married woman," Eric chimed in.

"Your old cheese," suggested Alec, fully in the spirit of their Darby-and-Joan wistfulness.

Kable laughed. "That's right, Alec. My old cheese."

Valerie said, looking Alec full in the face, "Soon we'll be making room for young people. Moving aside in the structure of things."

"Surely Byron won't be kept much longer," Lady Sadie said, perhaps to break up Valerie's attack.

"But where's the famous poet?" asked Eric Kable of Pelham.

"He's having dinner at some friend's place in town."

"Mrs Turner's," Ella told them. "The widow's. I believe he courted her at one stage." The information came slackly, but Alec was gratified foolishly as he always was when Ella behaved in a traditional womanly way—knew some gossip, for example, as now. "She keeps a sort of shrine to the man. Photographs and reviews."

Upstairs, distant but distinctive enough to betray Sir Chimpy's mortality, the cistern flushed.

Lady Sadie was well up to filling the silence so induced. "I hope the poet feels free to bring Mrs Turner."

"I don't think he will," Pelham told her.

In came the vice-chancellor, wiping excess water from his straight grey hair. From the days of international Rugby he retained a barrel-chest and a good colour, but age-lines had brought the old nickname close to the bone.

He greeted his guests and let Alec pour him a whisky. Everything now waited on the poet. Sir Byron took stock of the room and headlined a topic for discussion by saying to the Kables, "Dreadful thing for your friend Denis Leeming."

The Kables made doleful noises in the affirmative, a little like keening.

"Young Leeming's had his doctoral thesis rejected. On what you could call purely formal grounds." Sir Byron was bent on newsing up the rest of his visitors. "They said it simply wasn't geomorphology, as nominated. I think they were a little severe. 'Marks will be deducted if the question is not precisely answered'—that sort of stuff." He turned to the Kables, "They say he isn't taking it so well."

"Neither it nor anything else," said a deep voice: Professor Sanders'.

"But of course," said Lady Sadie, "young Leeming works in Professor Sanders' department."

"I don't want to be fatuous, Lady Mews," the professor said, "but I often wonder if he does."

"Oh, but Denis is a compulsive scholar, Dr Sanders," Mrs Kable claimed.

Until the past minute Ramsey had not known that the Kables and Denis Leeming were intimates. Neither, one could tell, had Sanders, who now shrugged as if conceding Leeming a good name for the purposes of the evening.

"And he had the devil's own job getting back from Canada," Eric Kable said. "He had two months in hospital over there."

Sanders shrugged again, regretting his earlier frankness.

Ella was the merciless one. "Took a token overdose, didn't he, Eric?" she suggested, for the second time that evening laying claim to inside information.

Eric swallowed. Anger came close to breaking up the team; and Valerie supplied for him.

"An overdose, yes. Token? No. Or at least, who could say?"

No one did dare say in so many words.

Ramsey could tell that the Kables' loyalty to Leeming had surprised the other guests, and Lady Sadie as well, to judge by the tiny bole of a frown she allowed to show between the eyebrows. Everyone presumed on the basis of this loyalty that an unlikely love affair raged between young Leeming and Valerie, and that Eric Kable was angry about that word "token" because he felt brotherly towards his wife's lover, as he had been brotherly to others of her lovers in the past.

With ersatz sweetness the door chimes tolled. "The poet," Sir Byron hazarded, while he and his wife churned about in the depths of their armchairs for leverage.

"Could I answer it?" asked Pelham, and was permitted to.

Meanwhile, restored to calm, Eric Kable threw a last opinion towards the vanishing question of Denis Leeming. "It does seem fashionable now to make catalogues of Denis's eccentricities. But most of us could begin our lists with oddities closer to home for us than that."

"Indeed, indeed," Ramsey chanted robustly, underlining Kable's opinion and drowning it in assent.

Then everyone began to take small urgent sips of their various liquors, fortifying themselves against meeting the bard. Ramsey watched sweet little Mrs Pelham take the alien sherry into her soft, shy, white body.

"Sorryumlate," said an entering voice. The poet's. The sober, mercantile face had gone turbid, a pink almost hideous: he had had drink. He swayed aggressively on his two unpoetic legs, like a beaten fighter whose instincts for footwork remain. Edging around his flank, capable but taut, was Morris Pelham.

"H'lo Chimpy, you ole bastard," said the poet. "Sorry-umlate."

The ceremonious Sir Byron went forward to test how the evening might unfold if he set an example by refusing to see the poet's sovereign and incontrovertible drunkenness. "Don't worry about that. Sit down. Oh, you know my wife and Mr and Mrs Pelham, Mr and Mrs Ramsey, Mr and Mrs Kable."

"Mrs Kable," he said, his eyes dilating in Valerie's direction. "God, wouldn't I like t'wind her in a strand or two."

"You've been doing well for yourself," Sir Byron went on, his eye on a deep chair towards which he was droving the poet. "With your verse. A regular subject of M.A. theses you are now."

"M.A. theses?" The poet stood with closed eyes and wavered, making and re-making a noise like a world-weary mammy. "Uh-huh, Lord! Uh-huh-huh, Lord!"

"There's a comfortable chair," Lady Sadie called, abandoning her own seat for the poet's sake and fortifying it with cushions. But her guest evaded her and fell into Pelham's place, forestalling the husband, abashing the wife.

"Wa's your name, darling?" he asked her.

"Sarah Pelham."

"Bloody nice, Sarah. Where's the old feller?"

He scanned about for Ramsey, as if he had to locate all parties before settling to an overly frank relishing of Mrs Pelham.

"The ole feller's present and correct," Ramsey assured him and toasted him in whisky.

"Def'nilly want a talk with you later, sport."

"Would you like something to drink?" Sir Chimpy was brave enough to say, consistent with his public good sense.

"Got a beer, Chimp?"

"Indeed I have."

Pelham said, "Might I?" and obtained beer hesitantly from the cabinet, ready all the time to drop bottle and glass and bound to his wife.

"And look," said Sir Byron to the poet, "most of the people here don't know me as Chimpy."

"Well what? *Your Excellency?*"

"No. Why don't you just call me Byron?"

"Isn't in character."

The lower part of Chimpy's face fell into a stoic pucker.

"Hey, Sarah, what about the garden?"

"It's very nice."

"Yeah. Prolific." It could be heard weaving prolifically in the night breeze. "But what about the garden for *us*?"

"There's no light," Sarah Pelham claimed failingly.

"I shall be, madam, your Lucifer and luminary. What about it?"

There was some indulgent tittering about the room. It was hard to damn outright someone who might well have had the future's ear.

"Behave yourself," said Ella.

"Umbehaving badly?"

"So far."

"It's that black mick bitch Turner," the poet urged in extenuation. He half-turned to Ella's flinty beauty and pointed at Ramsey. "Your voice of the turtle-dove, your flower in the crannied nook, your lean-and-chubby, your ole man? Et? Cet? Er? A?"

"He's my husband," said Ella. "He is not an old man."

"Well, Christ, I wouldn' want to be as old as he is."

"No. It wouldn't do anything for you."

Independently, the poet's hand felt with fair competence towards Sarah Pelham's knee. He still had the time to open a further front by saying, "Howsa career, Shelley, Byron, Chimpy—whatever they call you? Still at it hard?"

The vice-chancellor was off-balance sufficiently to say, "It's not a sinecure, you know. Not for a vice-chancellor who wants to *be* a vice-chancellor."

"To which I make reply, 'My Gawd! Chimpy's still the same old fraud,' " said the poet.

"Of course," Lady Sadie chuckled, wise to seem indolent, not to signal panic. "It's the frauds who keep the whole structure turning, the old fabric weaving."

"While the visionaries run to fat," added hard Ella. "Why do you think Mrs Pelham wants your hand on her thigh?"

Pelham worships language and forgives everyone by whom it lives, Ramsey thought. Any mere scholar or town clerk would have been punched by now. A very robust pink ran across Pelham's jaws as he whispered twice from behind into the poet's ear.

"Umbehaving badly?" the poet again asked Ella, whom he recognized, with artistic infallibility, as his public conscience.

The Mewses tried to laugh the plea off.

"You're acting atrociously," Ella assured the man.

"It's that black mick bitch Turner," he begged of the company. "She thinks it belongs to the Pope."

Everyone ignored the glaring pronoun, while he shook his head many times, his glass tilting beer in tiny libations on the carpet.

"Uh-huh, Lord!" he said. "Uh-huh-huh, Lord!"

For the febrile grey of a man about to die of sicking up drink alighted on the poet's face; he closed his eyes, emitting "Phew!" at intervals.

Ramsey felt unaccountable relief. "Come on, old fellow," he said, lifting the poet by the elbows. The company drew in their feet as Alec steered him across the room by the shoulders.

"Anything you need, Alec?" Sir Byron wondered.

Alec said no. He was pleased to be escaping with honour from a room that seemed to him to be dominated, not by the poet's drunkenness, but by Ella's willingness for fight.

"An utter change of personality," he heard the hard Yorkshire intonations of Pelham impress on Lady Mews.

The poet tottered and barked once on the oil-heating grid in the hallway.

"For God's sake, not here," Alec begged him.

"Not anywhere, friend," said the poet, and set his chin. He looked like a figure in a cheap recruiting poster. But certainly the sweat dried and he was garrulous again in the cool garden, by the cut crystal of Chimpy's swimming-pool.

Enclosed by rock-gardens, they sat largely beyond the reach of the wind, and could not hear the muffled speculation, the toned-down outrage of the company they had left.

"Those the offices?" the poet said, gesturing uphill towards the unseen administrative block and the union, one

26

of whose adobe flanks glimmered some hundreds of yards from where they sat.

"That's right."

"Christ. You can hear Chimpy's comptometers sleeping."

Their example appealed to him and he slumped on the hard slats of the garden seat. Ramsey stood to give him room for stretching.

"Your wife said um rude to people?" the poet confirmed.

"Yes."

"Then damn 'em, mate. They're lucky to have me."

"So you suspect you are—for want of a better term—a major poet?"

"It's a critic'ly def . . . *defensible* proposition."

"Yes, it is."

"But it isn't the poetry that's out of me, in print, that counts. That's all . . . *spastic* stuff. It's the poetry still in me that counts. Travellin' up the thousand-mile ovaries from the gut to the mouth. Eking down the Mississippis of creation. See? That's the *major* stuff." He stopped to sniff at the word and find it odious. "*Major? Major?* Ugh! That thousand-mile uphill river, see. Uh-huh, Lord! Uh-huh-huh, Lord! I reckon I've done about . . . five hundred and . . . ninety-six . . . point three miles of the journey."

He rolled his eyes in a way that signified what a rich day it would be for literature when his argosies came in.

"So you're not the humble bard, it seems? You're quite proud?"

"About the spastic stuff? Not on your life. I'm proud like a bloke won't get his inheritance till he's thirty. And at the moment I reckon I'm about . . . twenty-five years . . . eight months and . . . three days." He rolled onto his side and suffered again the alcoholic grisaille. At last he said, "Must speak to you 'bout that Dr Leeming."

"I think it would be wiser if I took you back to your hotel."

"Well, I didn't come to see you because of your bloody sagacity. See?"

"Suit yourself."

"Look, if um rude to you s'because I feel I know you. I got your picture at home. You and Lloyd and Leeming. All toggled up for the cold. You were a big ugly bastard even then."

"I've always prided myself on being a big ugly bastard."

"Well you might as well, friend. There's no getting away from it with them bulgy eyes of yours. Anyhow, now um going put 'em into verse."

"So you told me this afternoon."

"It must make you very happy."

"No," said Ramsey, meaning it. "It doesn't really."

"No?" The poet made noises of triumph like a detective at the dénouement of a bad thriller. Then, as if he had half-trapped Ramsey into some fatal admission, he feinted cumbrously.

"Your wife now. She's very. . . ."

"Young?"

"She's no more young than I am. Tense is what I mean."

"She *is* tense tonight."

"Now there could be two reasons for that. Someone tells me you were ill once—'ill' meaning 'psychywhatsit'."

"Someone was talking through his hat." Ramsey detested that anyone should know he had once confessed to, depended on, a doctor.

"I got a tenuous . . . you know, *tenuous* theory about that sickness."

"Good for you."

"All the same, it might be you're not up to her. On the couch. You know?"

"Look, I think we'd better fly you home tomorrow," Ramsey decided.

"Ah-hah! An admission." The bardic head thrashed about recklessly on the seat. It was a movement of pure gusto. "I like you a lot, Alec. You're an interesting old geyser."

"Instead of simply sordid." It was Ella's voice that dropped from the top of the rockery steps. Behind Ella the Kables bulked; and Eric Kable asked with knowing male solemnity how the poet was. The poet himself yelled his good health up at them and made eyes like a clown's at Valerie.

Then, "Hah! There's old *virgo intensa* herself."

"Both the Mewses are on the telephone at the moment," Valerie explained. "I think Mrs Turner is speaking to Lady Mews."

"Apologizing for people," said Ella.

"We thought we'd get a breath of fresh," Eric Kable said. "Sanders is talking earnestly to the Pelhams."

"The way that man is prejudiced against Denis Leeming!"

"Apparently," went on Ella, "Mrs Turner is telling Lady Sadie that some people are nice as pie while sober but proper pigs when drunk."

"Does she think that's news?" Alec muttered.

The poet sat up and performed a loose mimicry of Alec. "*Does she think that's news?* All right, you old poofter, here it is straight. You see little Miss Tensions up there? Say you're virile as all get-out, so she's not tense for that reason. . . ."

Ella gave a loud cry of revolt from the steps.

"Come on," Alec told the man. "I'll take you back to your hotel."

The acquisitive faces of the Kables seemed wide and blank as radar screens in the moonlight.

"No, wait a second, wait a second," the poet was demanding. "The altern . . . alternative. The alternative is that she's tense because you're psychywhatsit, and you're psychywhatsit . . . this is the . . . you know, tenuous part . . . you're psychywhatsit because of Leeming. And you're psychywhatsit about Leeming because . . . ah, because, because, because you and that Dr Lloyd. . . ! Well, question is, did you and that Dr Lloyd eat *of* Leeming?"

"I beg your pardon." If Alec was not straightaway outraged it was because the stressed preposition came to his ear with an almost biblical sound, innocuous to the sixty-two-year-old son of a Presbyterian pastor. *Unless you eat of the flesh. . . .*

"How did you get back to the coast then?" the poet was insisting.

"I hardly remember." Ramsey stood enthralled by the concept that had aspects of profound and oblique truth in it, as the improbable crimes have of which one is accused in dreams. His extremities began to sweat and, behind his back, Ella's resistance to the poisonous old subject of Leeming prickled him like something radiant.

"No one would blame you, but if the provisions are divided by the daily sub-sist-ence ration," the poet ground on, "you get an answer that ——"

Ella interrupted. "Now, Alec, don't take notice of the drunken fool." It was this voice of hers, so mandatory and fearful and taut with an inverted and poisonous pity, that furthered all his symptoms to the point where they became something like illness.

"—— implied you must have eaten of him," the poet concluded. Even he seemed chastened by the boggling heft of the idea.

Ramsey dared not move. That indigestible leader and unswallowable death flooded and exposed him at the one time; very like the similar vertigo and smotheration caused by the Antarctic phenomenon called white-out, when horizons are swept up into a murky opalescence that both coffins and threatens with infinitude. In such terms, in fact, almost visual, the accusation rebounded on Ramsey: such a whiteness, unmarred by dimensions, his fear took on now. On its coasts the skuas ranted and one's breath crepitated to ice with an almost electronic sound. The hideous plateau lapped close to him.

After a time he remembered that he had not in fact eaten Leeming, but the poet's suggestion seemed to him one that he must urgently blend into what he already knew of Leeming and himself.

As distant and quacking as voices at the far end of a cable, Valerie and Ella could both be heard. While he straggled a few yards along the edge of the pool, the skua-like hubbub climbed his blood and departed by the ears.

It had all been a shock. He shuffled his feet once on the delicious solidity of the pool's apron.

Eric Kable told him in a gratified way that he shouldn't let this sort of thing *get at* him.

"Ella," Ramsey said, "let's say good night to Sir Byron and Lady Mews and take this man home."

The poet urged himself to his feet, and the excess of his desire to be informed overflowed into a silly little dance along the rim of the pool.

"But you don't understand. You were *there*, in a bloody saga. How many poets get an inside seat on a saga?"

"I'm not interested," said Alec.

"None. Not. A. One. Because they're bloody neurotics, see? But what's the use of getting involved in a bloody saga if you won't tell a poet about it? It doesn't matter to me if you had to eat him. Do you think I'd judge you or something prissy like that?"

Ramsey called out, "Now listen, no more of that."

Ella could tell that that idiot of a poet was starting the whole cycle of betrayal obsessions running again in Alec.

"Get Morris to take him home," she ordered her husband. She sounded implacable: in her eyes Alec was the culprit for having reacted to excess. "I'm going now, if you want to come."

The poet appealed up the stairs to Ella. "Does he think I'd cast stones?"

"As if you could!" Ella ground out. The poet shied, as if her words fell downstairs with a physical impact. "Some people subscribe to the out-of-date romantic ideal of the artist as a man who is free to spew up on vice-chancellors' carpets. Of course, that's if you're any sort of artist to start with—a proposition that seems to be under debate in your case."

"You're a saucy bitch, aren't you?"

"I'm a poisonous bitch, Mr Bard. I hope you find that out. Well, Alec?"

"Please, Ella," Ramsey asked her, almost without dignity, "I can't unload him on the Pelhams."

"The trouble is," the poet mourned in monologue, "you Antarctic buggers can't be believed. You write your diaries and make it all sound like a Masonic Lodge on ice. Only, I admit you didn't write any journal, Alec. And you won't do his biography. See, to put it one way, you couldn't bring yourself to digest him all over again."

Ramsey told him, "If you say any more I'll kill you."

He was aware of yards of water to his right, their murderous potential.

"That's lovely," said Ella in one of her cold, hard panics. "I'm going."

That her husband stood mouthing murder on account of Leeming was a measure of the extent to which the memory of Leeming possessed him. She could not forgive this obsession, just as, ultimately, she would not forgive his death.

32

Lady Sadie now intruded speculatively from the porch. She saw the radically altered Ramseys and the engrossed Kables, and edged forward exactly like someone in a stream of uncertain depth.

The poet sat pretty, like an almost civilized person, one arm over the back of the seat, saying with aggressive good reason, "Whoa there, don't let her bully you, Alec boy. Wha's use of being in a bloody saga if you're going to let her bully you?"

Lady Sadie risked asking was all well. Ella tramped up to her, face shut, waspish high-heels jabbing at the cement; and said a colourlessly polite formula of good-bye. It had been pleasant, she said. And could Lady Sadie possibly ask Pelham to take the poet home?

Ramsey called out that no, he would.

"Then you'll walk." Ella's blind back was aimed at him. "I'm taking the car."

He imagined her cutting all the corners into town, chancing her outside wheels into the gravel, begging a skid, begging the ultimate demonstration, a death skid, crazily certain that the triumph of causing Ramsey to regret would outweigh the sharpness of laceration and lung-puncture.

Ramsey stood above the poet, the pink slewing face whose focus could not quite keep up with his now definite movements. "Get up. We're going."

The poet gave him fair caution, jiggling an index finger. "How about if you showed more respect?"

Ramsey pulled him upright by the tweedy coat's lapels; but the inadequacy of any devisable maiming kept him still. Pelham arrived, speaking softly, and removed the poet from Ramsey's grip. With a lemurine look of discretion, Chimpy helped the senior lecturer hustle the poet in through the back porch. For all the threats, Ella remained by Lady Sadie, back on to the poet's removal.

"I should help Morris," Ramsey told his hostess.

"No. No need. But I'll never read *him* again." For Lady Sadie thought that writers, so often indecent in print, should be decent in living-rooms.

At last they could hear the poet's voice rising in the wind at the front of the lodge. Then Pelham's choky old motor whirred and covered it.

3

Ramsey woke near Ella in the dove-grey morning, examined the graceless landscape of his bed with a muddle-headed conscientiousness, and rose in need of his morning newsprint lying furled, he could see, beneath an oleander bush outside. He longed for headlines and radio-pictures of distant violence: bomb outrages in Aden, earthquakes in Zagreb, mass murders in Ankara or Calabria—as if the insanity-level of the world were constant, as if the insanity of people and events at one end of the earth went to guarantee his own sanity at the other.

He remembered how last night they had so adequately exposed themselves to the curiosity and malice of three couples and Professor Sanders; and left the bedroom without a glance at Ella.

The worst that was happening in the wide world was that a millionaire had endowed the arts, brewery workers were threatening to strike, and General de Gaulle would visit the Pacific the very next month. He abandoned the newspaper and, resenting the world's wire services, straggled into the living-room. In the cabinets beneath the glassed-in bookcase, Ramsey's small Antarctic library was stowed away. Corresponding places in the homes of other university people were reserved for erotica smuggled home from sabbatical leave. The erotica of the Ramsey household were Borchgrevinck and Scott, Shackleton and Cherry-Garrard: the annals of all the Masonic lodges on ice.

He opened at page 27 a book called *Leeming's Last Journey*. Or the book furtively opened there itself.

The expedition's very capable dog-expert had the role thrust on him yet measured up to it like a life-long expert.

"Christ!" intoned Ramsey aloud. After the life he had had, he detested phrases such as "measured up to".

His name was Alexander Ramsey, graduate of Sydney University and recent Rugby international; and he first met Leeming on a train from the country during the winter previous to the expedition's departure. Leeming had taken an instant liking to Ramsey and, in September 1923, had regretfully rejected his application to join the expedition. The illness of the dog-expert Leeming had already chosen gave Ramsey his chance. During the expedition he became a fine skier as well as a superb dog-handler. Adaptability and physical strength were his especial qualifications. He was a quiet young man but never dejected. . . .

Ramsey was once more loudly blasphemous, and his large hand threatened the furry old page.

. . . and his regard for the Arts answered something in his leader's temperament. He and Dr Leeming would sometimes argue about the talents of poets whose names other expedition members had never heard.

In the polar night, from Lloyd's bunk and half a dozen others, obscenities would rumble. "—— Elroy Flecker." "—— Walt Whitman."

He would have blushed now for his callowness, except that Lloyd, O'Connor and the others had all joined Flecker and were one with Whitman.

Given Dr Leeming's friendship towards him, his out-standing strength and his capacity with the dogs, it was no

36

surprise that the leader paid him the final honour of select-
ing him as a companion for the dash to the South Geomag-
netic Pole.

The ineptitude of "final honour" irked him, but did not
have the power to bring on his symptoms. It was the sort
of serviceable term that blanketed reality, a ritual term
stolen direct from grammar-school annuals, absolving all
parties from considering the oddness of the relationships
between humans, advancing the story of miles covered,
specimens gathered. No, the old page did not hurt at the
beginning of this day in the sixties, with nothing worse
than a brewery strike threatening.

He found an ancient newspaper article yellowed in the
back of the book. Scarcely optimum archival conditions.
He began to read at the fold in the paper.

Meanwhile, he read, *matters went badly for the southern*
parties and for Leeming himself. His own party of three
had to turn back with the South Geomagnetic Pole still
two hundred miles off.

They had found nothing but high white plateau. Their
dogs were in a poor state, though they still had adequate
sledging rations. Though he lacked proper reference points,
Leeming had made a remarkably accurate calculation of the
height of this central plateau.

What he did not know was that, at the inland hut, a
member of O'Connor's support party was dying of pto-
maine poisoning from the adequate but tainted supplies of
tinned beef. This meat had caused some discomfort to all
the members of the party that had wintered inland, but the
consignment that had been sledged in from the coast in
early summer was the fatal one. It is said that a prominent
Melbourne merchant was in danger of prosecution in the
months immediately following the return of the expedition.

When Leeming reached the hut in mid-March, 1926, he
found that O'Connor with seven others, including the

37

three-man party that had surveyed the Victoria Land Mountains earlier in the season, had struck through the mountains for the Ross Sea. Only two of the eight were well; and they left behind them in a shallow ice-grave the body of a ninth.

There was a note in the hut for Leeming explaining that a Morse Code message from the Oates Coast had advised them to head for the Ross Sea, where the expeditionary ship Westralis would pick them up. The note further said that since O'Connor could not trust the meat he had had to take some of the sledging rations set aside for their journey home, but that if Leeming would consent to following them down the glacier to the Ross Sea, he ought to find that the pemmican and biscuit left for him was plenty.

Earlier in the summer the three-man mountain party had partly surveyed the David Glacier and found satisfactory travelling surfaces for twenty miles close in on the south side. Down this glacier O'Connor led his five sick men and two healthy ones, and marked the path for Leeming with bamboo rods. Their morale increased as they marched, and although two later lost legs, they all reached the ice-tongue and the Westralis.

O'Connor's necessary action of taking away part of the geomagnetic party's provisions compelled Leeming to follow the same path. Even if ice in the Ross Sea forced the Westralis out for another year, he and his two followers could probably survive a winter with the help of their tent and of the seal meat that could be found along the coast. All three men disliked the prospect though, and prayed that the Westralis would be able to wait.

Leeming therefore led his party east into unseasonably bad weather. He had slaughtered the four remaining dogs, and carried sinewy dog meat as well as sledging rations.

On a day of minus 54 degrees F. he collapsed, and Dr Lloyd told Alec Ramsey, the third member of the party,

*that it was a stroke. Though his speech was impaired and
one foot lamed, Leeming insisted on stumbling on and
became hysterical whenever Lloyd and Ramsey forced
him to ride on the sledge. But the stroke had made him
most susceptible to the low temperatures and his hands and
feet became dreadfully frostbitten.*

*On the evening of the fourth day he suffered a second
and fatal stroke. . . .*

"Have you got enough light for it?"

Ella had arrived bare-footed, firm shaven legs beneath
the nightdress. She frowned. The planes of her face were
out of harmony from long and not very happy dreams.

Ramsey didn't answer her. She walked softly to the
blinds and snapped them open with one swipe of the hand.

"Will porridge do you?" she asked, and prepared to go.
He had in some odd way forfeited meat and said that
porridge would do.

"I've a busy morning. Come when I call you."

She stamped out, no sylph without shoes The page
blew over in the breeze of her hard feminine passage.

He had admitted to Ella this much: that he first became
under a debt to Leeming at the close of 1924.

At twenty-three Alec Ramsey was large and soft-
featured and suspected himself of being ugly. He had
never had the valour yet to ask anyone whether the ugli-
ness was interesting or repellent, for if they told him
repellent he would have been properly landed with the
knowledge of his face for all the years to come.

That August he had already become an ex-international;
he had been teaching the whole year in a high school not
far from the Queensland border, and the education authorities had not been concerned that this made it impossible for
him to play. As his father had said, the education department was not run by even competent philistines. Ramsey

had eventually grown out of the way of the strategic straining and grunting of the ruck, loose or otherwise. He had been receiving in secret all winter a series of literary magazines of extreme viewpoint.

Now he was travelling south to Sydney. Somewhere, towards dusk on the coastal plain, a blunt-shouldered man with a tall man's thin and fine-wrought face and features boarded the train and sat in his compartment. It was hard to say what the man was doing, boarding in that unlikely town with a sawmill grinding overtime in the dusk and the breath of rainforests in the air.

This slightly microcephalic gent made Ramsey feel inferior, made him feel the brashness of his vestless suit and patterned sweater—the uniform of the unarrived. The man had stepped out of the timber town and onto the train in velour hat and raglan and cotswold suit of expensive insipidity, and was off-handedly in possession of some honour adequate to him. This was what Ramsey decided, asking himself, as a private but dedicated bourgeois, what two published Imagist poems (his own) meant beside the substance of this man?

So the man sat, inappositely placed but not aware of it, while the people you expected to be there, tradesmen and their wives from cow and banana towns, sheathed themselves frantically in blankets and made noises of exaggerated sensuality at the presence of foot-warmers.

The stranger read, but seemed to catch Ramsey staring at him. Ramsey was, in fact, trying to see the title of the technical-looking book in the man's hands. He hoped that it was something mean and soiled with trade, such as *The Double-U Drain Fitting in Modern Plumbing*. He saw at last that it was *Notes on the Glaciology of the Victoria Land Mountains*, and sank back once more into his humanist inferiority.

From which he was surprised by finding the man looking

at him in an intense and attenuated way. Ramsey thought he had once before seen a face balanced in exactly that way between taut and slack, between will and daydream; the face of a nut-brown businessman with plenty of pubic hair who, in the dressing-room of the Domain baths, had put his hand on Ramsey's naked thigh and whispered that he had a classic figure and such fine legs too.

This unutterable incident, interrupted by other bathers, recurred now to him. He began to read again. What sort of man, he asked himself in alarm, saw sexual messages in other men's eyes?

When he looked again the man's eyes were still on him. Or were they simply focused on the mid-distance, and would go on innocently focusing in this manner all through the night?

Ramsey rose and made for the corridor. Within a minute the man followed him. Ramsey's neck prickled, certain of the man's strange lusts.

"Can you ski?" the man said.

He had at least left the compartment door open; but an asexual wife, grunting in surprise at finding herself warm in a train, closed it behind his back.

"No," said Alec.

"Of course not." The man chuckled in his private intense way. "Very little snowfall in the dairying areas, eh?"

"That's right."

Ramsey read the grafted-looking head as a certain symptom of perversion.

"I've been looking for someone like you."

"I'll call the guard," muttered Ramsey, turning away.

Then the man understood Ramsey's idea of this confrontation and began to laugh.

"The penalty of monomania," he admitted and then, lying but to prove his bona fides, "No, I assure you, I keep a beautiful wife very happy." Perhaps he would not have said this if he hadn't thought that Alec was a boy from some primitive town where you could hear the cows mourn all night for the bull. "You looked as though you'd be very good at hauling a sledge, that's all. You remind me of my old friend Tom Crean. He was one of Shackleton's Argonauts. You may be too young to have known much about that."

Alec nodded. "I haven't heard of Tom Crean." He wanted to say, "And I bet the name of Ezra Pound doesn't mean anything to you."

Then the man said his name was Stephen Leeming. He was a university man on leave and was mounting an Antarctic expedition, the first post-war one. The sawmill Alec had heard rasping away at that country halt belonged to Leeming's family. He had been five days up in the Divide, marking the hardwoods he wanted cut for expeditionary buildings.

"I think aloud a lot. You get into the habit, putting on the donnish act for students. I suppose I came close to spending the night in jail in Grafton or Nambucca."

Alec introduced himself, and Leeming had heard of him as he had heard of Leeming. Alec hoped that Leeming read Imagist poetry; but no, it was Ramsey's vulgar reputation that Leeming spoke of. And, of course, Leeming was very much what Ramsey's mother called "physical", with the sturdy-based throat favoured in statues of Renaissance condottieres.

"I do some writing as well," Alec said with all the maidenliness of the newly published. "I have a friend who has promised me he'll introduce me to Norman Lindsay."

But Leeming, unbeaten on the score of clothes, reading-matter, and morals, wasn't now overcome by the prestigious name. "Oh yes," he said. "Remember me to Norman and ask him if he'd like to winter in the classic groves of Oates Land. My wife used to model for some of Lindsay's disciples, and ended by taking to art herself. Look, speaking of art, I could never understand why you literary chaps never exploited Antarctic material. Of course, Antarctic journals are rather physical records, nothing about what moves the men and what bigotries hold the work back. But the financiers of exploration don't like to discover that their good money has gone to subsidize faraway conflict of character. Perhaps the *bacillus antarcticus* will bite you if you read something of the continent. Why don't you apply when I advertise the vacancies? Not that I could promise a thing. But your shoulders would favour you."

And they laughed together about the earlier misunderstanding. Nor did Ramsey ever again have reason to suspect Leeming of sins against nature.

From his father's manse in Drummoyne, Ramsey made half a dozen raids upon Bohemia. He met Lindsay, and drank with companionable poets. He talked a full forty minutes with a painter who called him "Dearie" with intent, and felt himself to be urbane and tolerant of foibles like that; and woke one morning in a bed behind partitions in Darlinghurst to see two very pretty girls he could remember from the previous night racing out of doors half made-up, and apologizing to Ramsey and some man prone elsewhere in the big room.

He felt depleted and saddened, and wanted verification of his improbable memories. "What's happened?" he called to the other male.

"Last night's Caryatids," the other one told him, careless of mythology, "must become this morning's grade-two sales staff behind David Jones' toiletries counter."

"But what happened?"

"Oh." The other artistic young man chuckled. "Sick three times and scuttled her twice."

"You did?"

"No, you did."

Ramsey knew the effete boy exaggerated, but there must have been some basis for the overstatement. But he was no rugged sinner, and felt merely sad.

"I hope I didn't offend her," he said.

The one who hadn't recently read his *Primer of Mythology* guffawed.

That afternoon Ramsey found a penitentially large treatise on the Antarctic continent. So his Antarctic engrossment began in an expiatory key. This was because he dared suspect that a loss of innocence had taken place.

He thought of Antarctica in literary terms: a prophetic landscape begging a prophet and tailored for seekings and disillusionments of epic proportions. Yet none of the seekers had a literary style to bless themselves with, not the sort of style that counted. He was delighted with a book by Leeming: it took some small account of the gulfs between man and man.

He would have liked to revolutionize the staid business of Antarctic writing. But behind the desire was a more basic passion to see the continent. This had him by the heart at Wednesday breakfast in his northern pub when he found the expeditionary advertisement in the previous Saturday's Sydney newspaper.

He lied to his headmaster and caught the Friday train. On Saturday afternoon the line he joined outside the expeditionary office in lower George Street was stretched five hundred feet along the pavement, filled the hallway and two flights of steps. Most of the men seemed old soldiers, tested and sane. Ramsey waited just the same, and reached Leeming's office at six-thirty.

Leeming was tired, all the planes of his thin face sunken. As if he'd placed a bet with himself about the perverse way his quest would end, he asked and accepted questions with a sort of preconceived bitterness. He gave an impression of tightly controlled but almost hysterical testiness. It was with none of the geniality of the railway carriage that he said aloud as Ramsey entered, "Well, at least we know this one's motives aren't base."

"If it's hopeless my being here. . . ."

"No. Hopelessness and uselessness didn't prevent half the city milling on our doorstep this afternoon. Sit down please."

"I thought they all looked intimidating. A fine group of men. All those old soldiers."

"*Old* soldiers they certainly are. The war is six years over now. The expedition sails at Christmas, you know, and most of the places in it were privately decided months ago. I ask you, what men of that age would be able to abandon their careers and sail for polar waters with two months' notice? Only a man who has failed here one way or another and who wants a virgin continent on which to practise further fecklessness. No, I'm glad you've come."

Ramsey was disappointed that late afternoon by the aldermanic attitude Leeming had taken to the long line of applicants, and by the nasty classroom ring of "fecklessness". That evening Leeming seemed the last man on earth to whom you would confide any plan to revolutionize Antarctic literature.

He redeemed himself now by nodding at what seemed a long short-list on the desk. "There are exceptions among those old soldiers," he admitted. "But a certain amount of stability is primary. And I should tell you, Alec, that unfortunately mysticism and art can go hang down there. You said you were a poet?"

"But possessing broad shoulders."

Yet it was found he knew no geology, no magnetism, no physics, no meteorology, nor even the necessary zoology to at least get him to the Oates Coast. He was putatively a

45

churchgoer, and Leeming put stress on this although not himself orthodox. And he was very strong.

"I've put you on the short-list," Leeming said in an odd voice of complaint, seeming to be cursing himself for feeling bound to do it on account of their overnight companionship on a train from the country.

Still, no one had ever before shut Ramsey off from one of his horizons, and the éclat of an Antarctic destiny was his for two weeks. Erebus sat above his big shoulders and earned him more authority with his farmboys for less outlay of savagery. Then he received a letter of regret from Leeming. In revenge, he promised himself Bohemia and a world of more self-aware scuttling in the summer.

October turned to the first day of languid coastal summer. A telegram came. "If still Antarctically inclined report HQ Saturday latest. Nominal pay. Clearance arranged with education department."

"Are you good with animals?" Leeming wanted to know on the Saturday. His dog-man, survivor of two expeditions, had been stricken by a disease of the heart. "He always made much of the mysterious husky, as if to keep the proud scientists in their place. Now he's spent two years breeding huskies with cattle-dogs in the Alps beyond Cooma. We're going to take some of his cattle-dog admixtures with us. He's very sick, but won't be invalided. I'm sure you can learn the dog trade from him in two months. . . ."

Ramsey felt renewed. For you can't cease from Calvinism simply by going secretly rationalist at the age of nineteen; you still know by bone-knowledge that abasement and labour are the only fructifiers, and you look to the large intentions of men like Leeming to give your abasement and labour their grandeur.

At nominal pay.

With a facility learnt at businessmen's luncheons and

fund-raising circuses Leeming drew down the bold lines of his polar ambitions. They would start with a base on the Oates Coast, if a place could be found where the rise to the Antarctic plateau was gradual. In the first three months of the new year, supplies would be carried inland, and materials for a hut so that some of the party could winter in the interior.

"It hasn't been done before," he explained, but to avoid appearing a mere record-breaker: "It will put the scientists in a far better position to correlate magnetic readings and to take photographs so that the height of the auroral displays can be calculated."

Ramsey felt reverent and said he understood.

After the winter night one party would use the coast hut as base and go out to re-locate the shifting area of the magnetic pole. Another would survey the northern mountains of Victoria Land. A third would spend the summer supplying the inland base for the return of the further three parties who would range out from it.

Of this second set of parties, one was to survey the central Victoria Land mountains, another to move in the totally unexplored direction of the geomagnetic pole (with some hope of reaching it), a third to act as support party to the latter.

The demands of this schedule might well mean that they would need to spend a second winter in Antarctica.

Ramsey's awe burgeoned. "It must be the greatest Antarctic programme ever devised," he murmured, feeling silly at the grandiose sentence.

Leeming squinted at the rough map and ripped it up.

"You must get used to the idea that you and your dogs are indispensable," he warned Ramsey. He amplified.

They were to take four Fordson tractors that ran on kerosene, but a tractor couldn't adapt itself to polar conditions as dogs could. People had been at him to take an aeroplane, but he thought planes were a spectacle rather than a thing of value. "It is a contest that transcends mechanics," Leeming said; and the sentiment sounded emotively correct but, even to Ramsey, dogmatic.

Then the leader spent time urging Ramsey to be humble with the dog-man. "He'll resent you because you're educated and also because you're his replacement. He'll try to make a fool of you, and it won't be hard with huskies at his disposal. Be prepared to laugh at yourself at first, but keep asserting yourself and show him that you want to learn the art. He's a marvellous old man. Shackleton and Mawson both loved him."

The marvellous old man was perhaps fifty, but his wit was waspish and pulmonary as a ninety-year-old's. He was a retired seaman and lived on the edge of a village where snow-drifts remained on the ridges even in summer. Here he and now Ramsey shared life with three cattle-dogs and fifty huskies tethered in teams of nine. The cattle-dogs were friends at table and on the hearth, but those uncouth Siberians were never let into the kitchen, not even to whelp or die. The three-hundred-and-sixty pounds of meat needed to feed them each week was paid for out of Leeming's pocket, which luckily carried inherited wealth.

On the slopes with dog-team and sledge, Ramsey suffered from the man's wry sense of humour but learnt to drive a sledge in slush. The dying man had him chasing runaway teams, roaring the word he had been told (wrongly) meant *Halt*. The peculiar physics of the sledging-whip often wrapped nine feet of rawhide around his own head and shoulders. Yet the one vital hoax the wry and primitive man and dogs played off on him was to convince him that he too was a simple animal made for the large issues of Antarctic journeying.

The dog-man, pretending to be cautionary and resentful, lived to make Ramsey an expert, and insisted on advancing his own death's day by building a sort of dog-cart with axles of mountain ash to behave with something more or less like the pliancy of the runners on the sledge; for the sledge could never be taken far, and the ridges were subject to thawing except in the early morning. These were the sick man's pride, the dog-cart that Ramsey drove up and down on level land, learning the difficult control of the dogs; the élan of the team; and the fluency of the old sledge that had been preserved by his hand. And Ramsey knew that he was close to a phenomenon of beauty when he saw the gasping man, his digitalis unopened above the mantelpiece, nudge the runners with his boot and blink. "Boss Shackleton used 'im; 1908 'e got used by Boss, an' 'e's as good as ever and Dr Leemin's gonna take 'im south agin. Mountain ash, see. Lovely, bloody lovely."

Just before Christmas, they consigned the dogs by train. The old man wasn't too shattered but breathed morosely, choosing to show little faith in Ramsey when Ramsey shook the grey hand. In anticipation of the death, children had already broken into the yard and were playing admirals in the dog-cart.

The dogs travelled all night in box-cars, tethered by steel cables to the wall. At each stop Ramsey changed from one car to another for the welfare of his dogs. His boots would thump down on the gravel of country sidings as the engine emitted the sibilants of its rest and the dogs began their lovely ululations to the moonlight. He told himself then that all his contradictions had been jolted into unity by the simplicity of his new life. He would forever enjoy the sanity of his oneness; and even suspected himself of a type of sainthood. Yet his innocence was already forfeit by reason of his Antarctic motives.

Still the dogs chanted; their priesthood was of the moon; their science was selfhood, for Cybele was their goddess and of her order was the sainthood he felt to be imminent.

49

He knew that tonight there was not one spurious identity left in him.

He would have done well to listen to the angry milkcans of protestant farmers being taken on board farther down the train.

The next day was hard, spent in the goods-yards where his parents came to say good-bye. The dogs stood muzzled and chained, a team at a time, to iron rings in the floor. Hot and constrained against their nature, they flashed their mad canines at some neighbour dog's flank each time one of them was unmuzzled to drink. That morning Ramsey watered them twice, so that afternoon, being themselves, they slept while everyone else, even Ramsey, hurried up and down in the heat being decent British subjects.

Ramsey's impersonations in this direction took him to the expedition's office in lower George Street. Here a large man with a head very like Leeming's but more proportional to the solid rest of him, stood by the counter reading a letter. The girl in the office welcomed Ramsey and introduced him to the letter-reader, whose name was Dr Arthur Lloyd.

They said to each other, Ramsey and Lloyd, the wary things that strangers say when about to live together for a long time, but the letter was held in a very obvious way in Lloyd's hand as something the doctor could scarcely wait to return to. Eventually he said, "Do you know Leeming well?", patting the letter and then regretting this, since it gave its source away. Ramsey said he felt he knew Leeming well, but that this was probably an illusion since they'd met only three times. Lloyd said, "Don't misunderstand me when I say this, but do you trust him as a leader? I ask for interest's sake, that's all."

"Yes." Ramsey cut down on the fervour, seeing that Lloyd was a fairly prosaic man, disturbed by zeal, probably a returned soldier. "Of course."

"I don't suppose anyone could get Mawson and Shackleton to say the things they've said about Leeming unless they believed them?"

"That's right."

Lloyd filed the letter carefully in his breast pocket. "There are certain tests a man has to pass before he's a man in my book." It sounded as if Leeming had failed some sort of scout-manual test. Ramsey was grateful, despising such criteria.

In the end Lloyd shrugged. "Well, I don't pass most of the damn things myself," he said, to make little of his doubt. "I'm off to Melbourne with you tonight." The fashionably weathered face went into a smile that was mathematically even. Only shallow men had smiles like that; so ugly Ramsey had always told himself. "Two months ago I had my own practice and was a pillar in society. I used to travel around France in box-cars, and thought I'd seen my last one."

Ramsey thought *Christ* and foresaw an Antarctic night made merry with old soldiers' tales.

Lloyd turned to the girl. "Well, Stella dear, keep your heart warmed for me." From the back, minus the shallow refinements of the face, he was built like a wharf-labourer.

Ramsey kept from the meeting an inchoate willingness to distrust Lloyd based perversely on the very ceaseless reliability the man would be sure to be guilty of.

There was a short letter of congratulation from Leeming for Ramsey. As he read it the telephone rang and he heard the girl saying, "Very well, Mrs Leeming." Leeming's happy young bride.

"But no, Mrs Leeming, I can't leave the office because Mr Kable is coming in at half-past-two to do the correspondence." She was still rosy from Lloyd's attention. "Perhaps Mr Ramsey could help you." The telephone was given to Ramsey.

It was a direct, non-emotive voice. It said that a letter had come from Leeming asking her to gather some of his papers and send them to Melbourne with one of the expedition members from Sydney. At this late date it would have to be Lloyd or Ramsey, and Lloyd had already left the office to visit friends somewhere in the city. Dr Leeming had asked her not to subject these papers to the hazards of the ordinary mails. If she paid for his taxi. . . .

He explained that he had care of the dogs. Were they to be fed? Were they thirsty? Then so much for the dogs.

The taxi took him to a row of new bungalows above one of the smaller, not yet municipally barbarized beaches to the east of the city. The crude art-nouveau windows of No. 16 concealed very well that here lived someone of illimitable perspectives. There was probably a vistaed family fortress of stone forty miles out that busy Dr Leeming found inconvenient.

Mrs Leeming had also been busy in the bungalow. Opening the door, her hair hanging loose over a smock streaked with primary colours, she showed Ramsey down a hallway and into a living-room where crates of Leeming talent, his and hers, lay everywhere half-unpacked.

"You have to excuse the mess, Mr Ramsey. Anything serves Leeming as a city base, but I'm the one who has to live here. So I leave things in turmoil." She smiled back at him, shaking her head, impatient with her hair. "To create an atmosphere of transience."

She was no complaining wife, though; a businesslike talker with an unstylized gait, very like the one he would see in Ella fifteen years later. Ramsey was enchanted. She was an unselfconscious succulent, an ideal beauty. Her soldier's walk infatuated him by making her credible. In his chest he suffered a sense of evaporation from around the heart, which pumped something far more volatile than common-or-garden blood.

He had, of course, no sexual intentions. Not only was she sacred to Leeming, but the rings that were signs of maturing ran round her neck, which had pink in it and gorgeously threatened, but would never go over to, plumpness. She may have been as old as thirty-five, which in his funny mind made a relationship with her something worse than miscegenation.

On a table in the centre of the living-room were two ledgers and three or four folders of notes. They made up a manuscript, she told him, that a British publisher visiting Melbourne would like to consider. Dear Leeming would be very grateful.

"So, *you're* off to Antarctica," she said then, as if Antarctica were a vice he had picked up, after a long resistance, from his elders. "Why do you find it necessary to go?"

He told her; for the experience.

"What good is experience?"

He thought. "It enriches one."

She was doubtful about the validity of this. "How does it enrich?" Every time she asked a question she indicted you with her chin.

"Well, it extends the limits of the type of person you were before."

"Ah!" she said in a small, largely ironic triumph. "What type of person are you?"

He declined definition with a shrug.

"Then what is the use of extending the limits of the person you are if you don't first know what person you are? What is the use of extending the limits of something you haven't explored and exploited? How are you equipped to extend any such thing? It's like a railway porter promising to extend the limits of science."

He chose to do his puzzling smile with his big, easily discomfited lips.

"If you've decided to go," she admitted, "you might as well. The places one hasn't been mean a lot to the person who doesn't know himself. Would you care for tea?"

53

He told her no in something like panic, brought on by the image of her pottering about with tea-leaves like any old frump from the suburbs.

Would he like beer then?

The frosted bottle she brought seemed to express for him the naturalness of life, the savour. He was in a risky state of exhilaration, and fancied himself at the business of being a natural man, sitting drinking ale off-handedly with a woman who would have given a stone apostle a hard one; with another man's wife who had on her easel at that time a more or less finished, fairly curdled and radical-looking picture of Dido on the pyre. He thought of these facts as spectacular symptoms of the new man he had become in the mountains, in the dogs' and the old man's unvarnished company.

Meanwhile, Mrs Leeming seemed bent on sending him to Antarctica properly self-questioning. She veered from the question of self-knowledge to the subsidiary one of self-ownership. He sat through a steady grilling in this topic and could not help believing that on one level she was laughing to herself. He wondered whether it was this constant Socratic rigmarole of hers that had driven Leeming to the poles.

"It's not hard for anyone," she said, "to see Leeming as a great man. But he—and how much more so all other men?—has to beware of excursions like this Antarctic one *and* like the Great War, as highly organized attempts at getting round the necessity of self-ownership."

"You ought to tell the whole party that before they sail."

"The others wouldn't understand. But Leeming's temptations are hostile to his self-discovery. He often hides from himself in the almost frantic belief that the fates intend to humiliate him with disasters."

"What disasters do you mean?" Alec thought it was his business to know.

"Oh, climatic disasters, or trouble with his men, or being sold spoilt stores by some corrupt merchant." She smiled. "Or the dogs all dying at once. That sort of thing."

She stood and took her smock off. Beneath it she was wearing an old floral dress. Ramsey felt eviscerated by longing as she wiped her collar-bones with a small handkerchief. Saying, "But you'll think I'm some sort of crank. You'll have to attribute it to the fact that I'm about to lose my husband for at least sixteen months."

At this statement of wifely affection, Ramsey felt easier. The lady continued uxorious for a small while, giving her long hair an absent-minded pat that seemed to signify a conjugal and modest acceptance of Leeming's polar interests.

"But you see," she continued, "Leeming and I, both of us Christians, don't accept the concept that is condoned by our antique legal system—ownership by one spouse of another. All that too is a bar to self-discovery, because the business houses, the police force, the Oddfellows' Lodge and so on are all afraid of what might happen if we found our true selves. That is why the definition of marriage in our laws is feudal, and true marriage has outgrown it. So I don't make any complaint about Leeming's Antarctic infidelities; if they are necessary to him they are not infidelities. Don't you agree?"

Ramsey did, out of politeness.

"And since I am his equal, that raises the question of what is necessary to me." She walked up to his chair and removed the beer tray. Holding it before her, she seemed to, but could not possibly be, positing a relationship between what was necessary to her, and Alec. "What is your first name, Mr Ramsey?"

Strangely grudging, he told her.

She said formally, "Alec, I like you very much. You are humble and intelligent. You are innocent because you see the greatness in dear Leeming and because you expect a revelation in Antarctica. Do you believe in God?"

"My father is a Presbyterian pastor," he admitted. "Sometimes I believe in God out of politeness to him."

She laughed a compassionate laugh that began like a cry, with a low moaning noise. "But I didn't mean in your father's God," she explained, "though to escape *that one* it's worth taking off to Antarctica. I can't help but feel that Leeming's polar experiences have helped him become more theologically sound. Do I sound like a blue-stocking, Alec?"

He assured her, no.

She said teasingly, "Well, if it comforts you Alec, I love you in the bowels of Christ. You have heard that wonderful phrase?" But she cut the wryness down to solemnity. "No, I do, Alec, I accept you in the bowels of mercy. I sounded flippant because I was afraid you might think I was eccentric if I spoke seriously. But if you want you can spend the afternoon with me. Of course, although I feel a great deal of affection for you, I can't allow myself to take any responsibility for how your conscience might stand by four o'clock, say."

She looked at him with the sort of directness they tried to dissuade girls from in boarding-schools. Yet there was nothing that could be called specifically erotic about her. This was not only because she was dressed with bungalow decency and her face no more climatically disposed than if she were buying real-estate. It was that she too stood over in Cybele territory; or so Ramsey guessed. In Cybele territory there was no such extension of life as sexuality; sexuality was a European invention. Where she stood there was only the oneness of life; one trusted oneself all the time to the natural intuition, to the instinct informed by the phosphorus-flash of the click-exposure mind. In what he believed was such a flash, it seemed a perfectly

56

decent thing to hug and be hugged by Mrs Leeming and rake her long hair with his hand.

But the trouble was that Ramsey's mind was a respectable, businesslike mind, governed by deduction and authority. He could not cease to respect marriage nor to suffer sexual guilt as ratified by the churches and the breathless details of genital hygiene given one by one's hemming father.

So, by taking Mrs Leeming in his arms, he was committing himself to fragmentation.

"Wait there, wait there!" she said and fought free of him, taking her dress off with dignity, as if not to provoke him. The dress was put across an easy-chair and lay there like a mere statement of fact.

"I must get back to the dogs," Alec said fraudulently. He sounded as if he had run three miles.

She reproved him for a silly one. "It seems to me that concern on a summer's day for something that can sleep through a blizzard is excessive."

"The bulk of the travelling will be done with the dogs."

She laughed at him heartily, not at all like a vampire. Even to himself he'd sounded like a town-hall lecturer.

A bare, beige-coloured shoulder presented itself. "There," she said. It was not a moral being and to speak of it as aesthetic would have been cant. It was merely there for the kissing. He kissed it and felt the grotesqueness of his physical reaction. But she did not mock him. She respected him in the bowels of mercy.

"Do you think," she wondered, "it would be too disenchanting to go through into the other room, Alec? It's very much like every other bedroom in this city."

He asserted that furniture would have no chance of infecting him with impotence; and, febrile, trailed behind her. In the hallway he leant and mouthed her upper breast. She became angry.

"Come now, Alec." But she had blinked as if touched by desire. "You are not to withdraw from me into lust. Lust is as good a middle-class plot as any to prevent us from self-discovery. People who fear self-discovery through sensual love retreat into this subhuman state called lust. If you intend to do that. . . ."

He said how sorry he was. What he thought was that in the dreams of his puberty, of impossible encounters with ideal women, the dreamed-of woman never stood half-naked in a panelled hallway lecturing like an archdeacon.

The bedroom was full of standard mock-Jacobean furniture, but, as he had said, he wanted no inspiration. Now, self-conscious over the disproportions of his body, he could not look her in the face. He kissed her furiously but with respect.

"That's right," she said. "Otherwise there's no tenderness left for me when you've been satisfied." But it became almost too much for his home-bred prurience when she drew a hand over his loins. Later, he could remember being overcome by an anxiety to satisfy Mrs Leeming at this point; and the anxiety was as bad for them as any middle-class plot. He suffered an inconspicuous climax. Mrs Leeming seemed, above all, tolerant.

At breakfast with Ella forty years later, he sustained the fiction that it was this adultery he had never confessed to Leeming in person that now made him sensitive about Leeming's name. Fiction was how he thought of it. Legalistically speaking, it seemed to him perhaps half the truth. It was perhaps one-tenth of what his dyspeptic viscera accepted as truth deep-dyed and absolute.

Some years before the morning on which he sat locked at heartless breakfast with his wife, Ramsey had made much—before her and before a given doctor—of how dismaying it was to postpone a necessary confession and then find the one adequate confessor frozen (more or less) at your feet; of how dismaying it further was to find that he had died waiting for the confession. And though the word *adultery* no longer held the same Gothic prestige it once owned, to think of Leeming's knowledge of Belle Leeming's beddings iced up in Leeming's frozen brain could still make Ramsey sweat. But that was only part of his malaise.

In any case, Ella's profoundest demands were not for elucidation, though she frequently asked for it. She wanted the illusion dropped, the illusion that reparations were owing to Leeming. For it meant a withdrawal from her, and that she resented.

He slammed his spoon down. He heard it bounce against the breakfast impedimenta. Ella looked up in the pretended bafflement she never had any trouble adopting.

"For Christ's sake, Ella, let up!"

He got up and strode, and leant against the refrigerator. There was a sauce stain on its door, left there some days now in what was probably some upside-down protest against her childlessness and what she considered to be her widowhood. Both these were nearly exactly seven years old and had undermined her by now to the extent that she would leave stains about as a reprisal; and keep current accounts rafted across the refrigerator top. A similar dune of bills had covered some dark piece of furniture in his childhood. It appalled him to have come all those years and yet be ending life with the same set of old bills.

"Why don't *you* let up?" she asked him.

"We've made that exchange a thousand times. Just let up, for Christ's sake. Will you? Ella?"

"Listen, don't try to convey urgency by means of *for Christ's sake*." She was old-fashionedly averse to blasphemy. "You sound like something from an Edward Albee play."

"At least I have literary precedents then. But no one would believe your attitude, Ella." This he said in a man-to-man, rational sort of way. "You accuse me of disloyalty and of withdrawing. But loyalty is an action, not a state of the emotions. In what action have I been disloyal?"

She didn't answer.

"Ella, I need you to understand. . . ."

She grated her chair from beneath her and stood back shaking her head. Ramsey could see her full and beautiful left breast tremble, but nothing woke in him except the most abstract and inadvertent approval.

"*Me* to understand?" she said. "You'd think that by marrying *an older man* a woman would at least have some security of affection."

He had had enough of his age as a subject of low fun. "If that was your only reason, you shouldn't have married *an older man*. You should have married someone *virile as all get-out*, to quote the poet."

"Virility's the least of my worries."

Ramsey decided to misunderstand. "Ah, taunt the old bastard. That's right. Give the old man a mortal doubt or two."

She approached the table and said narrowly into his face, "You know I'm faithful to the death."

"Oh yes, you are. And you mean to point out too that there's special virtue in being faithful to an old man. And you're only faithful in the narrow, sexual sense."

"Oh yes, that's easy, that is."

"It *is* easy, for you."

"Well, it's nice to be valued." She was too angry to see that in the course of the one debate Alec had pretended both fear and indifference over the question of her fidelity. She turned her back and walked like a retiring delegation to the far wall, to round on him and call out, "I might have been justified in expecting myself to be matrix of Alec Ramsey's soul. Nothing like it. Guess who is? Someone mentions Leeming and you have to be sedated for a week."

"I'm not as extreme a case as all that. I can live with the idea of how much I owe Leeming. The trouble begins with your attitude." But even in a fury it was not worth his skin to suggest that childlessness had diseased her attitude. "Certainly I am disturbed by Leeming."

"Because of fun in bed with old Belle!"

"But it's because I dread your massive reaction to my minor one that the name gives me the shudders."

"Minor? *Minor?* I think there was something queer about you and Leeming." She gnashed her teeth. "The best of both Leemings."

"I wish it had been as simple as that." He kept snatching up the bills one at a time and scanning them. Her hostility stifled him, and the plucking-up of dockets was the random act of a stifling man. To a bystander beyond the window it would have seemed an argument about money.

Ella adjured him. "Well, *did* you eat him? You've never told me. *Did* you eat him?"

The question again angered and harrowed him as would any preposterous accusation that happens to be a fraction of an inch wide of the preposterous truth. On account of her cruelty and because the question seemed to threaten to stampede him towards the truth, he kept silent and crushed his head between his hands. It was a tough nob, though; no fissures in the old skull, no misses in the old heart; and blood-pressure scarcely a point or two above what was ideal for a man of his age. The odds were against his embarrassing her with death or even a small collapse.

"Listen, I have a surprise for you, Alec. This cannibal question raised by the poet isn't a new theory. One day, it must have been 1926, my father gave me nightmares by bringing the story back from town one Friday. That the survivors had eaten Leeming. So it doesn't matter to me what happened. Just digest him, as the poet says. Just digest him, that's all."

Ramsey brayed once, cuffed the enamel and sank to the floor. A small flurry of bills followed him down. To prevent herself yielding, to evade the terror of having brought her big man into an absurd and yelping squat by the refrigerator, Ella strode out with the hard masculine walk she had learnt carrying milkpails as a child.

She listened, pulling linen from the bed, for the sound of his gesture; he would put his fist into something. It was still a large, estimable fist. If applied to glass or panelling, it would bring another hardware account for filing above the refrigerator.

She waited and heard his grief periodically mount. It was genuine grief, within its boundaries. The boundaries were set by his knowledge that it often made her relent, that he knew it brought on a rush of pity in her from the base of the womb.

She looked purposefully out the window. "It won't prevail this time, mate," she said aloud. "It has to be settled." No cherishing each other's tears, no feverish caressings, no medicinal love-making with him dependent, unsure of himself, like a young man with an old tart. Not to mention any names.

She heard his fist strike some not very frangible target. "Christ," she said, clutching the dressing-table with all those futile beauty things that made her look enamelled and did not cure her saunter, "Christ, do the right thing for once and keep me away."

Throughout a dreadful January, Ramsey found that he could not grapple with any simple series of engagements, that Ella was frequently apologizing for his absences. He rarely met Pelham except at staff meetings and by way of the telephone. He imagined that there was something more overt now about Pelham's bitterness, something more carping about Pelham's loyalty. He read his own sense of moral hollowness into Pelham, and began to dislike him.

Late February brought on the last school, having to do with university drama groups, chaired by Eric Kable up from Milton. Valerie had come too, as an enrollee. Among the school's projects was a production by a Sydney director of *A Midsummer-Night's Dream*. It was to be avowedly kinky. Ella, sitting through an early rehearsal, heard the director say, "You see, no one has ever been brave enough to admit why Titania wanted to sleep with an ass." This he would attempt to say by means of Valerie.

The performance would be early in Orientation Week, which came now with a rush. Hundreds of defensively arrogant boys and girls, tacking perfervidly away from the close lee-shore of their schooldays, leapt from trains. As if

63

overweighted with its load of undergraduates, the Sydney plane flew low over the Extension building on one of the last mornings of February. The sky grated with its approach, the blare of its engines thudded over Ramsey's roof. Fate knocks on the roof, thought Ramsey in mockery.

Barbara came in to him. She said, "It's your friend the poet, Mr Ramsey."

She did not know why the poet had gone home early last October; she did not know he did badly with his liquor.

Ramsey asked her was she serious? Barbara drew breath into her large bones and gathered herself together into a very fortress of seriousness.

"You'll have to tell him I'm out," Ramsey said.

"But you can't tell lies to someone who wrote,

> 'Cleft by the gold karate of the sun,
> The elements swing back again to one
> And hallow home. . . .' "

Ramsey stared at the pretentious girl who had nothing but his weakness to feed her identity on. The fact was she was ashamed of her education; to prove her quality she learnt poets by heart; to prove her existence she quoted them.

"I've read that too," Ramsey told her. "I still don't want to see him."

Barbara again thought he was being flippant. "Well, as he says it's urgent, I'll send him straight in."

"Listen, Barbara. I may only run this place in name. But I won't see the man."

Barbara began to panic. "But you can't tell *him* that."

"No? Well, you've got too reverent a view of literary men."

But he found that the poet had already entered the

office. "Your manners are no more bloody suitable," Alec said, "than they were last time."

Very fluidly for such a big girl, Barbara slipped out.

The poet told him, "I'm sorry, but circumstances. . . ."

He merely stood looking sympathetic, his form discrete in a linen suit. He looked like a joiner, the sort of man who buys a lot of superannuation and does not believe in the subconscious.

Ramsey told him that they had nothing to talk about. The poet said very confidently that they had. But four months after the night at the vice-chancellor's, Ramsey was still frantic to humble this man.

"Look," he explained, "we have a very big fellow on the gate of the parking area. He's available for moving trespassers. I can either ring him immediately or do the job myself."

The poet actually sat down then, humbly enough but as if in humble possession. "I don't blame you for being angry, especially against a man of inaction. Even one who has taken two days' leave to come and warn you."

"To warn me?"

"Yes."

"Of what?"

"I can't tell you while you're in this state."

Ramsey sat up and began to dial the extension number of the parking area. He was afraid that if he didn't the poet might prove his credentials and evade the humiliation of being hustled down the hill.

"I know it will be considered a scandal to remove everyone's darlingest doggerel-merchant from one's office. But I'll accept that opprobrium. . . ."

"Besides, there's always time to cancel your request or tell him you don't really want me dragged down the drive."

Ramsey said into the telephone, "George, I have an intruder in my office. I'm sorry. Alec Ramsey, Extension.

Very well, George. Soon as you can." Looking up, he saw that the poet was gazing speculatively out of the window, perhaps to locate the threatened George. He spoke absently to Alec.

"You know, I have something to expiate with you, a bizarre suspicion harboured for the sake of its own oddness."

"You may stick it!" Alec articulated.

"Now something's happened that will be a pleasant shock to you, but a shock just the same. I believed I owed it to you not to allow this . . . pleasant, as I say, shock to be broken to you by someone unaware of your state of mind."

Across the top of a letter received that day, Ramsey pretended to be writing a memo. What he wrote was, "Cleft by the gold karate of the sun. . . ."

"You've won what you may consider a minus-quantity lottery at first. In fact, no horse ever came in at the odds your good fortune has." The poet seemed to have forgotten the expiatory side of his visit and to be enjoying the role of pundit. "I say good fortune because although it may take your breath away, it gives the lie to reckless bastards such as myself."

Ramsey hung his head, joining his large hands across the nape of the neck. "Come on, come on. What about this damned lottery?"

"Well, you're prepared now, and I swear there's no need for you to be shocked."

"God in heaven!" said Ramsey.

And while the poet dithered along the edge of the revelation George arrived, a lump of a man with the university badge on his cap. "Mr Ramsey?"

The poet swayed, making ready for the onslaught. Not all the geniality of George's bruin-like bulk would make him go peaceably.

"George," Ramsey murmured, "I tried to ring you again."

"We got rid of that fellow," the poet said. "He was a tough one."

"Not the fellow that I removed for Professor Meekin last week? Reckoned the world was flat? Tall, red-haired. . . ."

"Not the same one," Ramsey said.

The poet entertained himself. "This one was about my size. Smelt of drink. Wanted to be financed to do a lecture tour. The arrogance of the drunk!"

George unpocketed a notebook and took down the poet's solemn and incomplete description. Ramsey smouldered, assenting for the sake of getting George out of the room, when there would be a chance for private violence.

At last the man went, not satisfied but too polite to say so. Alec stood. "Get up," he said. "Little poet mocks big philistine. Big philistine rips the tripes out of little poet. You understand?"

"Don't take yourself so seriously, Alec."

"Stand up. No? Well, I've always considered your verse a proper fuck-up of decent sensibilities. And it seems there isn't much to you except your verse and a schoolboy sense of fun."

"Ah-hah, you're on to me! But are you ready for the tidings, Brother Alec?"

"Stand up and I'll write you over the wall like the genuine bit of shit-house humour you are."

"Very well. But I must tell you they think they've found Leeming."

Alec, confused, said, "What Leeming?"

"Leeming's corpse. They think they've found it. No need for alarm, Alec. I simply didn't want you to be taken by storm."

After some seconds Ramsey began to cry. He was

terrified of this emergence—or exhumation—no matter how little or how much it might mean to outside eyes. But he found he was weeping, in part, for poor Leeming. For it seemed to him then that he had always been consoled by Leeming's incorruptibility in the ice. It was as crude an intuition as this: he sensed that it diminished his guilt. Now he thought instantly that they must not force those pitiful remains to make any deferred payment of decay.

The poet had made a manly handful of part of Ramsey's right shoulder, and uttered soothing noises. When Ramsey quietened, the prosy little man said, "Understand they haven't actually found the remains themselves, but think they're likely to be no more than feet away, from certain . . . relics they discovered. They're going to wait for old Mrs Leeming to make a decision on what she wants done. She may well want to leave the remains undisturbed, sailing down through the ice-cap, you know. *That*, by anyone's imagining, is a fair simile for eternity." He sighed. "You see what I mean by odds."

Ramsey shivered. His fear of the resurrection, of the mere event, recurred. He fought it with his reason. There was no chance of pundits reading betrayal in the way the corpse was laid; there was, he admitted, some danger that the prismatic strands of his obsessions would be focused to lunatic unity by that eruption. Yet his dread evaded analysis and ran free.

"What are the details?" he asked.

"A gentleman—or rather, a public servant—from the Department of External Affairs arrived here by this morning's plane with a few items that were believed to be connected with the death of Leeming. If you verify this theory, then Mrs Leeming will be allowed to make one of three decisions. Fill in the pit again—in view of its having been so long. Or exhume Leeming and re-bury him in

Antarctica. Or exhume him and bury him at home. That is, of course, if they *do* locate the remains."

"You speak of a pit."

"Yes, in a place known to you, the David Glacier. The Americans took an ice-physics team there at Christmas time. I don't know what their purpose was exactly, but one of the things they did was to sink a deep ice-pit in what seemed a fairly open area. They sank it fifty feet down. They found two short lengths of ski-wood with initials hacked into the shorter length."

"Ah," Ramsey said. "Ah." Somehow his sense of Leeming having died had never been so pungently verified as now, by the poet's stating of these few crude particulars. "Sweet Heaven," he muttered, "the odds. The odds!"

"Yes," the poet admitted, properly reverent. For the odds were six million square miles multiplied by the depth of the ice-cap and divided by the length by breadth by height of Leeming in a sleeping-bag.

Ramsey decided, "This finishes me."

"No, not at all. Why don't you go home for a rest?"

"Yes." He felt frightened too that Leeming's reappearance would bend and incite him powerfully towards publicly saying *the truth*.

And he thought of *the truth* as of an unknown baggage that would be forced on him by this last ploy of Leeming's, this resurgence. He seemed to be afraid, therefore, of matters yet unknown to him, matters for which he would feel culpable yet which would surprise him as much as they would surprise anyone.

"What else do you know?" he asked.

"Nothing. I know this much because I have a friend who is secretary of the Antarctic Division. Griffith is the man from External Affairs who has been sent to see you."

"With the . . . items?"

The poet nodded indolently and rushed to other topics.

The things that Ella did for her sanity were lecturing somewhere between part- and full-time in the history department and a weekly potting class. That noon she had come home with a fish-gaping Inca face. It looked genuinely primitive, it looked an artefact. She hoped to hang it up in the living-room.

She fetched wire and, trying to plait it through the notches behind the face, ran it into the pad of her index finger. She swore, and returned to the damp box where Alec kept his tools. These were an immediate sign of Ramsey's diminishing powers of control over his life. The box was not often opened and had once filled with rain when left out in the weather, so that there rusted at the bottom hammers and braces which Alec had occasionally replaced with newer ones on top.

Ella could find no pliers. This had become a mark of their rare domestic endeavours; Alec's rusting box could be depended upon to provide a plethora of unwanted equipment.

She returned to the face, to torment the wire with her fingers. An understanding of the features diverted her in the dimness of the shed. Savouring the ovoid line she had given the mouth, and the emphatic eyebrows above shut eyes, she thought of Ramsey and told herself that this face was the face of a human sacrifice the moment the knife goes in. She wanted to ward off the omen by perhaps blessing herself.

Seconds later a university sedan, driven by George the university guard, wheeled fast in through the gate and propped at the front of the house. For some reason, it was clear, George thought an instantaneous arrival was of the essence. He jumped from the driver's seat, his big flank by accident toppling a staked hydrangea. Arrived at the off-side back door, he took delivery of Alec, who had been eased into the open by the poet. Alec seemed ill, and the poet and George began to convoy him up the pathway.

"God," Ella said. She suspected this was the ultimate, whose details she had been schooled in by a hundred widows. Poor Alec Ramsey, busy about Adult Education, stops in mid-stride and wavers. Barbara rises to help him, but his brain fades and his heart says enough of blood. He wakes blue-lipped and impaired and is helped home by strangers to settle down industriously to the business of dying.

She dropped the agonized face she had made in ignorance. The poet saw her sprint unevenly down the side of the house. She said, "Give me him!" and took him by the shoulders and peered into his face. Somehow he seemed chastened, but no older than he had at nine o'clock.

"Hullo, Ella," he said. "Ella, I'm finished."

"No, he's not," the poet pronounced. "He's had a shock, that's all."

"Yes," Ella said, inculpating the poet. "Yes, often. What is it Alec?"

"They've found Leeming."

"They think they've found him. The remains." The poet told his story and, wary of Ella, let her know the decency of his motives.

Ella accused him, just the same. "You brought this on." She believed in ghosts and the conjuring-up of ghosts.

"We mustn't be superstitious," the poet reasoned. "I admit to you I have no right to comment on the matter. But I think this is the best thing that could have happened."

Ella paused, for no adequate reason, on this hideous cliché by which both the indifferent and the grief-stricken reconciled themselves to somebody's lingering death or broken marriage. An absolute assent rose in her: it was the best thing that could happen that the incorruptible Leeming might now be removed from his preserving element and, in some municipal cemetery, made to come to terms with his mortality.

"Maybe," she told the poet, and pressured Ramsey's shoulders gently with her hands, telling him softly, "You're not finished. What makes you say that? This is a good thing, a good thing."

Ramsey widened his eyes in response to her sympathy, but did not recant his fears.

"Thank you, George," Ella said, and to the poet, "Will you be going back with George?"

Ramsey marginally protested. "No. Stay for a while." For he knew how her pity might sour.

Already she pretended to be more amused than she was. "Look how my enemies have become my friends."

Ramsey smiled a little, begging indulgence. "Yes. Well, he's acted as if he understands the matter."

Ella too still smiled in her strained way. "If I don't, it's not through lack of tutoring, eh? You'd better both come inside."

George was sent off with thanks. Ella led Ramsey and the poet in through the double front doors which the triumph of her entry from pottery class half an hour before had left open. With a slack hand Ramsey delayed her on the threshold. "Ella, thank God you're here." But he knew she would not be so easily bought off. Both men followed her penitently into the living-room, where, Alec could tell, she was torn between showing her anxiety in her indecorous and grudging manner and playing the hostess. She brooded in mid-room. Ramsey had recently grown beyond the desire to explain to outsiders that this was not the genuine Ella but a later version, beset by her definitive childlessness and her imminent widowhood.

"Ramsey," she legislated decisively this time, "this is a very good thing." She waited till he had found a seat. She

72

did not help to lower him; it was a dangerous ritual to help an old man before he needed help, to give his years and today's shock to his years official standing. It was the poet who stood by, discomposed by Ella's offishness and ready to fuss.

Ella continued, "Now you mustn't look upon this as anything drastic. I know you've suffered a lot on account of this man." She displayed the steely deference that an enemy shows for an enemy's ailment. "But this will allay it all, because he'll be put to rest, given a respectable burial. And that must mean a lot to you."

He had learnt that it was safer to ignore rather than mock her judgments. He nodded. But to his mind it was a dreadful resurrection that threatened. Not only did it edge him, as he had already sensed, towards the formulating of truth, but promised to finish him by drenching his evasiveness and fecklessness in such a flood of light that. . . . But he could not make out the results. (As for the truth, he did fear precisely its formulation, the task of utterance. Headlines and gossip around this town and any other could not touch him.)

"Don't you agree, Alec?"

"Of course, Ella," he said as if parodying marital submission.

"Well, what do you mean by saying this finishes you? You said out there that you were finished. Where does that put me?"

The poet insisted, "It's merely the shock."

"What might be finished are your Leeming tantrums perhaps. But to say you're finished is a tantrum in itself."

The poet risked probing at their apprehensions about Leeming. "If I might dare interrupt, you both presume that the remains will be found."

The Ramseys bore him with sullen politeness. For both of them, Leeming was a totem, a presence not subject to anticlimax. Some part of them believed that Leeming intended to emerge. The poet felt elated at making this discovery of a genuinely dramatic reaction.

The way they failed to answer their ringing telephone was also quaint. It persisted, though, and Ella rose to it at last. She said yes a few chary times and then clamped her hand over the mouthpiece.

"It's someone from the Department of External Affairs. He wants to see you urgently or some such thing."

"He'd be the man. Griffith," the poet told them. "From the Antarctic Division."

Ella belittled the knowledge with a cast of the eyes. "I see. Can he visit you here, Alec?"

The poet mumbled at Alec, "I'd rest for a time. Take a sedative and have a doze. He can afford to wait."

"Why is he coming here at all?" Ella demanded, but decided to ask the man from the Antarctic Division himself. "Why do you wish to see my . . . Mr Ramsey?"

An explanatory quacking prevailed for half a minute. "They want something identified," she conveyed at last to Ramsey.

"I know, some items," he said. "Tell him he can come." There was even a brand of excitement in his willingness to see the flotsam that would verify his fantastic memories; and Ella too was full of some form of anticipation as she told Griffith to come, and put down the phone.

"Alec, this could be a marvellous development, it could be the best. . . ." She realized she was repeating an enemy's judgment, the poet's, and left it unfinished. She steeled herself to be patient, now that a little of the wreckage of that holy saga had come to the surface. When Ramsey saw it it would show itself to be a few trite scraps of waste, a few silly mementoes. Transplant them to a cemetery in the sardonic landscape of Australia, in flat Pinalba or in suburban Sydney, and they would weigh anyone's ghost down with bathos; they would outrival the pickle-bottle borders in the graveyards of her childhood. Knowing this, she must tolerate for a little time any of his symptoms of shock—weeping, pallor, sense of dread. Professional undertaking would lay Leeming's ghost; the dust of a poisonous myth would pour up the vent of the Northern Suburbs crematorium.

She saw without warning that the poet was a blessing, so conciliatory, wearing the false clothing of his station-in-life, wondering whether he should remain.

"Would you mind staying?" Ella surprised herself by asking him. He would be a guard against hysteria; he could treat hysteria in Alec with all sorts of patient manly liquors for which Ella had no time.

"Griffith will think it's strange that I'm here. But I'll stay."

"Thank you. Alec—or rather, both of us—get very het up about things Antarctic."

Griffith was a brisk man; he moved into the Ramseys' hallway with the vim and command of a technician, of a man come to repair their television set. The items under suspicion of concerning Leeming were leant against the hall wall within reach of the living area. His strenuous face had no reason not to suspect that the fragments should be identified without an excess of emotion and followed by morning tea. They were wrapped in corrugated cardboard and sealed with the departmental seal.

Griffith's eyes lit when he saw the poet. They would have passed each other with a nod in Canberra, but Griffith made a bravura out of their acquaintance now, as if he were in a foreign country. The poet, obviously fearing a contradiction from Ella, claimed he was a friend of the Ramseys.

Ella and Alec stood palely by and were introduced. The man from the Antarctic Division set to work on Ramsey's hand. "What a pleasure this is. I've read the book, you see." He said almost accusingly, "You were superhuman, you fellows. Superhuman."

Ramsey frowned. He would have been happy with the fruits of mere humanity. He wanted to tell Griffith that the book might soon read differently. Behind his back, Ella sighed audibly.

"My husband isn't very well at present. I meant to imply on the telephone he doesn't altogether find this a festive occasion."

"I'm sorry. If you just sit where you are, and the public service bard will hold the parcels for me. . . ."

Fetching the first of the parcels, Griffith was aware of the dependent silences behind his back, silences more positive than a mere lull. He thought how interesting this was, and began to make a number of guesses, largely improper, about the connection between the three. Ramsey startled him by erupting in the face of Ella's stance of long-suffering.

"All right, Ella. The best of things has happened, so you say. Why don't you carry yourself like a woman to whom the best has happened?"

"You make it hard for me to believe in that proposition, Alec." The words rode in and out slackly on the breath, pretending to have achieved indifference. She was a very savoury bitch, the poet thought, but deserved to be beaten. "But we mustn't hold up Mr Griffith."

Who at that moment was opening a parcel laid flat on the poet's knees, easing the cardboard off with immense care.

The poet said wryly, "Are you responsible to the minister for that stuff?"

"Not at all." Griffith looked around for Alec. "There are Antarcticans down there still who know their Antarctic history. Fortunately someone on this ice-physics excursion that discovered these . . . well, what are they? . . . relics? . . . I suppose so. Anyhow, one of those Americans knew the story of Leeming's death in more than outline. If your identification is positive, Mr Ramsey, Mrs Leeming will be immediately contacted by our Sydney office. But I hope that all three of you will be good enough to regard this viewing as confidential until the news is announced."

All of them hostile, none of them answered. All Griffith did was to go on being provocatively careful with the corrugated cardboard. "Would you like me to buy you a roll of *that*?" the poet asked him.

"No."

"It wouldn't help you to take more risks with it?"

"No."

Neither did it end with the corrugated. Alec began to suspect Griffith of malice when it was found there was a final layer of tissue around the relics. It seemed an improbable act of delicacy on the part of the Antarctic Division for what had been forty years closeted in the coarse-grained ice.

"Two pieces of ski-wood," the functionary said at last, and held them up. "The lacquer's still in marvellous order, which would make some manufacturer very proud. You'll see the initials *S.L.* hacked in one arm and filled in with indelible pencilling, which still shows. Remarkable. Well, we thought they answered the description of the cross you made for Leeming. But that's up to you, Mr Ramsey."

Ella snorted when Ramsey accepted the pieces reluctantly, with a nearly rheumatic deliberateness. He felt bilious taking them, and the floor and the temperate latitudes swung out from beneath his feet for a second. What frightened him most was that the very taste of the morning returned to him. Lloyd standing by passively, all medical artifice suspended, himself pottering guiltily around Leeming. For a reason beyond his knowing, he would now and then chance the tip of his tongue out to his flawed lips—a racking thing to do—and taste his own death on them. His back to the mere thirty-knot gusts, he took off the mitts already frozen and sawed Leeming's left ski in two. The dreadful season first threatened to split, then anaesthetized, his fingers in their thin inner-gloves as he managed a bad knot of lampwick. With a knife in his good hand, he willed the lettering to happen on the shaft and, holding a stub of indelible pencil in a maimed way, began filling in the hacked outline. Here was a young man so baffled by winds and immensities that he believed all his atoning work with saw, lampwick, knife, and pencil gave Leeming some permanence on the face of the glacier.

Mr Griffith was busy with the larger parcel, and a careful shedding of tissue showed an aluminium cover, top and two sides, with lettering punched on one of the sides. Mr Griffith read it. "From the Worcester School, Sydney. 24/8/'24." Then he picked it free of its wrappings, while Alec inhaled noisily, fearing frostbite for the careless man, forgetting that all the voracious cold of the glacier had now gone out of the thing. Next he damned the Worcester School for writing its silly pride on the edge of the cover. Griffith, unlike the headmaster, was at hand.

"Why are you playing with me? Worcester School was Leeming's old school. Do you expect me to tell you that this was left behind by Vivian Fuchs? What fool thought it necessary for you to come all this way?"

"The director of the Antarctic Division is the fool in question. We're not trying to waste your time, and we don't think you want to look at relics of what must be a tragic day. But surely you remember that another party preceded you down the glacier? This may have been left by them. Anyway, we thought it kinder not to tell Mrs Leeming until we were sure."

Behind Ramsey's back the poet made a diminuendo

movement with his right hand, meaning "Don't be provoked. He's old, irrational and sick." Ella did not see this hint given; she sat astounded by the sight of concrete elements of the Leeming tragedy which had been so rarefied in debate between herself and Ramsey that one almost ceased to believe in it as something that happened in an ordinary material sense. This wreckage was to her, as to Ramsey, an amazing endorsement.

Meanwhile Ramsey was behaving very crochety. In the teeth of Griffith's reasonable explanations he muttered on. "Perhaps the director considers Magellan is an old boy of Worcester College, and suspects he wandered too far south, dropping a cooker given to him out of what could be bilked from small boys."

"But I've already explained how it's slightly more complicated than that. The question is whether you positively recognize these . . . *relics* . . . as the items you used . . . you and *Dr Lloyd* used in the burial of Leeming."

Ramsey glowered. He knew clearly that his emotions were exorbitant, but still had no control. "I did not allow him to be *buried*," he declaimed at Griffith.

Ella turned her head aside. She hissed briefly in disgust. "Give the man a chance, Alec. *Bury* was only a manner of speaking."

The man from the Antarctic Division showed he could be a diplomat. "Yes, Mrs Ramsey, but I can understand Mr Ramsey's sensitivity on that point. After all, the official history is very explicit on the matter."

Ramsey shook his head, saying "Oh!" in a tone that cast doubt on the sanity of those who believed official histories.

"According to the official history," Griffith persisted, "you used the cooker top as the basis of a windbreak around Dr Leeming's head. And after you had heaped up a mound, you drove the ski-wood cross in, wedging it with the camera you had decided to leave and with some

79

exposed plates. The director wants to know if the official history correctly details the . . . obsequies you performed that day."

Alec chose to stand on his dignity in a cockeyed way. "I like the bloody director's cheek," he said.

Ella found such bloody-mindedness insufferable in her spouse. "The director's not trying to impugn your truthfulness, dearie."

"Oh no!" Griffith verified. "But you can get winds of a hundred and fifty knots and more down those glaciers." Ramsey even considered sneering at the nautical pretentiousness of the word "knots" in the mouth of a man who, perhaps, sailed of a weekend on Lake Burley Griffin. "So that the question is, were the markers of Leeming's . . . resting-place blown away? Now you had no anemometer on the sledge, but the record says that on the day itself the wind seemed to Lloyd to be about thirty knots, and that the next day was still though very icy. Were these markers blown away, and if so, were they blown far? You were weak. How solidly did you ground these things? You can well understand that we don't wish to trouble the widow if the chances are that the supposed relics are merely winddrift."

Ramsey destroyed himself lightly. "They aren't winddrift. I planted these things very deliberately, solidly; a person does in Antarctica. Cairns, markers, mounds, and so on. You make them all to last."

He heard Ella utter a wry "Hurrah!" under her breath. He said, less grandly, "They may have been blown away. But the chances were in favour of their lasting."

"So you think Leeming is close to where these were found?"

"Yes," Ramsey said, and repeated the word, and nodded in a way almost ceremonial three or four times. This made

Ella lose patience, seeing an altogether too reverent and ritual a manner of acknowledging an old corpse.

"And there's no ritual significance in the thing," she told Ramsey. She sounded patient and minatory; her patience dwelt on each word and seemed to thumb-tack it to the ether. "He hasn't been in limbo, he's just been on ice."

"I assure you, Ella, I don't see this as a mystery of religion."

"What has us wondering," Griffith said smoothly, surmounting the family quarrel, "is that there was no trace of the camera and plates. Not that there needs to be, of course."

"The ways of glacial ice are no doubt strange," supposed the poet.

But Ella could not tolerate this sombre, parsonical axiom. She was up and pacing, but stopped by the window to gather herself. Seeing her, Ramsey wanted to cry out that he was the desperate one, he was the one who should rend garments, that it became her to stand by to soothe. He could have struck her for failing to see his need. "Ella," he said, "if you would like to go out for a matronly breath of fresh. . . ."

"Matronly?" She swept around. He could see the green, feline irises start in their peculiar way. "You said *matronly*?"

"I said it would be better if you went outside."

"You said *matronly*." She was frantic and triumphant; she had a pretext.

"Well, if I did. . . . Look, Ella, why don't you go and have some tea?" But he knew he had said one of the forbidden words and could not now avoid being made an even bigger fool of.

"Perhaps your admiring friends would be surprised to find that you mock me with that word. In view of my cancer of the womb. . . ."

"Christ!" Ramsey called. Both visitors stared. "Take her out," he told the poet. "For God's sake take her into the kitchen and hit her with something."

"You have rendered assault and battery superfluous, dear Alec."

"Take her out, will you," he ordered the poet again.

The poet made gestures of inadequacy: you might as well have asked the weather bureau to catch Valkyries.

Blessedly, Ella went herself, in a rush and probably ashamed at letting Griffith know her secret imagery.

In her electric absence Ramsey told the two men, "You mustn't take any notice of that cancer-of-the-womb stuff. She only means it symbolically. Childlessness she means."

Griffith was blinking, still wondering why the occasion hadn't been all wistfulness and reminiscence and how many lumps do you take.

Ramsey said, "Here's something for your epic, bard. Call it 'The Afternoon of an Argonaut. Complete with Sibyl.'"

The poet stared back. There was an air of righteousness about the man. Hadn't he given up two days' deferred leave just to expiate previous outrage? Yes, very much at ease he looked now; justified in his own eyes. The muse, Alec decided, provoked, might just as well have bedded down with Griffith as with this small accountant.

"I suppose you came for some such purpose," Alec surmised. "Or is Mrs T. less Papally aligned this month?"

The poet excused himself. From the door he asked Griffith, "What plane are you catching back?"

"This evening, ten-to-six. Connects with the quarter-past-eight to Canberra."

"Cool of the evening. See you on it. Good day."

Alone with Ramsey, Griffith devoted himself to re-wrapping the cover and ski-wood.

"You've seen enough of these?" he remembered too late to ask.

"Oh yes, enough is enough." Ramsey felt sheepish and wanted to re-establish himself in Griffith's eyes, in lieu of better ones. "I'm sorry for the way we've behaved. It's probably impossible for you—and in another sense, for my wife—to realize how close to the bone this whole affair cuts."

"That's understandable," Griffith assented busily. "You were very young. It must have been harrowing."

But Ramsey didn't want to be interpreted by Griffith. He shook his head. "No. The problem is that now I have to detail it all over again to people."

"I see."

"These events . . . *coerce* me in that direction." He slapped the ham of his leg. "Hopeless. What about the press?"

"They won't be told until we've seen Mrs Leeming. It will all be well handled by the minister's press secretary. After that, Mrs Leeming must be given a little time to decide what she wants done with the remains. In any case, this late in the season, a decision may be out of the question. She may well want a simple service held at the mouth of the pit, and no more. At her age that would be understandable and fitting enough."

At her age. Ramsey could tell that Griffith thought State funerals were best.

"Anyhow, Mr Ramsey, I regret very much that it's been so painful."

"No." Alec made a face like a victim, a face that asked, Why me? "But the odds," he said. "I've won an immense game of . . . of adverse chance. The odds are . . . prodigious."

Griffith, however, would not even let him have that much. "Not as prodigious as they seem, you know. Men

83

have always tended to travel on established routes in Antarctica. The David Glacier has been travelled by Mawson and Edgeworth David, by you people . . . and did Griffith Taylor visit it? Or Campbell? I'm not sure."

"You seem to have an interest," Ramsey said.

In Ramsey's house passion ran high enough without Ella and Alec resorting to the hearty sport of grudge-bearing. So lunch hour found them shame-faced and not very articulate, but forgivingly disposed. Ella prescribed that he should rest for half an hour, and he obeyed, spending his proneness on old magazines whose wiseacre commentaries and year-old political prophecies he could judge from a position of hindsight. Whenever he was in the furnace this sort of thing made his favourite reading.

Ella had gone to the history department's staff meeting, politely willing to call in at Ramsey's office and say he might not be in during the afternoon. It would have gratified him to prove her message nonsense by gusting in five minutes after she had been there, yet there was no validity any more in that sort of gesture.

He was still sunk in eighteen-months-old news from Saigon and Cape Town as someone—Mormon preacher, baker, insurance man?—rang the door-bell. He did not answer. Least of all he wanted to face some brisk creature who, wholesomely lunched, was already well into the afternoon's achievements.

The visitor persisted in pressing the chimes. Ramsey stalked into the living-room and up to the bay windows. Here a hatefully bright day filtered through the cretonne, and two of its most hatefully bright creatures could be seen from the flank, dressed informally, summer-school style, standing in the porch. The Kables. Mrs Kable, holding a sunhat fringed with carrots of felt, looked a cornucopian being, the impression of bounty heightened by very tight

84

slacks. Eric Kable, in science-fiction shirt, seemed a well-shaven Martian.

"Cool, man!" Ramsey muttered with an accent. He saw Kable ask his wife for something and receive from her a small pad and pencil on which he wrote something before lodging a sheet of paper under the door. Then they went back to the university sedan they had come in, Titania swerving through the gate with a carp-like flick of the hips.

It said, Dear Alec, that Mrs Leeming (and a fool of an exclamation mark after the name) had telephoned the office and been given his home number by Barbara. Mrs Leeming might not be immediately able to telephone but would be grateful if he could call her Sydney number as soon as possible. Mrs Leeming would accept the charges.

He knew how gratified the Kables would have been to deliver a message implying that Ramsey was not where he could reasonably be expected to be. No wonder they had minced away in that self-congratulatory manner, relishing the suspicion that Alec was hiding indoors.

But rather than indulge his almost religious hostility to the Kables, he telephoned Mrs Leeming in great haste. She had always been a most persuasively sane lady; and he felt that he would be comforted to find that she still was. As well, she had the say on what was to be done with Leeming.

He heard Belle Leeming's firm old voice say that she would accept the charges.

"Alec?" she wondered affectionately.

"Belle, how are you?"

"How are *you*, you poor foolish fellow?"

"Answer *my* question."

"Yes, I've heard from External Affairs, if you mean that. But I'm still the same woman as ever."

Indeed. The same proportions of disdain and irony and pretended solicitude. The exactness of the blend reminded Alec of sailing-time, 1924, when fogged by all the lifting and stowing and perilous overloading of the old Albany whaler that Leeming had re-christened *Westralis*, Ramsey had been found by Belle Leeming as he mooned around the kennels forward of the galley. The same solicitude: it was the departure ceremony; and to reach Alec she had had to climb onto the deck-cargo in a violet calf-length gown and a cloche, clinging to a parasol. The same banter: "Alec, I could tell by the spirit in which you left last week that you are determined to work through the conventional rituals of guilt."

He'd told her, not at all. To admit otherwise would have been to seem to recriminate. Apart from his small inroad into Bohemia, experience with girls, city and country, had borne out that it was somehow always the fault of the male and that the ultimate sin was recrimination.

Seas of moral difference lay, of course, between Mrs Leeming and the Bohemian girls. For Ramsey, hurt done against the man who would lead you into that absolute human state known as Antarctica partook of the mysterious sin against the spirit.

"I can tell," she insisted. "Alec, what we experienced won't have any benefit for you if you think that way."

"I didn't think it was intended to have benefit for me."

"So you think I was selfish?"

"No. I didn't mean not intended by you. I meant not intended by the scheme of things."

"The scheme of things? The natural law?"

"I suppose I mean something like the natural law."

"Oh Alec, you still are a rather horrendous Presbyterian."

He could remember having explained comfortlessly that he had said nothing to Leeming. Leeming had been so engrossed in business on the *Westralis* and so feverish with dinners and presentations and the need to say the correct things to businessmen in Melbourne. Leeming was frantic to begin, in fact. To make confessions to him would have been to savage him from the flank. But Ramsey may have had also a half-recognized fear that the lady told the truth when she said that she and Leeming allowed each other infidelities, accepting that if they were necessary they were no longer infidelities. To Ramsey's putatively free-thinking mind, one did well to be afraid of a leader who claimed to transcend the moral scheme, it being no less rigid than the physical or meteorological. He remembered keeping his face averted and knowing that she was smiling about this Protestant expedient that would save the gross memories from coiling out of him, save him from going aft to meet the Governor-General with a distorted trouser-fork.

He could remember her saying, before three hoots signalled that His Excellency was at the Williamstown dock, "Do you think I would commit a genuine infidelity against *Leeming* with *you*?"

Forty years later she repeated her claim into the long-distance line. "The same woman. And they tell me you viewed what the silly man from their Sydney office persisted in calling relics?"

Ramsey admitted it.

"Now this is no excuse for foolishness over Leeming." She was acquainted with the focus of Ramsey's ills. "You understand?"

The same Belle Leeming. The knowledge of her wrongs was deposited deep in Leeming's brain. *But no sweat, Belle, no sweat.*

He said the six words aloud.

"Not to make too much of the fact, Alec, it *is* characteristic of him, isn't it?" It seemed for a second that she too considered the event as the deliberate act of a revenant. For all her air of wisdom, perhaps she was afraid like himself. "The persistence of it, the staying power. If he's there, of course. But if he is, what are we to do with him?"

At that instant Ramsey's tongue seized. It was unprecedented. He had never had before this experience of some perceptive organ in himself, some subliminal wisdom for which he could take no credit, quelling intended sentences in his throat. He had meant to recommend that the pit be filled in or left alone. There were adequate reasons for leaving the prestigious corpse untouched. Someone in Antarctica even thought so, otherwise the digging might not have been suspended.

In the strictest sense, this opinion was unutterable. Being an answer merely and not a resolution of issues—what he most wanted and least needed—it would return him to the accustomed and strangely beckoning impasse of last week and last year. There seemed to be a law of almost metaphysical decency compelling him to see that this amazing epiphany should not be prevented. But if he was unable to save himself from it, he was too afraid to damn himself to it at his own word.

He said, "I don't know, Belle. I simply can't say."

"You know, I don't think Leeming had a very strong sense of funerary aptness, Alec. I mean to say, it *is* a rather suburban consideration. But in so far as he thought of it at all, I believe dear Leeming would have liked the idea of floating down the ice-cap for an untold time and reaching the sea long after all of us were topsoil."

"I think he might have, too," Ramsey ventured.

Ritually, she always called Leeming "dear Leeming" now. This may have been symptomatic of a growing cosiness of age. But it was not an affectation or the half-cynical accolade of the professional widow whose spouse has become a pallid god-of-the-hearth, worthy of a mild canonization.

She went on. "I don't know, though. You see, I'm like Leeming when it comes to these matters. I don't know much about what makes a fitting funeral. Here I have been, discreetly undermining society ——"

"From your plush Point Piper flat," he mocked her.

"Indeed. Discreetly undermining society and abstracting myself from the passage of time, which changes the fashions in funerals; and up pops dear Leeming and lands the undertaking problem of the century in my lap. Did he ever say anything to you, Alec? Anything that I can quote now as indicative of his wishes?"

"No. I can't remember anything. It was never presumed that what did happen would happen. It was never thought of as more than an abstract possibility."

"There's a family vault here in Sydney. It's still well tended. It holds his father and grandfather and sundry relatives. No need to tell you what the architecture's like."

Leeming's grandfather had established the family confectionery fortune. His burial place, which Ramsey had chanced on at the time of his first wife's death and burial, was in the spirit of his trade.

Ramsey said something noncommittal.

"I wouldn't put him in the vault," Belle mused on. "He warrants a grave of his own. Though that's what he's got, isn't it?" She said, as if it were a random fact with which she was not particularly impressed, "He was a great man. So if he *is* to be buried, he should have his own grave. Would the barbarity of the vault be cancelled by the decency of his lying near his fathers? I wish to God I had stronger apprehensions of propriety about interment."

He had no reason not to believe her confused. "This has tossed you, hasn't it, Belle?"

"It's so perplexing. And so unlooked-for."

He felt for her a petulance that was nearly pity. "I can't help you, Belle. I have no prerogative. . . ."

"But you have, you have," she insisted. "You were with him at the death."

The prospect of becoming an honoured mourner frightened him. "No, please, Belle. Can't you see I give you only those answers I can't avoid giving." He was still obsessed with the thought of his recent auto-censorship.

"Now Alec, you mustn't let it touch your health. Keep *that* inviolate." Her earlier doctrine of self-sovereignty had been withered by the years to a furiously defensive cherishing of self-health. Somewhere over seventy she had taken to leotards and yoga.

"Listen, Belle, there must be no pressure put on me to attend . . . whatever and wherever."

"Very well, very well. You know I'll honour that wish."

"Yes."

"How's Ella?"

"She doesn't understand. She makes scenes. I could control matters if she could only understand. . . ."

"She's mystified. You should tell her things."

"She knows about you."

The widow laughed. "About *me*? You make it sound as if we've been meeting at country hotels for the past twenty years."

"I suppose I do. But we've got no common sense in these matters. Ella hasn't. Ella is an absolutist."

During a silence they heard the twitter of the timing-device mounting up a bill for Mrs Leeming, whose decision would not be advanced no matter how long she spoke with Ramsey. Alec was on the verge of taking time off from his own anguish to think *poor old thing*. The silence grew around her loneliness and unwillingness to admit to it.

"I have a nephew there," she said. "I may wish to visit him at this time. I've no one to help me. Most of my circle are dead or dying."

"Please don't feel you have to have my permission to visit your own folk." But he was not fervent at the likelihood.

Belle continued to dither about her nephew. People fell out with him because they were mere technocrats while he was an Elizabethan, a Renaissance man.

Alec threw his head in a tortured arc, but ended by saying softly, "Belle, I wish I could help you. But it's beyond me. You have all my . . . unavailing sympathy, Belle. Believe me. . . ."

"All right."

"Belle, the truth is I'm afraid." Fear and the moist locked-up air of the house raised an itch on his arms which he raked with hooked fingers.

"Afraid of what?"

"Of the light it casts on us. When we thought we were finished with the business."

There was some more costly silence. At last Belle said, "Don't get yourself too involved in all this. Preserve yourself for Ella's sake. You'll live to eighty-five if you don't abuse yourself in this way."

"Mere survival is no triumph. Even if a hundred years of it are good for a royal telegram."

Belle tried a tougher line. "Behave yourself, Alec. This is no more than an unearthing. You mustn't seek overtones in it. Dead Leeming is merely dead Leeming. He died of his own necessity; and he would have had the insight to see that."

For what must have been the fourth or fifth time, the pips signified that Leeming's widow was up for another three minutes' worth. Belle seemed to be struck by a sudden thrift, and ended the talk. Even through his engrossment with Leeming, Ramsey could sense that she was being kind and loyal to an old flame.

Back at the Extension building by mid-afternoon, he shied away from Barbara's concern in the outer office. To defend himself, he was all briskness.

She sang, "I have a number of messages, Mr Ramsey. Do you want them now?" She was a little hurt as well as solicitous, the same blend as Belle and Ella. She had decided with his other woman that he wouldn't be working that afternoon, yet here he was, making a joke of their judgments. They were all earth-mothers, he told himself. Having eviscerated you, they nailed your hollow pelt to the wall and devoted themselves to seeing that it was never too cold, too hot, too tired, or in need of a cup of tea.

"Ten minutes, eh, Babs?" he called, very much like a man in control of himself. Inside, he shook from a bottle four habituating stimulant pills and swallowed three of them. He stared out of the window at the park. In happier days he used to make a joke out of pretending it was illusory with its British trees and rich lawns and arbors. You never caught anyone in the act of tending it or, perhaps because of its ambiguous position, between university and town, a rate-paying backside there seeking a garden-seat.

Beyond the park stood the bush-Gothic Anglican cathedral and, beyond it, an unflurried corner where an ancient department store called Jennings' retailed impassibly. Within five minutes his heart outdid Jennings' in pace by far. He felt tipsily fortified. He had never been able to root out the presumption he had that Leeming's corpse displayed auguries which, if they were ever read, would somehow be to his, Ramsey's, disgrace. With seventy-five milligrams of happiness beginning to besot his blood, he felt most convincingly that the world was merely a finite progression of parks and pulpits and Jenningses; that it did not particularly signify what was said of you on a limited and mortal number of corners. Some limited disgrace he could stand; and so could Ella, who would be challenged by it, whose potent motherliness would thrive on cherishing him in the face of the world. The drug helped him discount all the human elements that lay below his window: concrete, power-poles, red brick, all minced in with the native elements of the town: the river and willows and ridges to the north from which hulking stalks of red cedar came down to the town clamped on trailers. "Be at peace with the everlasting hills," he thought as the massed dose shook his heart, "and the towns will look after themselves."

But to say all that was to say nothing. It did not touch those certain elements in himself which were now busily gathering to crisis. He thought it was time for him to look at his mail.

"Only a handful," said Barbara, bringing it in. She began expertly to deal them, giving him a précis of each. Soon, he thought directly into the girl's gabbling face, you'll have a director who won't stand being directed. You'll become weepy and sleepless and lose weight (though not from the hips) or put on unhappy weight.

"And Sir Byron accepts our invitation to tomorrow night's performance, but regrets Lady Mews cannot be there."

"Ah, the old Chimp on the track of home-grown culture."

"And Mr Pelham rang up very angry because the drama group staged a party for some of the incoming undergraduates and the masters of two colleges have lodged complaints about it."

"Oh?"

"Mr Pelham blamed the director of the Drama School."

"He must have been angry! He isn't a man for recriminations."

"He said he was fed up. The whole summer-school programme is too much for one man to set up and supervise. That's what he said."

Ramsey felt, for a second, maudlin at having overloaded and alienated a friend.

"I'll telephone him, Barbara. And thank you. I'm very grateful."

She raised one eyebrow.

"For keeping the office afloat," he said as a penance.

Her eyes took on an intense and spurious chastity. "I only do what I'm paid for," she lied in going.

He sat nursing his pharmaceutical intoxication. Now and again the reality would break on him that they would indeed take that wronged and entire flesh out of the deep ice; the utter body, all the wronged blood solid in the veins, the brain frozen to that core of knowledge by which Ramsey had been known.

He was trying to telephone Ella at the history department when Barbara came again to the door. Beside her stood the poet. They waited in a concerned and polite stance; a surgeon and a nurse.

"I can't see anyone now," Ramsey complained.

The surgeon and the nurse swapped professional glances, as if a symptom had been handed them.

"Damn it all, come in and sit down then." He was not unwilling to have company that knew some of the rules. The poet qualified. Ramsey put down the telephone.

For some time they merely sat. Ramsey made the mouth of a man with acidosis.

"Stomach off?" the poet asked.

Ramsey believed he could afford to be ironic. "It's Leeming's hand. I shouldn't have gulped it down. It has me by the lower bowel." His jangled stomach felt very much that way.

The poet merely coughed and came across the room to put a new bottle of whisky on Alec's bookcase. "I thought you might need something like this and be too upset to get it."

"I'll give you the money," Ramsey insisted. He fumbled hopelessly in his fob-pocket. He must have had perhaps thirty-five cents there. "You were going home on this afternoon's plane."

"I may as well stop till tomorrow."

"Have some luck with the widow Turner?"

"I didn't come to have luck with the widow Turner. I think you'd better have a glass of this stuff."

Ramsey speculated about the effect of whisky on his already pelting system. "Thanks." Close to friendliness, he toasted the poet as the whisky was passed.

"As a matter of fact," the poet admitted, "I couldn't get a seat on the plane. And of course I wanted to see how you were this afternoon."

"There's nothing you can do, thank you." Ramsey held his glass out, none the less, and the poet obliged him.

"Do you think you should even be at work?"

"No. Certainly not taking up a chair in which a younger backside could profitably sit."

"You've always had trouble with Ella over the Leeming affair?"

"You can't be discouraged from impertinent questions, can you?" Ramsey stared at the blue hills. They quaked for a second in time with his heart. Liking to see the quake effect in an old, worn-down, settled continent, he drank again.

"You were very young though at the time, weren't you? The desirable minimum age for men working in Antarctica is supposed to be about twenty-five."

"You've been reading your American *Antarctic Handbook* or some such thing."

"Well, you were considerably younger than that, weren't you?"

"I was a big boy. I was dedicated. I was a polar monk and Leeming was my abbot."

"Have you ever *read* the official history?"

"I even wrote part of it. Not the part you're probably speaking of. But I wrote some. For Lloyd, who wasn't very literate. Like many not very literate people, he died rich."

"Have you read the official history *lately*?"

Ramsey claimed to have done so, and again held out his glass.

"Do you think it's wise?" the poet asked, meaning another glass. Ramsey claimed to think it was.

"I'll take your word that you've read the official history recently. Surely you can see it's no great human document? Reading that, you might come to see Leeming as a rather shrunken figure."

"Shrunken? Leeming?" Ramsey filled with glee to see the mountains shake again.

"He was a leader of talent, and single-minded. But single-minded people are limited, you know."

Ramsey leered without inhibition. The poet had made himself a flogging-post by his behaviour at Sir Chimpy's and his present extravagant exhibition of concern. "You're not single-minded then, you're trying to tell me?"

"No. My limitations are due to less classic causes. But leaders are not as rare as other classifications of talent."

"As poets, say?"

"I'm not a poet's wishbone. Poets *are* rare."

"Look, believe one who knows and leave it at that: Leeming was a moral giant. He walked and walked—after a stroke. He never stopped . . . testing himself."

"Indeed he was strong."

Ramsey groaned. "Don't expect not to be insulted if you keep on this tack." But he kept on it himself. "Don't believe the official history. Don't believe his journal. They both deal in the species of lies that are known as facts. Leeming was no conventional leader. The same as no great poet is a conventional poet." He drank again, and asked narrowly, "You're a pretty conventional poet, aren't you?"

"It might save you a lot of wasted irony if I tell you I'm not vulnerable on the score of poetry." And he topped up Ramsey's glass for vengeance' sake. "You mention his journal. It really is so limited. So plausible and untrue, just like Scott's as edited."

"Of course it was limited. The journey was potentially a saga. If he'd written too perceptively about anyone, it might stand against that man in myth and legend and school textbooks for ever." The liquor and his cavorting heart stirred him to metaphysics. "He seemed to believe that behaviour in the south proceeded on a different plane from behaviour elsewhere. Well, almost a different plane. He didn't see why his journal should be perceptive and literary just for the sake of outsiders who didn't understand the springs of behaviour in that other world. See?" From all this Ramsey lost syllables here and there; his legs were numb; his chest felt dissociated, like a balloon stuck in his hand at someone else's none-too-joyous birthday party. He said, more or less, "Leeming didn't do it for the titillation of dilettantes."

"Who merely wanted to write poems on the subject?" the poet suggested.

"*Who merely wanted to write poems on the subject.* Nothing personal . . . well, nothing too personal . . . but literary midgets are always attracted by moral giants. Moral giants are one of the things that help make up for the limitations of art. Another is death. Young writers are keen on moral giants and on death as a means of saving their talents from having to stand on their own feet."

"I bet you review in quarterlies. 'Mr Schmaltz introduces a new vein into the Australian novel.'"

"Yeah, genius. That'd be a new vein. Christ it would!" Ramsey took a long mouthful, as if the poor state of the native novel entitled him to this compensation. "But how many great works deal with moral giants? How many, eh? Scarcely a one. Let that be a warning."

Which the poet accepted with a pucker of the mouth. Meanwhile, Ramsey clucked to see that nearly half the bottle was gone. "Fast work," he said.

The poet corked the bottle.

"Mrs Ramsey will have a grievance against me."

"Mrs Ramsey? I don't know any shrew of that name."

"Ella."

"Ella? Married to the director of Extension?"

"Yes."

"Well, do I look like the director of Extension?"

"I think you'd prefer me to say no. So no."

"When are you going to go home, anyhow?"

"Tomorrow morning's plane. But I can cancel it if you feel you need me."

"Ha!"

"Your trouble is you don't pray."

"Pray? I pray in season, don't you worry. You couldn't find a nicer chap to pray to than my God. He's solid. He has collateral." Ramsey remembered. "He's secretary of Rotary. He reads an article a day from the *Reader's Digest* and fears the Yellow Peril. What else can a man ask of the merely divine?"

"Yes, but that's not prayer. That's social observance, not prayer."

Ramsey croaked venomously, "By Rotary means, in Rotary ways,/Help us, dear Lord, thy name to praise."

"You don't pray to your Christ."

"My Christ? *My* Christ? Are you some sort of revivalist? I assure you, dear bard, I wouldn't do anything so ill-bred as to claim proprietary in the Lord."

"Leeming is your Christ."

"And who am I? Just which Apostle?"

"I would say Saint Paul. The road to Damascus. Via Oates Land."

Ramsey whistled, a startling blast, the sort farmers reserve for their cattle-dogs. "I forgot. It's the mode to have a Christ figure. Any bumble-footed litterateur can spot one at a great distance. But I ask you again, how many great works feature Christ figures, Judas figures, Alphonsus Liguori figures, John XXIII figures or Archbishop of Canterbury figures? How many? Ah, a judgment on you literary people again."

The poet laughed; a man who had pre-judged himself as mediocre and needed no one else's crapulous judgment to fortify his sane sense of failure. Uneasily, Ramsey recognized the man's humility.

"Your Leeming," the poet was busily asserting, pleased with the literary neatness of it all, "fulfils all the puritan requirements of a Christ. He is morally perfect and divinely illumined . . . has a charism, as people say now and used to say in the first century. Besides, he has not fallen to the grave's corruption. He has died for virtue and for many, but his sacrifice is not properly esteemed. And you are very sensitive about his death. Eric Kable tells me a story relevant to that. I met him at the Drama School today. I believe we've met before, but I wasn't very self-aware at the time. . . ."

"Drama School!" Ramsey tried to bark. The poet's symbolist cocksureness made him furious, but he felt disjointed, almost glutinous, unable to direct an attack. "Mrs Turner?"

"I have to admit it. I was there with Mrs Turner. I give you permission to write 'The bard loves Mrs Turner' on lavatory walls, if you have to."

Ramsey gave up this right with a tiny movement of his hand.

"I was saying, you are very sensitive about his death, as if you had added dimensions to his passion and death. And now, behold, he will come again to judge the living—you. And the dead—Lloyd."

Ramsey stood at the second attempt. The mountains shivered again and there was actually a tranquil madonna with child and baby-carriage in the park. "That's clever," he said. "So you wouldn't care that it's so bloody objectionable."

"I'm sorry."

"You come to me waving a banner that reads, 'Don't jolt the old man, don't rub him up.' But that's only a blind for forcing your ratbag eschatology on me."

"*Your* ratbag eschatology, Alec. We're talking about the way *you* see the man."

Ramsey moaned through closed teeth, took up the stapling machine and hurled it at the poet. The poet raised his guard, taking the stapler on the pad of the shoulder. It fell to the floor with a pernicious clatter.

Instantly Barbara was rat-tat-tatting shortly and repeatedly on the office door. "Mr Ramsey. *Mr Ramsey!*"

"It's all right," the poet called. "Mr Ramsey dropped the stapler on his foot."

But Barbara was baffled, otherwise she would have been in the room by now. "Is it all right, Mr Ramsey?" she wanted to know from Alec's own mouth. She asked tremulously and as if she would never be taken in again by any gold karate of the sun.

Ramsey told her to go away. From the outer office came the shufflings of her considerable disillusionment.

At last the poet said, "Our trouble is that we're still capable of making firmaments and ultimates for ourselves, but have lost the gift of praying and making oblations."

"Oblations? To Leeming?"

"Yes."

"You sound like some sort of bloody queer."

"Said like a true atheist Manichee. But tell me what your

sweat's about, what's your shuddering? Acceptance, prayer, oblation aren't any more grotesque than *they* are. On the question of Leeming you have a fanatic's sense of reverence, a votary's hysteria. That's bad, because the man was interesting, but not without precedents. When I recommend you to undertake some ritual of expiation as a cure, you ask me with a sensitivity the gutter press would be proud of whether I'm some sort of bloody queer. Well, you may have doubts about me, but I know about you. You're just a poor de-mythologized Protestant being beaten to death by your own myth."

Ramsey, far gone in liquor and drugs alone, hissed, "And what are you, you smart Robert-Gravesy bastard?"

"I'm a poor de-mythologized Protestant whose main protest is that Mrs Turner won't take a tumble with me. But if I were in thrall, like you, I'd take a ritual way out of it. I would perform rituals of expiation."

"Are you joking?"

"Rites are better therapy than tranquillizers."

"And epigrams are no bloody use at all."

The exultation of his body seemed to have run on ahead of him, shuddering. The speed of the blood and the chugging of the heart went to create distances between him and reality: the walls, the atmosphere. He sat panting.

"It *is* no use my being glib, is it?" the poet admitted. "You should never have come back to work. A doctor should see you."

Ramsey did not answer. The poet composedly searched for and found Ramsey's number and rang it. Alec was surprised to hear his unhappy Ella chirp at the other end of the line.

At last, the doctor harried him to sleep with an injection. While he lay drowsing and relatively content with the postponement induced by drugs, the slow corners of his mind licked at one crucial memory of Leeming.

Ramsey was out along the ice-foot killing one of the hundred and fifty seals the dogs would devour that winter. It was no sport; the Weddells died negligently, receiving the bullet with curiosity. Hauling them uphill to the seal-meat depot was also no sport. To help him he had Steve, the base electrician who had meant to winter with his girl in Hobart, but who, when the regular electrician sickened, had been coerced into landing. Steve was twenty-one years old, plaintive, small help.

Steve and Ramsey were pulling a carcass up the contour of a hill when all shape and shadow vanished, all hint of rise and fall. Both men were affected much the same. There was a catch of hysteria in their throats; they wanted to break out. For they seemed to be locked in the belly of a muddy pearl; and further, the irrepressible conviction was carried to Ramsey that he was standing on a brink with a long flight of stairs threatening his heels.

Each man slipped off his harness and withdrew to the unavailing shape of the dead seal.

It quickly occurred to them that they must leave this poor point of reference. At every step Ramsey dropped the rifle ahead of them to see where the earth was. The shadowless length of the weapon floated at their feet in miasma. Grimacing, they took the step.

Somewhere to their left front and no more than four hundred yards away stood the hut. They must turn left at the crest of their hill. Having done this, but too early, they stumbled on ice slopes. Steve went frenzied at each of his falls, and Ramsey dragged him upwards to a better surface. In the south, where the uniformity of the vicious pearl was streaked with a threatened blizzard, they could hear wind brewing. Ramsey longed for the more accustomed blindness of the high wind to break on them. When it came, though at more than seventy knots, it soothed them.

Three hours later they were still raking the blizzard for their hut and both had the club-footed sensation of frost-bite. They shouted and cut the blindness diagonally, travelling what they guessed to be north-east, turning back to what they guessed was south-west, turning back again after what they guessed to be a few hundred yards. They were still busy at their besotted transversals when a line of men from the hut, roped to each other by the waist, ran into them.

Then the ravishment of warm soup and indoors, where decent shadows were thrown by everything, even the Bovril pot on the table; such a neat little belly of shadow that you could cry at its beauty.

They kept holding a hot-water bottle to Ramsey's nose, and took off his finnesko and the two socks on each foot. Leeming broke through the ring of attendants and made a mouth at the livid state of Ramsey's right foot. Then he untoggled the front of his union-suit and the cardigan and raked up the inner garments of Jaeger fleece to expose his chest. It was clear to Ramsey that Leeming intended to take the dead foot against his own body and, closing all the clothes again, nurse the blood back to the ghastly flesh. The concept was intolerable: for Ramsey to plant his foot in the black hair above Leeming's heart; for Ramsey to condone this intimacy which Leeming offered in ignorance of the true and sad kinship they shared in Mrs Leeming.

The ankle struggled in Leeming's grip, and in the end escaped. Leeming readjusted the layers of his clothing without question. Everyone fell silent, sensing a sexual reference in the refusal, but unable to define it. There was an air of assent in the hut that Leeming's motives had been questioned. Ramsey could read it in the men who continued to knead his frostbites. They felt none the less that after his morning in the blizzard he was excusable.

In a dusk of sleep forty years later, Ramsey was still

103

disturbed by his refusal to accept decently this mercy that, as he had later discovered, was knowingly offered.

Asleep, he dreamt of this same ritual. No dithering dream of subfusc colour and inchoate event, it was of the rare sort by which the wisdom of the mind that lies beneath articulation forces change upon the mind that speaks. The scene was broken ice on a glacier primitively caricatured into a white presence with pinnacles. Similarly caricatured was dying Leeming, whose face Ramsey looked at once only, shredded as it was into neat iced tassels of hanging flesh, the eyes stagnated to umber gluten of no meaning whatever.

Leeming sat as in his last days on what was likely to prove a sledge but was iced up, bolsters of ice encroaching round the sick man's thighs to give, sardonically, the appearance of a throne.

Into the dream was written the knowledge that Leeming had suffered stroke and that his extremities were five times more liable to the winds that prefaced the close of the sledging season. A love of religious proportions moved Ramsey and pardoned Leeming for his blunt eyes and bizarre face. The religious quality was inevitable, for Ramsey naturally thought that the sufferings of great men consecrated their bodies. So the threat of ice to the feet and hands seemed to Ramsey barbarous, not to be countenanced.

All was simplicity. It would take an exercise of courage and, above all, humility; and consciously Ramsey moulded himself to the exercise. He stripped Leeming's feet and opened his own clothing to that old carnivore, the polar wind. He unbuttoned the flesh of his chest as easily as any of the other layers of warmth so that Leeming should have the poor comfort of treading into the core of his vitals. So the leader, blind as an idol, trod about in Ramsey's guts.

The pain was sharp enough to wake him. "Christ,

Christ!" he began to moan at it, for blasphemy's sake and
not in verification of the poet's theories. By the normal
rules of sleep, he should have awoken and sat upright,
groping for a bedside light. Yet he clung with both fists to
the major reality of the dream. His heart burst like fruit
as Leeming tramped wildly as peasants showing off in vats
at wine festivals. Blood as thin and hot as coffee ran down
him and made steamy runnels in the ice. He uttered curses
against Leeming while the geyser of sizzling blood ate the
pinnacles down and sucked a moat deeper and riotously
deeper into the foundations of the ice-throne.

At length it was shown to be a church sedile of banal
make on which Leeming sat with a look of blind dominance
on his face. On either arm of the sedile was written, *I have
made my bed in the darkness. I have said to corruption,
Thou art my father: to the worm, Thou art my mother,
and my sister.* Ramsey was startled to read this, and looked
in question at Leeming. Were these words a profession of
preference on Leeming's part, or had some zealous parson
ordered them when the chair was still at the joinery works?

The face, whose monstrosities were actually arranged to
convey smugness, made no admissions.

Pain forgotten, Ramsey was still puzzling when the sedile
and its imperial figure began to slide in the wash of blood
and rode away, not at all like flotsam, rather like a barge-
of-state. He knew that it changed matters immensely for
him to have caused that unwedging. It occurred to him to
make a pun, he was so elated. "This is what they mean by
a solution," he said aloud.

When Ramsey woke the final time it was to the small
stutter of the drawn venetian blinds caught in a minimal
breath of air. There was something about the noise and the
air and the quality of the light that told him it was mid-
morning. This fact, and the busy noises of diesels at the

North Street depot, failed to reproach him for his late rise. He was refreshed and self-contained. He felt freed of obsessions, but was not: they had merely taken a more generous turn in his sleep.

He saw that the bed was medicinally tidy and tucked about, and that he lay in it tidily. Without anxiety, he wondered whether the dream had been heart-attack and if he was a patient.

There was talk from the living-room. Ella gabbling in drained monotone, and a specious lark of a voice tacking and swooping above Ella's: Mrs Kable; and listening again, he heard Eric Kable rumble out something interrogative.

He pulled on his bathrobe and stood performing guarded strong-man gestures before the full-length mirror, countenancing the gnarled calves below the robe. If the Kables had called as mourners, he would go in to them limbered.

In this spirit, dressed only to the knees, and all knots and nubbles below them, he passed into the hall. Here Ella's Inca head had waited gaping on the occasional table since the previous morning. The surprised Indian features had dust on them and didn't seem to Ramsey to be facing any more than a banal tragedy. He would not tell Ella; but he did make a mouth in imitation, and asked mockingly, "Anal thermometer broke, did it, friend?"

He lifted the face and took it in to Ella.

"You should hang this, dear."

She told him he should still be sleeping. The peculiar harshness of her voice, which only he could recognize as contrite, delighted him. She could not be loving in a facile way, and she knew that their trouble was likely to recur. Looking wistful, she put out her hand and squeezed his wrist.

He welcomed the Kables with the rich hypocrisy their act called forth in him.

"Eric and Valerie called in to see how you were," Ella explained. "I must have given them the wrong impression yesterday."

"How kind," he said. He was looking at Ella, who sat side-on and as if allied to him. Her loose summer shift, large enough to hide a pregnancy, gave her a Gauguin simplicity, and the sweet line of her shoulder giving on to her back and hips stirred his pulse. The legs, three-quarters visible and chastely joined at the knees, for once did not look too blatantly like the proud quarters of a dairy-farmer's daughter. Alec stood pulsing like an athlete beneath the bathrobe. "I feel a new man," he claimed, not altogether figuratively.

"You've had so much trouble, you poor old thing," Mrs Kable was telling him. "If it keeps up they may have to put you out to grass."

"Reserve me for stud purposes," he suggested. Everyone laughed. Mrs Kable twisted her hips at an excessive angle to the lie of her upper frame and appeared very much the sexual cliché Ramsey believed her to be. For proof he had Ella's infallible reactions. Ella, who could be jealous of Lady Sadie, was serene before Valerie Kable.

"But Barbara was telling us you've had some nasty turns," the lady persisted. Eric Kable raised joined hands a little from his stomach in a sort of antiphonal concern.

"Nothing symptomatic of decline," Ramsey told them.

"Will we see you at the *Dream*?" Eric Kable asked him. Alec wondered if, away from Valerie's direction, he might even have been provoked into saying, "If you're so bloody well then, come to the play."

"The *Dream*?"

"The Midsummer's-Night's one," said Valerie. "You've got no idea what the producer has made out of that old tissue of fairy-tales. It's as gay as a French farce."

Both Ramseys cringed marginally before chuckling.

"Ella, you should be in this too," Mrs Kable added.

Ramsey said, for the sake of having it denied by Ella, "The only role life with me has fitted Ella for is Lear's third daughter."

Ella demurred quite satisfactorily.

Then, giving no warning, Kable himself unfurled the morning paper he had been holding in his lap and offered it to Ramsey. "Have you seen this, Alec?" A fuzzy picture was indicated of someone in a dinner-suit. Though Ramsey's eyes were still good, he had to do the old man's trick of finding his focus by tilting his head and extending the paper. When he had, the face that formed and pounced on him from the blotty photograph was Leeming's. He had expected it would be, but was angered by so blunt an attempt to unhinge him. He felt pity, too, for what the bitch goddesses of the media might do to that thin, somehow private face. There were some indications in the headline to one side of the photograph. "Hopes of Recovering Famous Antarctic Corpse," he read aloud, showing the article lightly to Ella to prove that he had not been touched.

Ella relaxed into mere anger. Her voice quavered a little as she said, "Famous Antarctic Corpse! Next they'll be talking of eminent or distinguished corpses. *Who's Who in the Graveyard.*"

Ramsey took the paper from her and gave it back to Kable raggedly folded. "We've known for some time. Poor Leeming. The ghouls will be out in force."

And though Eric showed hints of being routed, Valerie jumped in chattily. "We knew too. Denis Leeming told us. Last night."

"Leeming is Theseus," Kable explained, to show that they had not gone hunting for the news. "In the *Dream*."

"He's extraordinarily excited."

"Yes, Sanders claims he *is* of an hysterical cast of mind."

"Sanders may simply be jealous. He was, after all, a mere senior lecturer until a year or so ago. A most insecure man."

"I don't know," said Ella. "I like people who are promoted late in life. It's a sign they do it by fair means."

After a chastened interval of silence, Eric Kable dragged the debate back onto its keel. "Anyhow, whatever the relative stabilities of dons, Denis feels this is a chance to reassert the value of his uncle's work."

And give him a sense of genealogical grandeur after his recent failure, Ramsey would have liked to add.

"Talking of promotion," Alec said, just to fret them, knowing they could not afford to ask him what he meant, "how are all you drama buffs making out with Morris Pelham?"

His face ever full of a commercial brand of candour, Kable now willingly allowed his eyes to go devious. Having so signalled that he was about to tell untruths, he murmured, "Excellently."

Valerie reproved the gallant lie. "Now you know, Eric, that that's not quite the truth, although you're hardly in a position to say otherwise."

"Oh?" Ella said. Ramsey could tell she was enjoying the way the game was going.

"The boy is very puritan. Tim—the producer, you know —is all inspiration. His discipline seems a little loose, but this is because he deals with professionals who carry their own private discipline with them." Valerie sighed a second, hankering for this nun-like capacity. At whatever risk, Ramsey winked at Ella. "Mr Pelham, not understanding the sort of talent that doesn't work to timetable. . . ."

Kable came in more moderately, lofting the ball to Valerie's forehand smash. "Morris does try to supplement Tim's deficiencies. He tends to round people up at the end of tea-breaks. . . ."

"Rounds them up? Corrals them! Which is an insult to Eric too, because Eric directs this particular school, even if Morris has charge of the entire programme." She accented "entire" as a reproach to Alec.

"He's anxious for the success of the enterprise, of course," Kable limply surmised.

"But it's deeper still than that, Eric. There's something dreadfully suppressed about that boy, something drastically misdirected."

"Perhaps," said Kable, and explained to the Ramseys, "Valerie's more perceptive than I am. I believe Morris does merely what he considers to be his duty."

"No reasonable sort of man would consider that sort of boundary-riding as his duty. I can tell you, Alec, the members of the school resent it."

"He wants to make sure, of course, that Tim's sweetness isn't wasted on the desert air. . . ." Kable again left his sentence hanging on a not over-subtle octave that bound his Valerie to "but's".

She said, "But you don't get the best out of strictly creative talents by timing their tea-breaks and seeing that the kiddies don't answer teacher back."

"Very well!" Alec said without warning and conclusively. Ella's quiet presence was full of applause. With two words Ramsey had given himself, although half-naked, the character of an examining magistrate who has concluded the taking of evidence; and exposed the Kables as over-eager witnesses. "I must go to the shower if you'll excuse me, Valerie, Eric."

"Of course." They would be very happy to see him go now.

"But if you mean by what you've told me that Pelham is guilty of the worst crime against education . . . I don't mean inefficiency, I don't mean lack of knowledge . . . what I mean is being out of tune with the spirit of the culture he's trying to transmit; if you think he's guilty of that crime. . . ."

Kable said, "Oh, I don't think we'd go so far as all that."

"But if you're implying it, say, I couldn't agree with you less."

Valerie smiled with rage. "But Alec, you're rarely there when these things happen, are you?"

"No, Valerie. To my shame. And my attendance record isn't likely to improve unless I wash and shave and get across to where the action is."

So he excused himself again and went to wash. He was ashamed that the load he had laid on Pelham gave an edge to the Kables' malice. He was saddened to find such concert between a notorious cuckold and a randy wife. But the congratulatory emanations from Ella's direction helped console him.

Under the gush of water, Ramsey heard Ella come in.

"Alec, you don't mind, do you? I have to get ready to interview freshers."

"Certainly," he said, like one polite boarder to another. It was not that they were in any bodily sense afraid of each other or that they made love, when they made love, through holes in shrouds. It was that their recent estrangement subjected the new peace they had made in confronting the Kables, the new peace Ramsey had made by showing a healthy toughness, to certain rules of etiquette. Unreal ones, since he knew she might well want him to bound dripping from behind the curtain and force her down on the tiles. And, soaping his firm breast and thinking how sixty-two was no more than middle-aged these days, he felt adequate to the feat.

Because he must get to his desk within the next half-hour, he turned from vibrant memories of Ella's summer dress and concise legs, and flesh the hand threatened to skid on; he turned, for abstention's sake, to memories of the odious Kables.

"Something suppressed about Pelham, eh? Something misdirected. Perhaps old Valerie considers herself the panacea."

"Yes, perhaps."

"And they're very strong on young Leeming."

"Yes. A funny assortment, that."

"Do you think la belle Valerie may be currently favouring young Leeming?"

"Leeming perhaps, though he's a pallid boy. Perhaps the poet."

"The poet?"

"He has all the qualities. He's distinguished and he's sexually silly."

"But you can't judge him in terms of Sadie's soirée."

"Yes I can. You, drunk, would never reconnoitre up ladies' thighs. You'd insult everyone, but your hands wouldn't stray."

Talk of thighs and straying hands did little for his self-control. "Anyway," he told her in haste, "the poet's only been here since yesterday."

"Of course."

She sneezed, and dropped some bottled beauty aid in the sink.

"Ella," he said. "I'm well again."

"Then I am too." But she sounded tired. "Alec?"

"Yes."

"I get angry because I don't want to lose you to this unbelievable thing. I get angry to think of the possibility. I won't tolerate this . . . decomposition. In fact, I can't tolerate it."

He turned the taps off and asked for his towel. Ella passed it to him without violating the modesty of the drawn curtain. "I'm sorry, Alec. It will all happen again though."

"No. It's the way you said. The best thing, Leeming turning up."

"Turning up?" she questioned, as if she didn't herself think of Leeming in active terms. "Being found. In either case I don't know what dangers are involved for us. I never do. All I know is that dangers there are, enough to do for us, Alec."

"No, it's the solution. But you must accept the solution in my terms."

"What do you mean?"

"Would you mind if I left this university?"

"For another?"

"I fear not."

"To retire?"

"Not in the azalea-growing sense. I can think of two or three journals I could review books for. Even a daily paper. I could lecture for the W.E.A. I could even teach in a school."

"Today's youth?"

"I'd rein the little bastards in. Well?"

She said flatly, "Whatever you like."

He heard the bathroom chair pulled out from beneath the towel rack and the moan she made in sitting. At length she said, "Two days ago you were hysterical. Now you're happy as a young buck. None of it's any good. It all comes from the one central lunacy."

"Oh no." He came out dressed in a towel and stood above her. "Has this old, old trouble ever manifested itself before in *happiness*? You don't need for me to be director of Extension, do you?"

So endearingly and provokingly young he seemed then to Ella that she laid her head against his towel-girt belly. She meant to signify that she had despaired, but wistfully.

"Before I knew you," she told him, "I used to be always meeting boys who because of a dream or a chemical shift in the blood would assure you their lives were changed, that they'd beaten themselves, that they were fated to manipulate lesser men, to become moral giants or mystics or extend the limits of the novel. Over beer, in town, at the Imperial, they'd tell you these things. Prior to stumbling out the back. You remind me of them."

They argued this point for ten more minutes with rare sanity, until even Ella began to hope that he might have become substantially less vulnerable. There were things he could utter now, he said, things he could remember, that he had not been able to utter or remember before, but he mustn't keep her from her freshers. He assured her that he would not lose his power to articulate them.

For the sake of being punctual they broke off some likely love-skirmishing. The young, he said, the eager youths she would advise all afternoon, deserved a sight of her cowled shift.

They could even speak of Belle Leeming and the likelihood of her coming to the university; and, clinically, of Ramsey's forty-year-old adultery. She asked could news of it, one quaint way or another, arise out of Leeming's emergence. There was a list of names that Dr Lloyd had had. What had become of that? Alec said he didn't know, but that a list of names was merely a list of names and had no meaning in itself.

He explained how what he feared was the reappearance itself. The eroded deity that dwelt in Ramsey's consciousness was a force of irony that would bring ironic consummations to his life. He supposed that the modern equivalent of being "saved" (in the sense the term had once been used in the Drummoyne Manse) might well be to see and accept this one pattern of which a life was capable, a pattern of irony. This completed, a man was at last his own man; but he could not then sit at the same desk as before.

"Well," Ella told him, "to presume so completely that Leeming will be found and base your future on it . . . that's insane." Yet they both knew that she was willing to compromise and accept this less virulent madness.

So he was hopeful and cubbish. She must shake her dislodged breasts back into their buckrammed cups and insist on going. From the door she said wryly, "Perhaps if I didn't ask questions there'd be time for you to say those unutterables you mentioned." She could see that he was still frightened by them.

"Not now, Ella."

She made a chirping cynical noise. "I'll give you odds, Ramsey, that after all this secrecy and posturing I won't even be shocked."

Seven years before, in the summer of 1956, Ella had—in that quaint term implying inadvertence—fallen pregnant. She began to bleed dangerously, as often as once a week, from the time her state was confirmed by a doctor. There was never any soothing her when she found herself bloody. Ramsey stood in the hallway calling comfort to her while she evaded all his clichés of hope and cleansed herself in private. It was her grief as much as her sluicings that were too intimate for him to intrude upon.

The rate of bleeding increased, yet the embryo continued to develop. Fearing a monster, Ramsey began to insinuate the idea of abortion. In view of her long sterility, Ella saw such talk as a betrayal.

At five months, the doctor could hear a heart-beat, but bleeding went on. Ramsey was told that whatever frantic hopes Ella held the child could not be born healthy and would probably come before its time. The doctor suggested a city hospital. In the seventh month, in a vast baby-farm of a hospital, the child died in the womb and was released by Caesarean section.

Ella did not mourn the loss in any accepted sense of the word; she was gay at visiting times. Yet it was the end of her youth. She had, until that time, worked at a career in the history department, gathered material for a doctoral thesis, been stung by ideas, and otherwise favoured the illusion that the future was without limit. Now she saw the apparent but specious infinitude of her mind narrowed down—to one dreary lumber yard of cut-rate ideas—by the very excesses of enthusiasm she had committed when young.

Her primitive nature rejected the idea of adoption. This she thought of as redressing the balance of her own barrenness by calling in someone else's fertility. It was futile to tell her that within a few days the child would seem as if born of her, that to ensure it was fed it would ingratiate itself frantically. Ella might well have had a doctorate planned, but her pride and shame were as basic as those of a tribal woman cursed with a dead womb.

Ramsey already felt that he provided only the poorest vistas, yet Ella persisted in even more intense hopes of possessing him as her universe, her race, her tribe, her brood.

Stepping at that time from a Castlereagh Street boutique with a present for her, Ramsey was struck on the ham by an electrician scuttling into a café, swinging the compartmentalized tool-tray that had done the damage. The electrician turned his small eroded face back to Ramsey. Ramsey found it at least evocative.

"Hey, it's Alec Ramsey."

"That's right." Alec strained after the name. "Steve. Steve?"

"Steve," the little man admitted. "I was base electrician, remember? Used to help you fillet the seals. Real cordon bleu job. Me? The place finished me. Ain't over it yet. Ulcer, see." He whispered. "Not enough tart. You know. I need tart. Regular. I did then, anyway."

"You don't look past the need yet."

"God, I'm not neither. But that place . . . I get night-mares about it."

"Not many of us left to have nightmares, Steve."

While Ramsey chatted with the dyspeptic little elec-trician he wondered what Steve was doing, hustling over Sydney's rabid pavements to fix fuses in Greek cafés and Magyar coffee houses. Didn't someone in Canberra know he was an historic relic, one of Leeming's last men?

"How's Dr Lloyd?" Steve asked Ramsey.

"I think he's well."

A fretful young Greek came to the street end of the café's counter. "Ey, we got today's holl milk goan bad."

"O.K. Adonis, keep your feathers on."

"Thas awright about feathers. We lose the business while you chatter-chatter."

"Who do you think you are? Bloody Onassis?" And to Ramsey: "Didn't you know about Dr Lloyd? No? He's full of cancer, poor old bugger." He enjoyed being able to alarm Ramsey with Lloyd's fatal state. He would have been disappointed to have been limited to saying that Lloyd was merely half full of cancer. "They opened him, but there wasn't anything left untouched. So they sewed him up again and sent him away to die of it. I thought he'd just been sick, you know, and he used to do the wife's eyes and hardly charge us anything. So I sent him a get-well card, not knowing. And I got this toffee-nosed letter back from some junior bint in his family, Mrs Sherwin-Lloyd, saying it was feared Dr Lloyd wouldn't recover, so they hadn't given him the card. But I don't think the old Arthur would've minded, do you? I mean, he was never morbid."

Not knowing he had said it, "I must go and see him," Alec said. At wide intervals over thirty years he and Lloyd had made what would be called conversation, but there had always been an undefined urgency in Ramsey to speak bluntly and at length. It was a demand that had been, up to now, always postponable. But he and Lloyd had been fused by the very fact of survival, and would ultimately, like two spouses, have to speak the truth profoundly.

He telephoned Lloyd's house at Rose Bay and explained to the woman who answered why he had some right to visit the death-bed. She went away. At the end of the crackling line came the peculiar resonant silence of Dr Lloyd's big house of stone. The woman returned, sounding unwilling in saying that Dr Lloyd cared to see Ramsey, but giving all manner of reminders about the man's weak state. Ramsey would need the reminders more than, making faces in the phone-booth, he imagined.

On the street he was struck by a distaste and lassitude at the thought of seeing Lloyd again, and of seeing him dying practically, ruggedly. So he kept missing taxis and it took a sly one, nosing along the curb for victims, to catch him.

A desultory woman who called herself Mrs Sherwin-Lloyd met Ramsey at the door and left him in the vestibule for ten minutes. She returned with a middle-aged nun of some obscure order whose entire work was the nursing of terminal cases. Then she led Ramsey back upstairs.

The room was shaded by holland blinds drawn to knee-height. Two parallelograms of light nuzzled in under the blinds and reached for Lloyd's big, grey hand. False sweet smells, the sort that come from cans, overlaid the stink of the alien organism that owned Lloyd now.

Ramsey had seen Lloyd rarely enough since 1926. He remembered a man as tall as but broader than himself and who, bearded from the South, resembled Tsar Nicholas II.

This sunken face was a parody of that one, though the eyes seemed still vainly addicted to survival.

"Here you are, father," Mrs Sherwin-Lloyd said, and left.

"Alec," Lloyd uttered with a real warmth and raised two fingers of one hand off the bed.

"Arthur." Ramsey shook the two fingers.

"I'm sorry if I smell," Lloyd said because he meant it, not because he was trying to play the marvellously brave old patient. "These synthetic perfumes are no damn good. I asked Sister Antoine to bring along some of the incense her people burn in their ceremonies. She thinks I'm pulling her leg. I tell her I've never been anywhere near a nun's leg. She laughs. She's a good sport, that Sister Antoine."

There was actually a copy of the *Australian Medical Journal* open on the bedside table. The page said, "Medicinal Control of Pterygia: a New Treatment". Ramsey was disconcerted into privately acclaiming the bravery of keeping up on pterygia when you would never see another one.

Lloyd's breathing came hard but the speech very clear. He was weak, but his concentration did not waver. Ramsey hoped to God that he was not so excessively valiant as to refuse pain-killers.

"Are you in much pain, Arthur?" he asked straight.

"A little. I don't get my morphine until five. But it scarcely makes me drowsy now. Never mind. I'd rather go out in mid-sentence."

It was true that the doctor seemed moribund, but very toughly so, and Ramsey resisted admiring him, remembering that the toughness was of the man's fibre and went hand-in-hand with less likeable insensitivities. Lloyd demonstrated the major one immediately, by asking with his all-boys-together brand of malice, "Seen old Belle Leeming?"

"I'm afraid very little."

"Yes. All the sting went out of knowing Belle, didn't it?" There was an element left of the hard, intolerable mockery of Ramsey and himself that may have been the blunt man's way of expiating. But the mockery faded quickly. "I'll tell you what, though. We haven't seen nearly enough of each other, Alec."

"That's right, we haven't."

"Of course, you felt under an obligation to me. That was bloody ridiculous."

"I suppose it was." He didn't want to hurt the dying man, but suggested, "We weren't the best of friends in 'twenty-six."

"But that was Antarctica, Alec."

"Maybe, but I don't think Antarctica is a substantial state of existence on its own, as Leeming used to seem to think."

"Do you really think I ever gave a damn for that sort of poetic balls? We should have seen more of each other, that's all."

Then Lloyd had a spasm. You could see how nearly dead he was by the feebleness of the head that wished to strain back into the pillows but lacked the strength. Like something wrung, the face shed gobs of sweat. Ramsey looked about for a bell, and thought of going to the top of the stairs to call that good sport, Sister Antoine. He was halfway to the door when he heard a loud snort of release. Lloyd was better, taking whooping mouthfuls of breath.

"Shall I call someone, Arthur? I hope I didn't cause that."

"Don't be silly," Lloyd told him in a reduced voice. "Funny thing, this cancer. I don't think they'll ever find a cure for it. A special cancer, all his own, for each man."

"You're probably right."

"I am. There's something very much like a compulsion

about the way man goes on growing these dirty things. What did you think of my garden?"

"It's a garden to be proud of."

Lloyd was occupied with getting breath for some seconds, but Ramsey could tell he wanted to speak, and so waited for him.

Then Lloyd said, "You don't have to talk as if you're humouring me. I won't act up if you didn't like the gardenias."

"I thought the gardenias were fine."

"That's what I mean. You only want to tell nice lies. The bloody gardenias aren't even in bloom."

In fact Ramsey had become inattentive through anxiety. He had come to test his own uneasy memory against Lloyd's apparently commonsense one; Lloyd was the one point of reference. But how could Ramsey begin to use him for reference in the midst of all this talk of gardenias and smells? And even if an opportunity came, Ramsey would fear it. For one could beg off any apparent facts cast up by an infected memory, but there would be no begging off Lloyd's sanely offered reminiscences.

Not that Ramsey even had, at the time he came into Leeming's death-room, any coherent fears.

Meanwhile, Lloyd seemed to be growing paler. Soon crisp little Mrs Sherwin-Lloyd would come and decree that they had spoken enough. Now they chatted on for two or three minutes, with intervals of hard breathing. Ramsey felt alarmed when Lloyd said without warning, "But I guarantee you came just to talk about Leeming."

Ramsey admitted it.

"What about Leeming?"

"I don't know. I thought there might be something you wanted to say."

"I suppose you think I shouldn't be leaving you in this situation. I mean, leaving you to your own silly judgment."

Ramsey's feet went cold; it all sounded like something from a familiar and compulsive dream. He said, "That's a dramatic way to put it."

"You've got a taste for drama, Alec. But Antarctica was in real terms. So will the Judgment be."

"The Judgment. I wish I believed in the Judgment, capital J."

"The very one I'm talking about. It must happen, Alec, otherwise the Mrs Sherwin-Lloyds of this world would prevail over the Sister Antoines. And in a world where quite a few sensible things happen, that would be against all good sense."

"You're probably right," Ramsey supposed, falling silent. He could not help allowing the onus of talk to fall on the breathless man.

In any case, Lloyd had much more advice. "Men are judged on a real basis, not on a poetic one, Alec. You see, God hasn't read that literary rubbish you have. You can bet your bottom dollar the Judge is nothing like you. My advice is, forget Leeming. I'm dying, Alec, yet he doesn't preoccupy me."

Alec nodded at every sentence as if it was all a help. It certainly cost Lloyd an excess of pain. Ashamed, he scarcely heard Lloyd say, "Accept it that Leeming was virtually dead when we left him."

The sense of the sentence occurred to him slowly, and even then it was merely a crystallization of his dreams, a crystalline formula for thirty years of unshapen moiling.

He said quietly, "You said . . . *virtually* dead?"

"Dead in any real sense. Deader than me, and I'm not even my own man any more. The crab owns me."

"But *virtually* dead?"

"I'm saying it explicitly, damn it all. Not for my sake. I don't need it said."

"What is it you don't need said?"

Arthur Lloyd did his best to be patient, though there was a hint of the spasm again. A knock on the door proved to be Sister Antoine, saying that it was time he rested. Indeed he was plainly tired and probably in pain, but said he wanted five minutes. Sister Antoine looked regretfully at Ramsey, and obeyed. It occurred to Ramsey that Mrs Sherwin-Lloyd probably made life hot for Sister Antoine.

Lloyd's pajama'd shoulders were quivering imperceptibly in the bed, a casting-off of what he thought was Ramsey's unwillingness to talk turkey after so many years.

Too loudly for a death-room, Alec called out, "You mean he wasn't dead when we left him?"

Lloyd told him dryly, "You're looking me over to see what are the possibilities of a death-bed confession. By me, I mean; prejudicial to you. Well, there's no need to fear that."

Alec was angry at this suspicion. "Are you planting a joke on me, Dr Lloyd?"

"All right, Alec. I was the surgeon. My responsibility." Lloyd gave an impression of nursing his strength now that Ramsey had gone hysterical. The eye doctor had that wisdom for knowing one's limits which is essential for journeyers. Meanwhile, Ramsey kept telling himself, "At least I'm innocent of that abandonment." Yet he felt forced to admit his certainty: he had known, and had let an argument that Lloyd was the surgeon and Lloyd's the responsibility, excuse him from finding Leeming alive. He could remember the massive gratitude swelling in him at Leeming's death, and an unwillingness to look at the amply-wronged body. Whatever obsequies he had done had been done with face turned aside. But more compelling than his memory was the drift of his dreams, secrets carried in the blood.

Lloyd was honestly perplexed, there being indeed terrible

accusation for Ramsey in the perplexity of a dying man of action. "But Alec, you kept away from me for thirty years. Thirty years your eyes have been slewing off mine. On the morning itself I saw your eyes slew away." He gathered breath and further evidence. "You wouldn't let the head of the sleeping-bag be covered."

"And you would have?"

"No. Your zeal made any decision of mine on the matter unnecessary."

Ramsey's mind stretched out to re-interpret the facts. "You even rifled the body," he said brutally, referring to a sachet, containing a list of names, that Lloyd had taken from Leeming's throat.

The eye doctor murmured, "I took the poor man's halter off. If you don't believe me, you can go to hell." There was a pain and an anger in Lloyd that he could not afford to voice. It shocked Alec to think that perhaps the doctor had always been hurt when he avoided more than perfunctory meetings.

Ramsey was still priding himself uselessly on being free of the treachery. Though it might unbalance the dying man's conscience, he could not prevent himself from saying, "In Adelie Land, Mawson stayed by a dying friend for two days, feeding him food that couldn't be replaced."

Lloyd gave a small shrug that meant *different circumstances*. "Our man was past help, past pain. It would have been a silly piece of good manners to wait for his breath to give out."

Lloyd's invincible conscience chafed Ramsey. "Mawson's friend was *virtually* dead, but kept climbing out of his bag and convulsing."

"It didn't happen that way with Leeming."

It was invincible conscience, it was capable, it dealt in realism as Ramsey's could not. And what unedged Ramsey was that he knew it loved Leeming while his, Ramsey's, was directed to himself, to some destructive demand his own nature made on him.

This pattern had been set years before in a gale at about fifty-seven degrees south latitude. The stoke-hold of the *Westralis* began to flood, and the steam pump and the hand pumps seized for long periods. After twenty hours, water lay in the engine room. When this or that pump became operable, Leeming, classically enraged, would dare the thing to give out. The failure of pumps and the weather he took as personally offensive to him and as proof of their aim to make him ridiculous or uselessly dead. So Leeming worked up and down the octaves of his stoical hysteria by a hand pump on the port side where Ramsey himself spent part of the day, catching Leeming's tone, working in a fury, furiously accepting death and the spurious aggrandizement death offered. It did not occur to Ramsey, and may have ceased to occur to Leeming, that the pumps were not sibyls but worked on a vacuum using reparable parts fabricated by machine.

It had, however, occurred to Lloyd and the engineer, who had cut a hole in the engine-room bulkhead and climbed into the flooded pump shaft to remove the clods of oil and coal-dust that had done the choking. They went further, climbing in and out of the black stew, and cleared the suction roses and covered them with a hand-made mesh of wire.

Leeming and Lloyd became genuine friends that day, for Leeming had atoned for his mysteriousness by his hysteria while Lloyd had washed off, in the cold stink of the bilges, the aloofness he had shown, the clerkly business-letter brand of speech he had till then used with Leeming, when Leeming all along knew him to be a gay, honest, and profane man. So Leeming shook the doctor's hand emphatically. Whereas Ramsey was left high and dry with a skinful of irrelevant emotions.

There was a second soft tap on the door and Mrs Sherwin-Lloyd appeared.

"Really, father!" she said, but looked directly at Ramsey.

"I'm not finished," Lloyd told her, though in another sense it was precisely the way he looked. Mrs Sherwin-Lloyd made visibly, even ostentatiously, the decision to indulge his age and the hopelessness of his case.

"You must make it very quick, Mr Ramsey. You can see he's exhausted."

When she had gone, Lloyd made a wry mouth by which he meant that he would rout Mrs Sherwin-Lloyd except that his prospects made that futile. Ramsey himself moved to the head of the bed.

"Arthur. . . ?"

"I take the whole blame. Before God." Lloyd was fortunate, having no doubt that God was something to be argued with man-to-man. Ramsey sought the right hand and began to weep. At one period, from the age of fourteen to thirty-nine, he had never wept. Ella had more recently liberated him from the male fetish of dry eyes.

"I didn't know," Ramsey said. "Not about Leeming."

Lloyd seemed to believe that. "You're an innocent then. No wonder Mrs Leeming found you easy fodder."

"But you know I'm telling the truth."

"Ah yes." The word was ambiguous, but Ramsey had to be satisfied to get any word out of this body subsiding into the mattress. "It doesn't matter. I take full responsibility."

"I would never have left him."

"Not necessarily a virtue," Lloyd murmured without breath, his eyes closing.

Ramsey felt terrified; it seemed that his blood had got onto the secret of Leeming sleeping but not dead and had raced away accepting it; certainty was therefore deposited like alluvia in the pit of his stomach. He made a formal, even sentimental, good-bye.

Sister Antoine wondered what he had done with her patient. Mrs Sherwin-Lloyd was cold on the stairs.

"It is not too much to say," the minister ventured two weeks later, Arthur Lloyd's casket stately on the conveyor that would speed it into the furnace, "that Dr Arthur Lloyd was one of our very finest contemporaries, a man of wealth and accomplishments, yet of simple faith and kindness. These qualities combined to make of Arthur Lloyd a superb Australian."

Here the preacher, who hadn't taken the opportunity to know the superb Australian called Dr Lloyd while it lived, shuffled the biographical notes supplied by the family. "His name defines ice-bound Cape Lloyd in Antarctica. On that testing-ground of a continent he survived a perilous attempt on the South Geo-magnetic Pole from a base in Oaten Land."

Someone in the family needed to be more careful with his s's.

"He saw his leader, the gallant Leeming, die of complications from a stroke, and then, supporting another man . . ."

"Not worth naming," supplied Alec, *sotto voce*.

". . . won through to the sea and the rescue ship. This in a land where it is often easier to die than to live."

Funnily, this had been one of Lloyd's aphorisms in an argument he had had with Ramsey in the autumn of their survival.

"In this land, in which it is easier to live than to die, Dr Lloyd faced the necessity of death with the same positive courage with which, thirty years ago, he faced the arduous necessity of life."

The sentiment, unlike most occasional ones, was not

false. Ramsey remembered a four-day blizzard on the high plateau, some time before Leeming's stroke; the tent full of a chill clamminess, temperatures reaching up into the plusses; and all the ice they had accumulated in baggage and clothing, all the moist that had hung frozen and tolerable in their gear, their boots, the folds of the tent, melting and seeping through to their skin. Lloyd's answer to the swampiness of their existence was to be droll about it. The twice-daily shedding of socks, for example, was a chance for Lloyd to go all hearty and chat with his feet as if they were two of Rembrandt's less erogenous ladies caught bathing at Manly. It was a method that did a great deal for anyone who did not have an itch within to match the outer one. By the third day Alec's left hip was, from secret scratching, pink and raised in small violet-purple pustules; and he worried not so much at Lloyd's dogged slapstick as at the fact that Leeming didn't bind him to silence. As Lloyd himself said, there were certain tests. . . .

When Lloyd had gone from the tent for a few seconds, Leeming said to Ramsey, the thin head sticking up conspiratorially out of the baggage of polar clothing, "I know you find Lloyd's method of tolerating these conditions hard to . . . tolerate. But he's a good man. If you need proof of that, I don't. Might I just say that when Nansen wintered in Greenland he chose as his companion a Norwegian petty-officer who matched all the deficiencies of his own temperament. Who was practical where he was nebulous . . . not that Nansen *was* nebulous . . . who was blunt where he was artificial. In fact, the man came close to sending Nansen off his head. The point of the story I won't make explicit, except that I'm very pleased to have you, Ramsey, for reasons quite other than your strength and your ability with the sledge. But I am very pleased also to have Lloyd. I don't think I'd be well served by two Lloyds or two Ramseys, as you wouldn't be by two Leemings."

The point was that two Ramseys would not have survived while two Lloyds would have. Certainly Ramsey had had invigorating daydreams, himself become a man to be taken most seriously by Leeming, the man to whom his wife fell, and, after his initial anger, an equal and special friend.

At other times he innocently accepted that Belle had no other lovers, or that she had others from whom he would capture her, or that she would be rendered down to docility by his love. He believed he loved her, and once imagined Leeming painlessly dead, and himself the strong family friend taking the widow's troubles on himself. He dreamt sometimes that she was his woman whom he protected. At others the authentic Belle imposed herself across him. His thighs drew heat as if from hers. His troubled seed woke him.

These dreams were negatived by the mere fact that he never told Leeming about Belle and himself. The expedition *seemed* to be the reason. The overall impact of an expedition on the mind of an outsider is of a mystical unity and compactness of endeavour. But the fate of a leader is to face one banal detail after another. You could go to Leeming with your will to confess formed, and he would ask you, straightaway and with urgency, about sores on a given dog's flank, or shrinkage of a cork liner in some tin or other. How could Ramsey then say, "By the way, I've been meaning to tell you. . ."?

By this neglect, and by his dreams, he was not well set up to face Leeming's illness and death.

So Leeming was declared dead.

After his first collapse, Leeming lived six days. He was irascible, resisted being loaded onto the sledge like baggage, tried to march. Often they let him. They too were weary, Ramsey wearied for life. And Lloyd thought that to struggle with Leeming to make him accept passenger status on the sledge would be more dangerous to him than to let him march. Ramsey suffered from finding himself aggressive against the leader who shambled through those days, the sort of brute wreckage that makes you want both to succour and lash out with your fists. Ramsey could sense perversity in the dying man's stamina, and condemned himself for sensing it, whenever he ceased hating him totally.

He felt liberated on the man's second and lethal collapse.

It was the end of March, 1926.

They were on fairly open ice with ridges running west-east. This counted as a good travelling surface: in fact, someone had surveyed the glacier earlier in the summer and recommended it as such.

Ramsey had loaded the tank on the sledge while the polar wigwam still stood upright, and had to work pieces of cooker and Lloyd's and his own sleeping-bags and the provision box up the funnel-entrance to the outside. He worked in this overdone way so that he could find it easier to build up a good head of resentment against Lloyd.

The canvas box they called the tank was frozen and the tank strap no more pliable than, say, a medium-tensile metal.

There was a terrible flesh-eating wind and he began and kept on whimpering for his fingers in useless inner gloves. The drift was beside the point, since they had to travel.

Without cease he swore against Lloyd.

The reason was that Lloyd was a doctor and had the, for the moment, soft work of attending Leeming inside and nodding over Leeming's feet. These had become especially liable to frostbite since Leeming took his first stroke.

Lloyd was competent, and called the strokes cerebral vascular accidents. Ramsey told himself that Lloyd used these terms to give a technical grandeur to his reasons for not strapping up the tank.

When he had packed, he wormed back under canvas, full of bad weather news.

"There," he intended to say and show Lloyd his mitts. "Freezing up already."

Lloyd was toggling Leeming's sleeping-bag at the neck and face. Ramsey could see through for a second to the face within. It was livid and elsewhere canvas-coloured. Shredded skin hung from the lips like a moustache.

He asked if the man had moved. Lloyd said he had died. Lloyd seemed self-disgusted, as if his lack of skill had brought on the death. He was, in fact, an expert physician.

Ramsey's scalding hands engrossed him. Therefore he postponed any grief. It would have been better, he could remember thinking, if he had had time to speak to Leeming about his wife. And he had a woolly sense that Lloyd was wrapping up a wronged body. He felt that to be sure he ought to listen to Leeming's heart, but that meant a job of untying and untoggling and un-press-studding Leeming's clothing—the zip-fastener era had not dawned—and he was still bending over his hands, which were stuck into his clothes against his Jaeger fleece, returning to life and to their million daily pains that were all to do with chafing and split skin.

He was afraid besides that he might find the heart had begun beating again—and then they would have had to put up with his shambling again and waste food on him.

They removed the tent from him and folded it—it took forcing, and went together like a metal concertina. Ramsey thought Leeming looked hateful. Exposed like that in his grey sleeping-bag, he looked like some animal's hateful excreta.

Lloyd said they mustn't waste strength by the body. But he ran through some of the service for the dead—he'd learned it in France and knew it was the acceptable thing at such a time, as one sends cards at Christmas.

Then he went to the sledge and stood stiffly looking east, where, the maps had it, was the ice-tongue and the sound still ice-free (perhaps) and the *Westralis*. If the *Westralis* had not been there they would have made a hole in the ice and lived off seal-meat. And Ramsey would easily have gone mad.

He found he could not leave Leeming straightaway. Though he avoided looking at him, he put some markers at his head.

Lloyd was patient. He said nothing at all that day that could be remembered.

But at night in the tent he took out a small leather sachet and let it fall in front of Ramsey's face as if he would immediately find significance in it. He didn't. Lloyd said, "My God, aren't you just an innocent? Did you ever speak to him about Belle?"

Ramsey felt sick: he hadn't known Lloyd was privy to the fact of Belle and himself. He had to say no, he hadn't spoken to him. Lloyd stared at him and he stared back, warning the man to keep those eyes of superior morality off him. Lloyd had a wealth of the sort of virtues that have social value. While Ramsey hated him he was also encouraged about their chances because of Lloyd's straightforward moral anger of the moment.

Lloyd took a wad of paper from the sachet. It was rolled tight. He unwrapped it for Ramsey.

The paper began with a quotation from St Paul, the one about lest St Paul consider himself exalted by the abundance of revelations, a thorn was given him in the flesh, and so on. Belle had speciously used this text and put beneath it a name list, a who's-who nearly, except that Ramsey was included. And Lloyd. There were politicians and writers and others—Ramsey felt first sick, then hollow, then brimmed with revulsion.

Lloyd said it wasn't right of her to send her husband that

sort of bloody thing and it was beneath Leeming to wear it. He said this was the greatest wrong, as if the two of them there had practised many wrongs on Leeming but couldn't match Belle. For a second he wanted blood and attacked the interests Ramsey and Leeming had shared. But he instantly returned to sense and the question of survival. While Ramsey thought of Leeming's perverse endurance and suspected that the husband had, too late, decided to settle accounts, Lloyd spoke of the same suspicion. "He travelled with me and he travelled with you, with both our names round his neck. Makes you wonder whether he wanted to travel or was making a bloody pilgrimage." He reminded Ramsey that he'd said once there were certain tests a man had to pass before he was considered a man in his, Lloyd's, book.

Ramsey said yes, he recalled that.

Lloyd told him, "Well, that bastard hardly passed any of them."

Ramsey had no idea what his own intentions were at the time, whether to live or die. He was, above all, tired. Books and ideas would never have for him the same bouquet. He wanted to protect his hands and feet. Lloyd's bullying brought him home.

As the burying parson was to say, Lloyd's bullying was a great gift.

When the undertaker's men came forward from the aisle to strip the casket of its florals—including a band of lilies inscribed, "To the memory of Arthur Lloyd, who led me to the ship, Antarctica, March 1926"—Ramsey felt the claustrophobia of the corpse, and was unable to stay.

Once outside, he smoked, as if for antiseptic reasons, what was for him a rare cigarette, while the fumes of Arthur Lloyd scudded south from an imitation belltower chimney.

The parallel between the ice's possession of Leeming and

the fire's of Lloyd made him whimsical, but also brought to a point the numbness of a funeral earlier that month, when his child had been buried.

Mourners began to emerge, signifying a swift end to matters involving the late Dr Lloyd. Arthur Lloyd's son sought out and cut off Ramsey's line of departure to tell him how touched they all were by what had been written on Ramsey's tribute.

Ella quickly became his woman again. It was Ramsey's attempts at tenderness that were characterized by wavering followed by a hedonist roughness by which he meant to emphasize that although he thought himself less than a man, she was none the less his.

Ella read another meaning into Ramsey's harsh physicality: in losing her child she had been diminished in his eyes to merely one other woman; all purpose in their mating had been abridged. His new fierceness took her into areas of sensuality she had always coveted; yet she woke in the middle of nights feeling scarified by the gymnastics of excess.

By the light of day, Ramsey lacked force, postponed staff meetings, failed to fetch an electrician for two weeks after the water-heater broke down (thus questioning the right of his body to warm water), ceased to read, wallowed in cryptic crosswords in the small hours. He let loose his previously well-controlled talent for fecklessness, mislaying documents, breaking most of the rules by which the records were kept straight. Letters from every State begged to draw his attention to proposals that had been made by neglected letters two months before. Since order was an image of a moral rightness he could not pretend to, his desk became a documentary abattoirs.

Again Ella reacted to his decline and withdrawal as if they were reproaches on her barrenness. Ramsey tried to placate both Ella and Leeming's ghost by sketching his unworthiness in abstract terms—calling himself talentless, treacherous, slothful. But nothing could be expiated or fended off in those terms. On her parallel line, Ella became so insistent on the question of barrenness that when he was driven past endurance, it was the first stick he took up to beat her with. Which all the more convinced her of his contempt.

Within four months he was sicker than he would be again until the poet told him of the Antarctic findings. While Ella hastened to misjudge the cause, his colleagues rushed to excuse him on the grounds of his stillborn. Cornered by doctors and the visits of his wife, he threw them at last the news of his historically real adultery with Belle Leeming. Both Ella and the doctors were variously enriched by the confession; and, the doctors in particular, diverted by the neatness of the pattern made by Calvinism, Belle, and the dead child, ceased to press him for worse news, news of deeper than mere historic strength, news of Leeming left sleeping.

On play night they ate a fast dinner together. Ella did not trouble him about his hint of further admissions concerning Leeming. Even if she had not had a taste for the tranquillity of the moment, she believed that all she could possibly be given would be some new face of his abiding hysteria.

Meanwhile, Alec thought of what he had to say as *deep* truth; but it was at last accessible to his tongue. There was no need to gabble it out. So they both felt a frail gaiety when the Union Theatre, beleaguered by undergraduates, loomed through their windscreens.

Ramsey found that the evil aspect of meeting Pelham when he was feeling well was that he felt twice as guilty for what seemed unnecessary burdens he was putting on the boy. Pelham greeted them in the foyer; there was certainly a brand of tolerant resentment in him now. He said, with a seeming lack of purpose that probably meant he was testing Alec, "I wondered whether you wanted to meet the cast."

They made for the side door. Ella whispered to Ramsey behind Pelham's gratified back, "We can show the Kables how well we persist in being."

Yet what had they against the Kables except a tidy revulsion over Valerie's sexual nomadism, and Eric's behaviour at a university dinner a year ago when, tipsy in Valerie's absence, he had called on Ramsey to resign? The outcry had eaten into Ramsey at the time. But hadn't it since given Ella and Alec many an hour of delightful antipathy to Mr and Mrs Kable?

Professionally speaking, Eric Kable was an unflinching worker graced with wide interests and even (Ramsey would have denied it if he could) sound literary taste. Why should he feel as passionately as he did that Kable should not succeed to the directorate he himself had ceased to care about? Kable would sharpen up the office; the names of Pinter and Modigliani would thrive in the living-rooms of distant farms, together with a thorough understanding of the future for self-government in West Irian.

But he sidestepped the demands his reason was making on his prejudices. He told himself that in the hierarchy of his present mind Pelham was a son of light, Kable a yokel. There was no arguing it; a man as harassed as he had been could not afford to tire himself arguing the ground plan of his mind.

They found, in any case, that Kable wasn't available for baiting. Beyond the props table, he sat (a little pink in the face and wearing a cravat) on a stool before a battery of dimmers. He called to someone on stage, "Number-seven has to be put straight onto three-quarter power then." A man of wide interests, polishing up his lighting plan. His concern for number-seven rheostat convicted the Ramseys of their own pettiness. But Pelham firmly led them on.

In two bunker-like rooms at the back of the stage, Athens lords and ladies and diverse supernatural agencies were nearly dressed for their play.

"Have you met the gentlemen of the cast?" Pelham asked the Ramseys formally. The gentlemen responded by swinging away from their mirrors to front on the visitors. Their faces shone with a more than cosmetic radiance, these men who had taken their annual holidays to come to the drama seminar and act in a kinky performance of Shakespeare. Ramsey felt reverent before the staying-power of their zeal. Since his own range of enthusiasms had been intimidated out of existence, he could no longer understand the ardours of the very people on whom his department relied for its being.

Ella, a traditionalist, called out, "But the costuming!"

A boy with a pitted face said votively, "Yes, nothing conventional. That's why it's such a privilege to work under Tim."

Puck wore tight pants of tangerine, a paisley shirt, polaroids, a septic-looking beard. He did not seem especially credible as one who could put a girdle round the earth in forty seconds; but a stagily large hypodermic on his dressing-table seemed to imply that anything might be possible on lysergic acid. Next to him Oberon fondled a ten-gallon hat and filled out a tuxedo and sequin-studded cowboy boots. The Athenian lords were dressed in dinner suits, the Athenian workmen in khaki shorts, blue singlets, sweaty-brimmed hats.

Ramsey felt exhilarated by all of them, and humbled as well. They proved that, however he neglected his department, someone he'd never met would be going to the trouble of being thorough and invigorating and zanily original with the material at hand. He wouldn't hesitate to bet that they even knew their lines.

Then he saw that nearest the door was a vacant place, and on the make-up table a heap of three books. The top one said *Ice Motion—Its Constants and Variables*. Ramsey, waiting on Leeming's re-emergence now as on a liberation, had forgotten how liable he was to that same touchiness that had ruined an evening with the Pinalba Rotarians some months before. His best social grin strained as he bent to find the titles of the other two books. The second, opened at the graph of an ice-grid, was *The United States Ice Physics Manual*, the third *Antarctic Glaciation*.

For a second Ramsey's face tended into lines of mad affront; for it seemed that this roomful of men dressed for a high form of practical joke against the cash-paying customers had been encouraged by dear Tim's flippancy to make a fool of him, Ramsey. Yet after a second, sanity asserted itself physically, with an almost muscular sensation in his chest. So he smiled in time and remarked, "Someone studious missing?"

"That's Denis Leeming," Oberon told him, and went on perfecting the dents in his Stetson. "I believe he's down the corridor."

The concept of young Leeming boning up on his uncle's physical environment revolted him. Pelham and Ella wished the cast success and began to leave, Ella still easeful, unaware that Ramsey had had his surprise.

Outside, near the ladies' dressing-room, they found a phantasmagoric Mrs Kable, apparelled to within a millimetre of her life. A jaguar-coloured leotard defined her lower limbs; a silken cummerbund held her waist. A white shirt with bell sleeves combined to further the erotic image, which was perfected by a pith-helmet and a stockwhip held in the hands.

Morris Pelham winked sombrely at Ramsey; Ella made choking sounds and pleaded her sinuses. Valerie loomed towards them as if she had been waiting there for no one else. They praised her costume, and she performed for them one fairy-twirl. Alec knew that young men in the audience would lie awake tonight thinking of the brashly sweet concordance of her hips and belly as shown off by those jaguar pants.

"Oh, Alec," she said, "could you keep an eye out for

Denis? He's running about in a state of acute excitement bordering on lunacy."

Her concern for Leeming seemed uncoloured, something more valid than a mere preparation for scoring off people. Even the words "acute excitement bordering on lunacy" were a surrender of extensive information to the enemy, and therefore a gauge of her uneasiness. Ramsey concluded again that there was an affair at the basis of her concern. "You see, the aunt is here. Mrs Leeming."

Ramsey knew that Belle might be coming to the table-land, but had not told Ella. Now she searched his face for the hazards the news raised, while Alec choked an instant on the maniac resentment he had not felt for the Kables that morning, when their news-carrying had had an edge to it.

"Here in the town?" he asked lightly; but the likelihood of Belle's nearness did give him a squeamish feeling of being encompassed.

Titania pulled a face that gave her a frazzled look. "She's even staying in Denis's flat at Parker College. Of course, he must put her up. . . ."

Ella and Ramsey and perhaps even Pelham thought, "Ah-ha. One sports arena eliminated." How ironic that Mrs Leeming, a wide-range lover (on quite subtle grounds) of past decades, should now be curtailing Valerie Kable in her bloom.

At this point the much-bruited Tim came hustling down the corridor, calling crisply, "Good luck Valerie. Seen him?"

Mrs Kable let her respect for art-on-legs, and her sense of having touched the golden bough with a small hoist from this man, generate a gush of special laughter. She intoned, "Bless you, Tim!" as huskily as Bacall. "We're still looking for him," and when he had gone, reverted instantly to the banal Ramseys and that quaint Englishman, Pelham.

140

"I wouldn't worry," Pelham said.

"I don't want to pester Tim, but the truth is Denis isn't to be found. Eric has been hunting for him, but he isn't anywhere here, front or back, and he isn't with his aunt. And the fact is, he's in this lyric state of excitement . . . well, we simply wonder where he could have got to."

Lightly teasing, Ella said she had never known anyone to come to harm in a lyric state of excitement. Perhaps she was taking revenge on Valerie for changing her evidence thus after beginning with "a state of acute excitement bordering on lunacy".

"I can't leave here," Valerie went on, bound by her own ingenuousness to fail to notice the malice of others, "but I wonder if you'd tell Eric to come and see me if he's still at the lights. And if you should happen to see Denis. . . . I don't know what sort of performance we can expect from him tonight, after all this unrest."

Ramsey knew he should not ask, but failed to curb himself. "What exactly is the cause of all this hithering and thithering?"

"He may be going to Antarctica," she whispered, eyeing the corridor up and down for eavesdroppers. "Just for a few weeks. All to do with arrangements for the uncle. If you could do the small favour of looking out for him. I know it's presumptuous of me to requisition the director of the department and his wife and a senior lecturer. . . ."

No, they said, it gave them pleasure. But first they must give their best wishes to the ladies.

It had been hot in the quick forge of backstage, so they took a breath of the fresh evening on their way back to the front of the theatre. Pelham and Ramsey smoked, Ella stood breathing the unstressed night. Pelham was friendly again, and a good friend.

Ella proposed a stroll, since they had seven minutes plus

any delay that Leeming might be able to cause. There was an undertone of urgency in Ramsey—to meet Belle Leeming if she must be met. But his urgencies did not compel him any more; or so he hoped, commencing to saunter under the cool of the trees.

He said, "Morris, there's no need for you to say a word when I tell you that I intend to resign. Ella already knows."

Won over thoroughly, Pelham said he regretted it. Alec shoved such valedictions away from him with both hands and, checking on Ella, found her face peaked but acquiescent in the moonlight.

"You shouldn't look on this as a formal declaration but as a nod good—or so I hope—as a wink. At one stage I saw myself lasting until you got your doctorate, but you say that won't be for a year yet. You see, I wanted you—and not certain persons unnamed—to take my place. I shall certainly make it clear to the vice-chancellor that you're my choice, but I shan't have a formal choice, you see. It's up to the selection committee, some of whom will think well of a man considerably senior to you. Again, no names."

"But he has a formal connection with someone in panther's pants?" Pelham suggested, sounding dour and rueful in the authentic Yorkshire tradition. Ella and Ramsey laughed frugally, for Ramsey was playing with Pelham's career and Morris could not, at his age, consummate the ironic patterns of his life by retiring.

"There's an assistant directorship vacant in Queensland, so they tell me. If you looked like being passed over here ——"

"I won't work under Kable." Pelham said it with fervour and with a margin of censure in Ramsey's direction. "I couldn't take all that bedroom politics buggering up the works."

"Morris, I hope you'll treat this as confidential."

"And as far from irrevocable," Ella, who had been so understanding, still felt forced to add.

Perhaps this waiver was lost on Pelham, though, for he began to point to a form below them on a hip of lawn beyond which stood the gallows shape of the stage put together for the graduation ceremony which would be held . . . "Christ!" Ramsey said below his breath, "tomorrow." Meanwhile, there was certainly the outline of a well-clad male lying athwart the curve of the bank. He seemed to have taken up the primary position for relaxation as suggested by yogis or women in black tights from the Workers' Educational. Perhaps he had been neatly spread-eagled, no less. Eric Kable, wronged once too often, pays off his wife's lover with . . . possibly a sandbag from backstage. So, at one bound, Eric gets life and Pelham gets promotion without having to resort to Queensland.

In the spirit of this whimsy rather than from any certainty, Alec said, "I think it's Leeming."

It took a young man, Pelham, to walk down such a slope. There was no movement in the shape until Pelham was practically on it, when it rolled on its back, making such an abrupt change from slackness to control that Ella yelped.

"Good night . . . who is it? . . . *good night*, Morris," it said.

"Good night, Denis." Even Pelham had caught the national tradition: first names to the very death. "Are you well?"

"Oh, yes." Leeming got to his feet. He too wore dinner-suit as an Athenian gentleman should. "I fell asleep."

"You're lucky we didn't have a love philtre handy," Ramsey called to him.

Ramsey could see the scholarly Leeming face transmuted onto the skull of a very different man from uncle Stephen. The line of the mouth looked particularly long when broken up by Denis Leeming's abiding sense of being threatened by lesser men.

Ella explained how he had been missed by Mrs Kable, and the four of them turned back to the theatre together. Young Leeming seemed a little chagrined by Valerie Kable's motherly fussing.

"I felt I might have trouble with lines unless I could get away for a good bout of concentration. As you know, there are bigger things afoot in our family now than amateur dramatics."

"Now then!" Pelham contended. "The Extension Department has gone to expense to see that they're more than amateur."

"Just the same," Ella conceded, "you must be considerably disturbed."

Leeming ignored the censure and the appeasement. He chatted copiously about himself, seeming proud of his ability to fall asleep at curtain time while beset by aunt, uncle, and Mrs Kable's overstated concern. "I took up the turtle position and lay there forcing everything from my mind. You see Arabs in the Levant do this—it sometimes stands them in stead of hours of sleep. Hess used to do it too—you know, the German leader who made that inexplicable flight to Scotland in 1940 to offer peace terms? He was a remarkable man, even though a Nazi. He could still handle a fighter plane at the age of forty-five."

"Hope yet, Alec," Ella said while Leeming harangued on like a man under pep drugs. The reports of his enemies said he always conversed this way.

"I had a Chinese friend in England who was given hell by his college tutor. When this uncouth Welshman had my friend properly riled, my friend would simply join his thumb and second finger, thereby making a closed circuit of his tensions, or some such thing. I don't quite understand the physics of it, if physics is the word, but it used to do wonders for my Asian. So, combining these three exercises, I'm afraid I fell asleep."

"It sounds like a hybrid process," Alec said. "Yoga, Arab, Chinese."

Leeming murmured, "Culture is always a cross-breed."

Ella approached a new topic, an adventurous one. "How is your aunt just at the moment?"

"She's inside now, in the theatre." He turned to Alec. "I hope you won't upset her."

Ramsey let a silence signify some measure of hurt. "Who told you I was likely to?"

"Oh, Aunt Belle doesn't give away secrets. But you've always been affected by my uncle's death. That's known."

"By the Kables, perhaps."

"No, generally known."

Ella told Leeming in a tight voice, "You can at least depend on Alec to attempt more tact than you seem capable of."

"They tell us you're going to Antarctica," Pelham intervened.

"Yes. To be at the diggings." Leeming said it clinically, as if uncle Stephen Leeming were a Greek vase on the Turkish littoral. "Nothing is definite yet, but I've applied for two weeks' leave. The Americans have told us that if the weather lifts there's to be a flight from Christchurch to McMurdo Sound the evening after next. It's nothing more than proper that a member of the family should be there," he ended chastely.

Yet another silence rose around the masticating sounds their shoes made on gravel. The theatre hove before them, its foyer still thronged. On the edge of the night and in the open stood a roué at work, the rangy, elegant shape of Professor Sanders who had shared with them the discomfort of the poet's night-out at the vice-chancellor's. A pretty girl, her eye-sockets emphasized to the diameter of saucers by misery and the uncertain light, faced him. It was a private confrontation, so much so that instinctive decency had the Leeming rescue party skirting round the two, who scarcely noticed them in spite of the noise of trodden gravel. Sanders' voice, level and intense, carried to them.

"Look, I'm a man of principle. Anyone who lives beyond the normal rules has to be. Consistency of conscience. All I ask is that you should have a consistent conscience."

"It's not the same sort of thing," the girl muttered.

Sanders put his hand to his forehead as the Ramseys and Pelham and Leeming passed. But it was the movement of a man in genuine puzzlement rather than of someone merely trying to hide his face. They heard him say in a scarcely lowered voice, "But how can I be expected to afford. . . ?"

Ella whispered, "The womanizer unmanned."

It appeared that the sight of his departmental head, Professor Sanders, debating some personal matter with a young scholar, possibly an undergraduate, had exhilarated Leeming further, almost to the point of geniality. He thanked them for waking him, patently convinced that he could have slept a long time on the methods of Rudolf Hess. They wished him well as he went off to lend his fairly inadvertent talents to Tim.

As Ella and Ramsey came into the theatre through a side door they each searched earnestly but with mutual discretion for the aunt. Neither had succeeded by the time the lights were dimmed.

Alec found it sweet to sit in the dark and whisper patronizing things about the production and the acting.

"So much for the Reverend Bowdler," he hissed as Mrs Kable whirled through fairydom exploiting double-entendres she wouldn't have admitted to knowing in her offstage pose of guilelessness. "She isn't saying it according

146

to the verse pattern," Ella complained. But a joyous audience didn't give a damn.

There is a point in the play where Lysander, whose eyes have been anointed with love-ointment, pursues Helena through the forest and awakens a similarly anointed Demetrius-Leeming, asleep there for the past two hundred lines. At the words "You love her not" Leeming was meant to rise and besiege Helena from her blind side; and the two upright actors implied that this course should now be taken by inclining their heads minutely towards the prone Leeming. Who still did not move. Encouraged by the lightness with which Tim had laid the play down before them and by the fluffiness of the acting, a group of students began to sing advice, and Leeming woke to find that his crossbred art of relaxation had betrayed him again.

Yet he might have heard the prompter and made a recovery if he had not dropped the correctness of Athenian gentleman and classic lover and begun to argue with the youth who was Lysander. Lysander kept to the dramatic illusion and tried to argue in character, and so fought at a handicap.

Ramsey, who had often enough made a fool of himself and gone on to compound the matter, still blushed for Denis Leeming. Yet there was at least a doggedness about the nephew this evening that reminded Alec of the uncle. Meanwhile, even the students fell embarrassed, and in the hollowness of the audience's sense of shock, laughter and catcalls rang false.

Then the curtain fell, but no lights came up. People began to chat and wait on explanations; which came from Lysander, breaking the curtains open and coming forward in a rush, as if either impelled or braking the momentum of a sudden escape from someone's hands.

Lysander begged their pardons and said that the delay followed an error of which he himself was primarily guilty.

Someone's voice, not necessarily Leeming's, was heard from within the curtains: ". . . bloody hero of himself. . . ." When the curtain came up again, Leeming continued his Demetrius with a knotty sort of vigour; which made it impossible for people to forget that here was Leeming acting Demetrius with a knotty sort of vigour to show that he wasn't intimidated by people's opinions. Ramsey wondered whether the lapse hadn't been caused by the thought of ice grids.

Suddenly the interval lights were on, exposing Alec to the necessity of meeting Mrs Leeming and showing her to Ella. In a foyer full of undistinguished youth a sole old lady with classic face gone rather leonine and britannic with age was easy to locate. As was the due of so imperial a lady, Alec saw her. She did not, or did not seem to, see him.

"We have to speak to her. You don't mind, do you?" After all, he could have said, if there was argument, that at the time of his coupling with Belle Ella had been five years of age.

None the less, as Ella advanced, her eyes were brittle with a good will alien to her. It was certain that she saw the physical grandeur of the old woman as something worth mistrusting.

"Belle," he said simply, conversationally, careful against sounding nostalgic.

She rounded, uncertain. For forty years they had met only by accident, at intervals and never for long. "Alec," she guessed now in the face of this rugged old man. "Yes, Alec. And this must be. . . ."

"Ella," Ramsey told her. Ella stood back a little, foolishly believing herself cheapened.

"Oh, Ella," Mrs Leeming said, and searched Ella's face with the same direct brilliance that had undermined Ramsey decades past. Ella was saved from anger by seeing that

148

one of those incisive irises was rimmed by an ugly yellow growth. "I've always wanted to meet you."

"And I you, Mrs Leeming." Which, despite Ella's best efforts, sounded like something said at a showdown.

"At the risk of being thought a mere flatterer," Belle Leeming said, "I must comment on your complexion, dear. How many of these eighteen-year-olds can match it?"

How many of them could match Belle's? Ramsey thought. Her cheeks, mouth, and throat were startlingly shapely, her complexion even, though her temples gave a hint of sinking to purple basins. All this looked false on what was (it was somehow obvious) a very old lady, so that cynics would have incorrectly written it down to extreme care before the mirror, recourse to cosmeticians and even to cosmetic surgery.

Ella was looking sideways at Ramsey, to see how the compliment had registered on him. She was too suspicious of mockery to attempt graciousness in return.

"You're afraid I'm being insincere," Belle startled her by saying.

"No, no," Ramsey denied on her behalf. "For some reason praise always takes Ella by storm."

"Do you think I'd try sarcasm, Ella, when my closest relative has just made such a fool of himself?"

Ella felt like the delinquent schoolgirl caught out by a meticulously just headmistress. It would have been preferable to be insulted. She seized on Belle's proffered weakness.

"You mean Denis?" she said.

"I wish he didn't have these unfortunate public mannerisms. It embarrasses his friends, but worst of all, it embarrasses him. So that he's committed, then, to further inanities."

Ramsey tried to gloss the question over. "It's simply because he mistrusts himself. And don't we all?" he added for luck, in case the words might turn on him.

"That's characteristic of Denis. But living in the groves of Academe helped do this to him. The people who are so toffee-nosed about him now fêted him as the child-wonder once. All the laurels were his for the picking up, and pick them up he did. It's ludicrous to see the letters after his name. Three master's degrees, no less. Did you know that, Ella? Three, one of them honours from Oxford. Half a dozen diplomas. It's freakish. When they go to so much trouble to shore the poor boy up, to stir him on to become a latter-day Da Vinci, the least they could do is finish the job properly and make him a doctor. Though I suppose he'd want a Ph.D.(Hons. Oxon.) then. Is there such a thing, Alec?"

Alec thought she dealt with her nephew at such length out of mercy towards himself. He had this and a great amount of other evidence to prove that in her singular way she was a loyal and discreet woman. Yet he wondered if it was even possible that she was being merciful to herself. Less rabid and doctrinaire than she used to be, she might also be a little less impregnable.

Ella did not care to leave the matter tacit. She asked without warning, "Mrs Leeming, how do you feel about this discovery?"

Belle did not pause. "My husband?"

"I'm sorry, but Alec suffers a great deal for his memory." She felt contrite to see the old eyes, the one with the growth, flicker for an instant, as if altering focus.

"You've got every right to ask, Ella."

"What will happen, then, Mrs Leeming?"

"I don't know. I'm an old woman, you see. I want to be advised by Denis."

"He'll go south?" Ramsey said.

"We think it would be a good idea." The widow shut her eyes.

Ramsey's own eyes made one conspiratorial sweep of the

room before he gave her advice. "Perhaps I should tell you, Belle. Those who know him seem to think he's a little unstable at the moment."

Belle remained in an aloof stance. "Denis? I trust my own. There's no one else to call on."

Yet Alec could not believe that the old woman relied on any vein of good sense in Leeming the younger; nor could he imagine her as the fond aunt-by-marriage, blinded, in the face of her own decaying, to the oddities of her kin. As for her being an old woman beset by events in which she needed a mediator, he could see no evidence for it other than the mere statistical evidence of her years. And age came as close to being an irrelevance in her case as it could possibly be for mortal woman.

Again he found it intolerable that Leeming, immune up till now at his improbable latitude, should be required to rot in the earth to make a circus for Denis.

"Indeed there's no one else to call on, Belle," he affirmed. "For God's sake don't fail to do what's needed yourself."

The widow stared at him. The stare was read by Ella as something to do with pain; but such a reading was provoked by her belief that a funeral under the aegis of Leeming the younger was the very thing to exorcize Leeming the elder.

"Alec," she pleaded. "Be decent."

She was herself startled then to find the old lady's hand on her wrist. "No, no, no, Ella. He's within his rights." It was toneless: the old lady thought Ramsey's rights funny ones.

Alec refused to be shamed. "You're the widow," he insisted.

"It's a precise description," Belle admitted.

"I don't think you of all people should consider that your age excuses you."

The two women referred to each other's eyes. Ramsey's

brashness had made Ella forget Belle's past whorings; they were entrenched in sisterhood, happily misreading each other.

"Alec, if I were senile and had lost control of my bowels, as thousands have at my age, you would certainly excuse me. But what you could never forgive is that a robust woman of seventy-nine years should attempt to preserve her health."

"You surely don't mean that Mrs Leeming should go south herself?" Ella challenged him.

"Belle knows what I mean."

Ella was reminded by this that Mrs Leeming and Ramsey had shared more than meanings. She resented Alec's flaunting of Christian names as token of intimacy, and did not know that he had always called Belle Mrs Leeming until they had again met by accident and innocently in a restaurant in 1938.

The old lady said, "Ella asked me what I thought about this discovery. Let me tell you that it's all grotesque and alien to me, as Leeming's ambitions always tended to be."

Alec might have said some such thing as "So it seems". But Belle still retained her asbestos air of candour, of the heroism of the straight talker. Before it, liars felt intimidated. Ramsey was a liar.

"You can't tell me there was any need for that last journey. Ella, if *you* had been his wife—a better wife, that is, than I was—you would have seen the nonsense in it. Oh I know, man's irradicable thirst for knowledge is invoked. But who can say man's soul does actually thirst to know the height and latitude of mountains in Victoria Land? That isn't knowledge, it's fact. Void fact, too. There is no human significance in the configuration of the hindquarters of those mountains."

Ella blinked, but remained loyal to the old woman. She knew that she was not herself tolerant of Ramsey's fantasies. Yet she could not conceive of her intolerance extending itself to the dishonouring of Ramsey's memory.

"Now the ludicrous and tragic nature," Belle continued, "of what was done by Leeming was that it could all have been done from the air within a short time. Quite a number of people have seen his abhorrence of aircraft as something odd, as if it was important to him to reproduce the conditions of earlier expeditions. You know yourself, Alec, he was offered a Hawker aircraft. His motives all had to do with some sort of self-testing. Let me speak bluntly about my husband. His death was in some ways less meritorious than if he'd drunk himself to death, because drinking wasn't in his nature. It was an excess that he would have had to work hard at to acquire. So you see, I was out of sympathy with him then, and feel alienated by what has happened now. And I won't be bullied in the matter, Alec."

A handbell rang, calling them back to the enchanted forest. The Ramseys had nothing more to say but waited each in private possession of his belief, Ella seeing a nice funeral as salutary, Ramsey suspecting it as a sacrilege; Ella wanting bathos, Ramsey the revelation, both out of the same eventuality.

"Shall we go in?" Belle asked. The students hustling might have noticed her as one notices a town hall, something placed to encourage old-fashioned proprieties. A sweet old girl, the young might guess, fat with years and marital wisdom.

They had stood waiting for the press of people to thin. Now there were three or four couples left, making haste with cigarettes, although the unhappy girl who had been seen earlier in debate with Sanders was prominent, causing gentler but equal misery to a handsome boy talking low with her.

"Now that we're alone, Belle, when are you going to stop lying?"

"Alec, control yourself," Ella barked. For she had seen the eyes change quality again; almost like a shift of pace, precisely managed. Yet perhaps in ten months or ten years the tensions that commanded such shifts might split the old brain.

"Would *you* feel hostile towards giving *me* a fit funeral?" Ramsey asked Ella.

"If I had been hurt enough."

Ramsey grunted and kept to himself his opinion that Belle was invulnerable. But even the old lady herself belittled Ella's melodramatic claim.

"Alec believes I'm not easily hurt. I think there's evidence for such an opinion. But perhaps Ella has been hurt, Alec, by your silly concentration on my husband. Ella is a beautiful woman. You can't expect her to consume her life on an ageing fool whose mind is three-quarters on what he considers to be debts, ancient and forgotten ones. Ella deserves you entire."

Ramsey filled with the kind of annoyance a non-believer might feel if a pontiff changed doctrine. "You didn't believe in private possession once."

"Neither I did. I was an absolutist then. A lot of people fall apart without serene possession of someone else."

He continued ungenerous. "But morally inferior to you, these people? Aren't they?"

"Imagine my apologizing for Denis!" said the widow, raising her eyebrows.

They were the only group left in the vestibule now, and heard the audience hush as music burst out inside. When Ramsey looked back to Belle there was a tear on each of her cheeks, utterly unheralded, apparitions. Her face was just as passive yet as vital as before.

"I so wanted to see Denis in this second half," she said levelly.

Ramsey refused to honour the tears, but Ella whispered

before them, "Of course, of course, Mrs Leeming," and without blushing, put an arm around Belle's shoulders for a second. "Get out of the road, Alec."

"There's no need, darling," the widow muttered, shaking Ella off, finding her own way into the dimmed theatre. But Ramsey had held Ella back too.

"Let me tell you," he whispered. "She's no member of any sisterhood of wronged women. She's tough, a loner, a regular monolith."

Ella defied him. "She's a genuine lady. I like her style."

And she holds it against me, he thought, that I fell to a far more rousing Mrs Leeming.

He knew, however, that she would forgive him his mere rudeness if he gave her time. Acts III and IV should suffice.

Leeming presences had dominated the night, and it was only when sherries were served on stage that Ramsey saw Sir Chimpy had attended. Awarded a glass each by Pelham, the vice-chancellor and the cast eyed each other with some mutual shyness which Ramsey was surprised to see, especially on Sir Byron's side.

Ramsey stepped up to him and hoped he'd enjoyed the evening, being sorry only that Lady Sadie couldn't have come.

"She isn't well," Sir Byron claimed. He seemed a little furtive, as if unused to telling polite lies for Lady Sadie. The stealthiness was replaced by an amazingly frank-faced and legible desire to confide his worries.

"I'm concerned about Sadie. She always knew what it was to be . . . well, to be the wife of a vice-chancellor. She's refusing a lot of the customary jobs now, and she's very neurotic. Hostility. Tears."

Ramsey was amazed to see that Sir Chimpy possibly had had no experience until now of women reacting to their chemistry.

Alec took on, partially self-deceived, a pose of male stability. "I wouldn't worry, Byron. Their biology must get them, sooner or later."

Seemingly conjured up by the word "biology", Mrs Kable burgeoned at their side, demanding Sir Byron's just estimate of the play. Faced with a woman whose chemistry was on the sunny side, he said, "You really were splendid, my dear." So, honoured, she left them, and was succeeded by Pelham.

"Leeming isn't here," Alec remarked.

"He's taken his aunt home." Pelham frowned. "I believe he intends to come back."

Sir Chimpy asked, "Who was the boy he quarrelled with?"

"He's a law clerk from Pinalba. I think he's waiting for an opportunity to spring on Leeming with apologies. He suffers from a now nearly extinct disease called reverence for academics."

"Silly boy," Sir Chimpy laughed, but as if approving of the basic condition.

"I hope you told him not to dare be abject to Leeming," Alec told Pelham.

"Indeed," said Pelham efficiently, in a manner from which it was possible to suspect that the unfathomable Yorkshireman had read too much of a command, command late and irrelevant, into the stricture about the boy Lysander. To turn the talk, he drew on his small experience of stages.

"It's like acting to a hostile audience, isn't it, standing up here on the stage, lights on, performing in front of all that dumb upholstery?"

They were all three outstaring the theatre's vacancy when the door of the treasurer's office at the front of the theatre opened and Mrs Turner stepped out, chattering to someone over her shoulder. Someone proved to be the poet.

The question of cosying up the party by bringing down the curtain died. In a state that could almost be called a renewal, Ramsey yet felt as little patience as ever at facing that catalytic gentleman. But the poet was doubly unwelcome because a walking souvenir of yesterday's frenzies.

"Wasn't he going home?" Alec asked Sir Chimpy and Pelham, who may not even have known of his arrival.

Sir Chimpy ignored the question. "I'm pleased to see," he said instead, generously enough to suggest that the poet had made peace with the Mewses, "that Mrs Turner seems more receptive."

From across the room, where Tim was retailing his theatrical stories, Ella tried to gauge Alec's response to this portentous entry. Her mistrust sharpened him against the poet.

On the edge of the stage Mrs Turner was held up in business with the president of the town's dramatic society. The poet came on alone and stopped before Sir Chimpy.

"Well, you seem to be doing well for yourself," the knight, all hearty, told him. It was obvious that Sir Chimpy considered the poet a wild boy, his lack of orthodoxy balanced by his talent; a lovable prodigal. There was no evidence for this reading in the poet's industriously vacant face, scraped ruddy with a sedulous morning razor. Nor was Mrs Turner any artist's skirt but a pleasant and pretty matron rasped by the sun and a little blowsy from the hard diet of widowhood.

Ramsey said, "The people who arrange reservations at the travel agency here . . . you must be getting to know them very well."

"They're quite tolerant."

"You're staying longer than you thought?" Sir Chimpy asked, to make talk.

"I *will* have to go the day after tomorrow."

The vice-chancellor went sly. "I suppose you didn't want to miss our graduation ceremony." The histrionic sentence called for nods and winks and nudges, which luckily Sir Byron did not sink to.

"And I suppose you're looking forward to resuming your *own* life," Ramsey suggested.

The damned poet was amused. "No, I remembered to bring it with me."

From Pelham came a small grunt of indefinite significance. "Well," he said, "I never liked watching duels. I must go and mix. Sir Byron." He went off. It was equally likely that he was showing tolerance and discretion or retiring piqued at the energies Ramsey spent on hostilities.

They talked about the play, but Ramsey was in a fever for the vice-chancellor to move and share his presence around the stage. Against the poet, who had ever appeared only to augment the pitch of his mania, Alec must measure his new health. It could not be done with Sir Chimpy yammering at them about a West End production of *Oedipus Rex*.

". . . but altogether I rather disagreed with the interpretation," he said at last. "Well, I must mingle, gentlemen."

He commenced mingling with expert grace.

The poet said, like an intern on rounds, "Well, how are we?"

"We're very well. I hope you didn't stay on for our . . . *my* sake."

"Ah, we don't need soothing till next time," the poet mocked.

"You call it soothing? Never mind, I am grateful. You've been very kind up to now, but if you try to be kinder I'll take it as an interference."

"You have failed to preoccupy me for the past twenty-four hours, Alec." The poet looked around to see how Mrs Turner's diversion was shaping. "One of the reasons I

158

stayed is that I have an interview with Mrs Leeming tomorrow. I know it isn't a felicitous time, but she's seventy-nine, poor old thing. You never know when the chance will come again."

"There are no signs of last gasps at the moment." He asked narrowly, "Why should you want to see her?"

"I want to see the sort of woman Leeming had at home, that's all. The ruins."

"They're not ruins, damn her eyes. Not yet they're not."

Someone made an impact between Ramsey and the poet. It was like the transposition of film. First a tranquil horizon of the poet and people's backs, then, in mid-sentiment, Denis Leeming's lozenge-shaped face flooding his sight with overintimate views of this or that (largely clean) skin-pore.

"What did you say to my aunt at the interval?" Leeming called out, but neutrally, so that if others heard they would have thought it conversation.

"You can't expect me to answer if you're going to hustle me." The cutting tone of rationality that belongs to a man who keeps his temper was, for once, Ramsey's prerogative. He took time to think how characteristic this style of anger, impassive, unemphatic when seen from a distance, was of the dead uncle; the slow-combustion hysteria that no one ten yards away could have identified.

"She is the man's widow, you know. And even you make a show of being sensitive about him."

Ramsey corrected him. "Even I *am* sensitive about him."

"You think you own him. Don't you think she's plagued enough at the moment? The unequalled situation. . . ."

"I didn't know I had upset her," Alec said. He felt contrite and meant to be seen to be. "How is she now?"

"*How is she now?* She came to me after curtain call."

"Was she crying?"

"She isn't a crier. I thought you knew that much. She

looked exhausted, grey, and she wanted to be taken home. On her way home she said something about your being a hard man."

"She's wrong. We're all upset and at sixes and sevens."

"I don't understand you. No one has asked you to take any part. Or worse still, my aunt has and you've begged off."

Ramsey nodded; a risky impulse formed in him. He found the boy's eyes set beneath a small frown, the vacant brand of eyes that turn up in royal houses through over-breeding. "And you should beg off too, Denis." He wanted to say how alien nephew and uncle were to each other, but that was offensive and a fantastic way to talk; as if the dead man had an aura in need of solace. In a fever, he ended with the worst of puns. "You're poles apart."

Leeming sniffed, equally for sinus as for contempt. "I can't help my limitations." Genuine passion was there now, streaky on the partially made-up face.

"You're angry now. But I wasn't talking about your limitations."

"You're willing to admit I have them, though. By the gross." He was exploring the vein marked *failed doctorate* —one could tell.

"Denis, we've enough to discuss ——"

"Yes, let's discuss genuine failures." There was no misreading his state now. Sir Chimpy was aware too, his head at an askance angle. "Aunt Belle called you hard. . . ."

Ramsey wanted to ask did she mean the word in the sense she had favoured it in her youth.

". . . I said no, not him. He's no Iron Chancellor. He's certainly no Iron Director of Extension. . . ."

Alec's big hands threatened to fly to the lapels of Leeming's dinner-suit; the poet stood by, making noises of disgust, but those of a man who enjoys being in at a con-flict. Alec announced that he was very remorseful at offending Mrs Leeming and that he would not risk doing it again.

But Leeming, touched on his paranoia, was looking for hidden barbs in everything that was said. "That's an ambiguous enough statement," he surprised Alec by saying. "Though they tell me ambiguity is built into you. I hear Morris Pelham and Eric Kable think so, anyhow."

A dissenting Pelham and Sir Byron had begun to move in. But that creature of vulpine loyalty had already prowled up on Leeming's left. She opened her mouth at the same time as the poet; there was a garbled outcry from both.

"No, no," Ramsey said, restraining them. He actually feared a scene and had time to marvel wanly at this sign of new health.

Ella murmured, "Go away, Denis." All the silent cast heard her, enslaved by her voice that, rarefied in anger, hinted at the gods of electric eloquence who preside over any stage. Then Sir Chimpy was there, calling on their good sense. The air of good sense he himself gave off diluted Ella's Medusan presence. Then Pelham, telling Leeming he would make his own complaints, thank you. And the poet saying Ramsey himself hadn't been well lately.

Leeming questioned the adverb.

Ella's handbag was of a soft metal called Oroton. Hefty with a large part of Ella's current bookkeeping, with brushes and toiletries and an old paperback novel, when swung against Leeming's temple it stunned him and raised a few parallel scratches on his forehead. He stood back, cherishing one side of his head in both hands.

Ramsey was the first to him, and grotesquely sympathetic. The poet smiled discreetly; Sir Chimpy's jaws fell away into bags of incredulity at this further instance of woman abusing man's good faith, while the Kables frowned, eyes feverishly significant, swapping the ocular equivalent of a nudge.

Mrs Turner brewed up peace with the tea, and carried both to the wings where Sir Chimpy, the Kables and the Lysander youth were tending Leeming. The decent mercies of tea were then extended to the people on stage. Ella held cup and saucer stubbornly. "I won't go home," she warned Ramsey. Not till she had shown everyone that she didn't blush for Leeming's injuries.

"You know *young* Leeming?" the poet said, coming up fondling his cup in a confidential way. They could hear Valerie clucking over Leeming's forehead and see Eric standing by, frowning in enchantment at this latest Ramsey atrocity. "*Young* Leeming is over thirty. One forgets that, hearing people, even people in Canberra, speak about him as if he hasn't yet come into his estate, as if he can be expected to soon, and as if it will be *some* estate. People are continually saying, 'When he learns. . . .', and going on to mention this or that social virtue the marvellous lad still lacks. Well, how many social virtues do you pick up after thirty, unless they're already there in germ? I tended to lose all mine."

Ramsey said in self-judgment, "If you had you wouldn't joke about it."

Some minutes later he went himself to check on Leeming's state and, finding that even Mrs Kable, her face rapt with a votive anguish, could not manage to predict worse than mild concussion, asked Sir Byron's permission to go home. Given it, he felt bound by office to speak to these people. "Ladies and gentlemen," he called.

"What right have you to stand, even, on this bloody stage?" Leeming was well enough to say. "How have you contributed?"

Ramsey prepared to fend Ella away, but she remained, a bleak lady, midstage. The shabby peace-making of these academics deflated her; she would have been a tower in the days when resentments were hoarded and written off in blood.

"There was a time when I did contribute to most things that happened here. I suppose that's why I've been allowed to last beyond what a lot of people would say was all reasonable decline."

Pelham rumbled a denial; Sir Chimpy swept the admission aside with a motion of his hand, seeming to think it not so much untrue as irrelevant. It was of course, as Ramsey could see, a mean sample of public self-flaying, designed to force his enemies and disadmirers back onto their hind-legs as they thought, "He's culpable maybe; but at least he's honest." He thanked, in the partially successful hiatus he had thus created, the actors and Tim for the evening of enchantment they had created. This phrase pleased Sir Chimpy, who raised it to the level of legislation by fervently grunting. Ramsey ended in hoping they would excuse him.

He and Ella had already made the corridor when Leeming, trailing his nunlike Titania, caught up with them and placed himself in front of them. He had strangely reverted to his earlier, deep-frozen brand of anger.

"I'll be looking after Aunt Belle's interests in the matter," he told them. "There's the press and television. . . ." Like many scholars, he invoked the names of the media as hostile gods yet worth placating, present holders of the horn of plenty. "The funeral—presuming there is a funeral—will get a wide coverage." Somehow he knew that Ramsey would be hurt by this news. "You'll be expected to attend without causing trouble."

"Indeed," Ramsey told him, "the world will remember your uncle for unreal causes. Because his body surfaced intact after forty years. The world is interested in that sort of stunt."

"I simply wanted to warn you," Leeming claimed tolerantly. "We won't tolerate any tantrums at the graveside."

Valerie took him by the arm. The womenfolk led their knights off in opposite directions, uncertain of the extent of their injuries.

As he should have expected, Ella had forgotten her handbag, and now remembered that the theatre was used by the English Department during the day. It was reasonable enough, she argued, that she should not want to lose to some undergraduate such an item in her armoury and the papers it contained. Ramsey hoped he merely imagined that the bag seemed to have endeared itself especially to her on account of its having started Leeming's blood.

She insisted on being driven back to the university. At first Alec suspected her: what woman ever forgot her handbag, such an intimate extension of herself? Ella raised both arms and flapped them, so that even under her coat the bag must have been most cunningly disguised not to rattle or drop.

Back at the stage-door, she refused to be taken inside, like someone under suspicion, by Ramsey.

She met Mrs Kable in the dressing-room corridor.

"I have to get out of this drag," said Valerie. She sounded friendly, as if she was actually grateful to Ella for her having behaved true to form. "*These our actors as I foretold you. . . .*"

And on the fading pronoun she idled with regret into the ladies' room.

Everyone on stage helped Mrs Ramsey in her search for the bag. They could tell that she was one of the people whom they must be rid of before a hard-core party could start. Sir Chimpy could not be seen, but Pelham was still there, tenacious, restricting the affair to a mere sherried function. It was Pelham who found the bag, against the leg of a table. It and an impression of gruff exhaustion Ella received from him.

Rounding the prop table into the corridor, she saw Denis Leeming edge out of the men's lavatory and blink up and down the passage. She halted and breathed low. Her hip knocked Bottom's ass's head over, but she caught it as it fell. Its papier-mâché noises did not carry to furtive Denis Leeming.

By one of the dressing-rooms was a small properties cupboard. Leeming opened its door and entered. In lieu of the bedroom of his fellowship flat, Ella thought, occupied by Aunt Belle. She even muttered in the shadows, "Ah, Mrs Kable, I'm onto one of your earths."

A fast survey of the ladies' dressing-room showed it empty. Conclusion: Valerie had preceded her lover into a dusty tryst. And, given the unhelpful milieu, would not waste time becoming impassioned. Ella decided to wait two minutes and blunder into the pantry, an ingenue enlisting them for a search after her handbag, which she would leave here on the props table.

In childhood she had learnt to measure time by how long it took to say a Lord's prayer. Even in her agnosticism she still used the method, seeing little that was absonant in prayer used as a rein on impatience until Titania should become ignited.

She was close to the pantry door, in the open corridor, without cover, when doubt found her. It suggested that Mrs Kable and Leeming, at love, would not be simply antic; there would be the strident physical realities to be faced which, when matched with the lovers' flaws of personality, could or should bring one closer to nausea than to laughter. So she saw with some self-disgust that she was doing something less than supporting Ramsey by bringing discomfort to his enemies, that she was less than loyal; a mere rampant sense of grievance seeking an object.

This sense of grievance was, of course, keyed to break in on the male-female grotesqueries of Titania and Demetrius. It found in the first place darkness, and then, taking some seconds to locate the switch, two half-naked blinking males—Eric Kable with his cravat at least intact.

Her primitive sense of morality, bred matriarchally in a dairy farmhouse, saw this coupling as worse than sickening; she was horrified to the womb—horrified authentically and not in the sense in which some people use the word to mean mere moral titillation. Though their hairy, knotted, pallid-to-tan legs stood before her, it was a conviction of her own nakedness in front of their intention of seed directed away from the womb that set her running in her cowgirl lope directly out-of-doors. In the open, she remembered that her bag was still at the far end of the corridor, by Bottom's ass's head; but damned it to remain.

Next morning the small hours turned cold, and Ramsey, early to work, spent his time till ten secretly ordering his papers for a successor. Sometimes he heard people downstairs dimly braying about the weather, or loudly predicting a hard winter as they passed each other in the doorway of Extension. Despite these hints of the lateness of the season, it failed to occur to him that decisions about Leeming the elder would be made today, even the venomous decision to give him a home burial with honours. What most diverted Ramsey was Barbara's shufflings in the outer office, Barbara serenely shuffling in the sure hope of at least another three years out of her figurehead. It was a pleasure, petty but sharp, to suck on the truth: that the king of Extension was withdrawing from the top, leaving Barbara a pygmy figure staring up through the slats of a vacant throne.

About ten o'clock, when Ramsey was relishing the triumph of having stopped Barbara from feeding him buttered bun with his tea, the poet appeared again in the outer office. He came in wary and amenable, rather like the poet Ramsey had met in the first place, on the steps downstairs last October. Today he would leave the office at Ramsey's word if it were given; leave without any silly demonstration of power on Ramsey's part, such as calling for George from the parking-area gate.

"Would you believe me if I said I was going home tonight?" the poet asked.

Ramsey laughed, on guard. He feared the man's presence as something that would force him back to urgencies he had been free of that morning. "I'd take your word," he said.

"You may hear rumours in the coming weeks that Mrs Turner and I have been . . . betrothed. It's true. I'm coming back at Easter to marry Mrs Turner and raise our long-odds offspring as—of all damn things!—R.Cs."

He waited for Ramsey to mock the news and point at the doubt it threw on his motives for visiting the tableland. But Ramsey was, as always, mutable and held silence.

"Now," said the poet, "although my journey ended with Mrs Turner, it began with you."

"And I've benefited by it," Ramsey admitted, and was surprised to find it the truth. "You're a meddling bastard, a real church elder. But I've benefited."

"I have to admit I was hoping for a reward by the way. I was hoping for the drum on Antarctica, I was thinking you might cough up some Antarctic quintessence, something that can't be learnt from the journals."

"I won't be giving you that."

"I know. But at least I'm on my way to beard old Mrs Leeming. I believe there was a time when she would have given me some sort of quintessence with a vengeance."

"Oh yes. But the worst thing she's ever done to Leeming is this abdication of power over Leeming's remains. Of course it's for reasons that are adequate on paper. But utterly unbelievable."

Ramsey thought suddenly of the mid-winter dinner in 1925, Leeming rising from the Swallow and Ariel pudding and holding up a glass of non-alcoholic cider. "To wives and sweethearts," he had called.

Nettled by the memory of Leeming's vulnerability, he picked up the nearest letter and was delighted to find it a weapon. "The Council," it said, "is happy to tell you that it is willing to provide travelling expenses for the visit of Simeon Harper, English novelist and critic, to Australia. . . ." This Harper, Alec knew, had once published in the *Observer* a parody of the poet's work. Ramsey flung the letter across to his guest.

"I hope he gets caught in Chimpy's filtration system," the poet said. Which was honest and blunt and therefore disappointing.

It forced Ramsey to admit, "I could never finish any of his, except one. And that didn't have me with my legs in the air, begging for more."

He received the letter back from the poet, who said, "You're very busy. I'll go."

Suddenly ashamed at his own pettiness, Alec began to be helpful.

"Listen, there's no such thing as this Antarctic quintessence you speak of. It's a common mistake to think of Antarctica almost as if it was a moral state on its own. Man's motives don't change in those latitudes. After all, the latitude of the Oates Coast is seventy degrees south. At seventy degrees north, in Norway say, there are town councils whose perceptions, you can bet, don't differ from those of their brethren further south. Anyone who has ever been either cold or prickly hot among snow, and anyone who has ever been ravished by hot soup after a day in high wind. . . ."

168

The telephone had been bleating for half this speech and Ramsey here gave in and picked it up. It was the exchange, with a call from Sydney. A quiet voice introduced itself as a feature writer whose name and prestige were known to Alec. It said it had been talking to Leeming, who had been sure that Mr Ramsey would have nothing to say about the location of the uncle's remains.

"Mr Leeming was quite right, I'm afraid," Ramsey told the man. Who began to press the idea of a Saturday feature on Ramsey himself, survivor for forty years; on the emotions let loose in him by the finding of what the journalist called "these pitiable relics".

Ramsey became disrespectful. "There's an account in the official history. I'm only a common-or-garden man-on-the-glacier and have no right to add to it."

"Would you be pleased to see the body returned to its native soil?"

"Which is its native soil?"

The man was patient. "Pardon us. Fine weather is expected at the digging site."

Alec felt immediate constrictions in his throat and belly; in this way paying for the spaciousness of earlier that morning.

"When?"

"Twelve to twenty-four hours."

He had surmised wrongly that he might have ten days, and now could not imagine how he had come to such an ample figure. Umpteen times, he had presumed, he would stifle and his vision fill with blood before Leeming dreadfully came; but at least there was also room for leisure in ten days; he wanted time for leisure, for feeling wistful or grudging towards people like Barbara and the poet. But if they were raising the corpse now, this afternoon, the very pace of it would suffocate, engorge him, split him open.

"So young Leeming doesn't intend to visit the site," he suggested.

"Oh yes. I believe the Americans have been asked not to raise the body, even if they find it, until Mr Leeming and the photographer arrive. It seems that this is very late in the season and that people at the site would normally have left ten days ago."

It seemed to Ramsey that he had been given this much to provoke him to an interview; as if even the journalist found the detail concerning the photographer callous.

"What photographer?"

"A staff one. From *Life*."

"My God!"

"And I believe he has employed an agent to sell the film rights in Dr Leeming's journal."

But Ramsey would not be interviewed. Every question he answered with the anonymous brand of stupidity shown by people pounced on in the street and asked their opinion of the effect of the European Common Market on the local dried-fruit industry.

The feature writer gave up abruptly, and Ramsey was drawing breath to tell the poet of the idiot nephew's plans when the idiot nephew himself came in. Barbara, closing the door on them after Ramsey had asked Leeming in, gave the wry impression that she was doing it to foster Ramsey's illusions of privacy.

Although he must have known that Ramsey would have heard of his dalliance with Kable, not one centimetre of his dominant presence stooped to taking account of it. Why should it, since his loves were sacred to him? Not so plans for putting uncle Leeming across to a hard world.

He had come to see the poet. "The girl on the desk at the hotel told me you'd mentioned you were seeing Mr Ramsey and Mrs Leeming. I'm sorry to say you'll have to limit that to Alec here. My aunt will have to be excused."

"I hope she isn't ill."

"No, but frantically busy and under a massive strain. This morning's mail alone included nearly forty letters of what looked like condolence but turned into invitations to join or preside over or address this or that group when she had recovered from her nasty shock."

"We live in ghoulish times," Alec muttered, with acrid intent.

The poet asked, "And your aunt has to attend to that sort of thing? Mr Leeming, if a woman of your aunt's age says she's tired, she's tired. If she says she's sick, she's sick. Might I plead, though, that I was interested in your uncle long before he became fashionable in this grotesque way? I was one of a small knot of true believers. I needed no imprimatur from the news services, like the people who are trying to waste her time now."

"Well, of course, we shan't answer these people, except cursorily. But there are more important demands to be met."

Ramsey said politely, "I believe you wish to make your uncle's name widely known."

"How do you mean?" Leeming said it as if waiting for the inevitable insult, one more flat joke from a tired old comic.

Not to disappoint him, Ramsey spat it out. "Popularize him. Aren't you trying to sell him to the films?"

The poet whistled. "So much for my epic," he murmured.

"If you mean that a literary agent approached me and offered to try and sell film rights in my uncle's journals, and that I couldn't see any good reason why not, then you could say, however unjustly, that I was trying to sell him to the films."

Ramsey announced, "Ramsey can't play himself. I thought I should tell you."

"If I may say so," the poet ventured, "it seems a pity to take your uncle out of the ice and subject him to the banalities of a modern funerary orgy. He's native to the ice and alien to the other."

Leeming smiled for the poet's simple-mindedness. "The concept of my uncle seeping down gallantly through a glacier is at least as crudely sentimental as anything an undertaker could dream up."

The poet considered this. "No. No, I don't think it is. It's sentimental, but not crudely so. It has style. On the other hand, I've never been to a funeral that didn't fill me with morbidness. . . . After all, this familiar old body that I'm always giving little presents to, they're going to file away in a horrible little socket of red clay. Funerals demean you, make you hate institutional religion and the climate. The climate." He murmured, implying an imminent risk to Ramsey and himself, "Most old men die at the height of summer. Blowflies desire them. I think Dr Leeming is lucky to have the ice."

Ploughing his own furrow single-mindedly, "There will be a state funeral," Leeming told them. He seemed certain that the information made the poet's arguments about clay and high summer irrelevant. Then he began to detail, with a gusto that would have fitted a public-relations man, some of the other arrangements: *Life* photographers, television stations approaching or being approached on matters preliminary to the finding of the corpse. It was hard to remember that this young man flushed by his encounters with the media was a career monk in the groves of Academe.

Ramsey governed himself, ignored his own hysteria, choosing not to believe it. It demanded such things as bullying Sir Byron into preventing Leeming; it condemned the widow to persuasion by the fist. His fingernails dug into his palm, aching to strike the widow for her malice towards her husband.

He said, "And Professor Sanders has given you leave to attend to all this?"

"I haven't heard officially. But I have what the army calls compassionate grounds."

Though one might wonder why, the poet was the most frankly angry of the three of them. "You've surely 'been approached'," he suggested, mocking the passive verb that Leeming had used, "by a tin-plate manufacturer with a tender to press a few thousand 'I love Leeming' badges."

But mockery did not bring even a silence.

"I hope you understand about my aunt," Denis honked. "As it is, I should be leaving for New Zealand this afternoon, but whether I get away or not depends ——"

The poet went blatantly admonitory. "This business of emerging so many years after death does seem to add a poetic roundness to your uncle's story. But its dramatic aptness in any refined sense may not be what primarily interests the people who are pestering your aunt."

"Pestering?" Leeming shut his eyes; he specialized in gestures of withdrawal. "Notice from them pesters somehow, while notice from you somehow dignifies. Even though *they* so often offer cold cash."

"Leeming Polar Manifestations Inc.," the poet muttered to himself.

Leeming had news for the poet. "If that's satire, it's of a crudity you seem to think properly belongs to other forms of communication than poetry."

The poet blinked and claimed, "I talk about what is patently decent for your uncle."

Denis continued sharp. "You mean some such thing as artistically decent, I think. Unfortunately, life isn't all art, neither is decency all art. The Americans, for example. The tone of their dealings in this matter is based on a presumption that the most natural thing to do with remains is to bury them at home. I suppose that as a race they spend more on military funeral arrangements than we do on our entire defence. You must have heard the story of that American aircraft carrier that plied between San Diego and Vietnam carrying nothing but bodies. Who is to say that their suspicions about what is decent aren't the right ones? Anyhow, you'll have to excuse me, Mr Ramsey. This visit begins to defeat its purpose."

When Leeming had gone, Ramsey and the poet glanced at each other, more or less offering to share the quiet, heady fury they each felt. Ramsey was the hesitant one, suspecting that the poet's anger would pass, was of the haphazard type that might come close to stinging a man into writing a letter to the editor; while Ramsey had abiding reasons for opposing the boy. Besides the abiding pressure of dread, he had a sense that the crisis of resurrection on which his newfound balance hung and from which his liberation would date depended on conditions as stark and free of foolery as those under which he and Lloyd had deserted Leeming. And apart from that he cowered from taking a place at the panegyrics and rituals of Leeming's home burial and from the lies he would have to tell to be exempted.

"It's simply not appropriate," the poet said.

But Ramsey wasn't soothing his urgency with rhetoric. He hunted in the university gazetteer for the number of Leeming's fellowship flat. He found and dialled it.

"Why should you be so upset?" he asked the poet, while the far end of the line rang and rang far longer than it should have, even if Belle had been tottery, even if she had not had the makings of a centenarian.

"I'm a conservationist by profession," the poet explained. "Besides Leeming, Antarctica itself—I'm fascinated by them. And I *am* writing on the subject."

"Yes, but how seriously do you take that?"

The poet was hurt, or pretended to be. "How seriously have I taken you?"

"It's Belle Leeming that has to be shifted. She's being either mad or perverse. Guess which? She was always a woman of principle. Perhaps she is acting on principle now."

"Even though," the poet said on the basis of rumours and anecdotes that must have been common in Canberra (old Belle and this, that, and the other distinguished old man), "even though in exercising her principles she sometimes took away those of others."

"Hello," Belle said then, from Leeming's flat.

"Belle, it's Alec." He abstained from bluntness. "I said hurtful things to you last night."

"Yes. But I can forgive you, Alec. While you can't reverse the favour."

"Belle, we've just now had a strange visit from your nephew."

"We?"

He told her that the poet was there.

"I hope he didn't mind my not seeing him."

"Really he's been writing about your husband. A long poem."

"Oh, Alec," she said secretively, "what a bore."

"Belle, the more freedom you give Denis, the more painful the whole affair will be. For you as well as me."

"We've already spoken about this, Alec." She seemed to be about to put the phone down.

"Belle, neither of us wants to be a guest at his funeral."

Then he told her of a conversation from their first summer in Antarctica when progress had astonished, even alarmed, Leeming.

Four of them were running dog-teams into the latitude at which a hut was being made for the inland wintering

175

planned by Leeming. The hut would be base to a party that would survey the hindside of the Victoria Land mountains and to the party of eight that would attempt a less valuable but more pressworthy journey to the South Geomagnetic Pole. The weather was excellent, and this further disturbed Leeming.

The four dog-sledgers were Leeming, Lloyd, O'Connor, Ramsey. O'Connor was a surveyor, gentle, wise, articulate, and sometimes pithy. He was devoutly Catholic without making too much ado about eating pemmican on Fridays or missing Mass. But if time allowed he read his Missal on Sundays. Leeming, who knew theology, respected him as a seemingly rational believer, but passed off this respect by teasing him for being very much like Cardinal Newman for someone called O'Connor.

A brief snowstorm kept them to their tent one Sunday. The four of them being crowded into a tent built for three, Leeming, Ramsey and Lloyd became engrossed in O'Connor's reading of his Missal. The book that each of them had brought had scarcely been chosen for the ennui of snowstorm, but ennui was irrelevant to O'Connor's reading. They all kept glancing at the rapt Papist. Lloyd stole snatches of ritual from over O'Connor's left shoulder. They were all doomed by these means to talk religion when O'Connor had finished.

Lloyd began respectfully, asking O'Connor some honest Masonic type of question about the consecrating of bread and wine. O'Connor answered well, too well for Lloyd, who was frightened off by all this talk of real distinctions between the substance and accidents of bread and wine. Not that Lloyd was easily intimidated, but there was danger of argument over such an exotic belief and, since they were jammed hip to hip behind plosive canvas in a gale, nowhere for offended parties to stalk off to. So Lloyd remained sensibly unprovocative.

In the same spirit, Leeming told O'Connor, "I can see that a belief in Christ's presence as something that is achieved by the performance of the act of social ritual called the Mass is justified. But why must you persist in this old form of the belief?"

"Old form?" said O'Connor. It was an old form for which he would have died. "All our beliefs are in the old form."

Leeming placated him. "What I mean is the belief that there is a Real Presence in the consecrated bread, that the accidents of the bread remain the same while the substance becomes the substance of Christ. Such a belief answers the needs of an age that is now dead and is expressed in terms of a philosophy, Scholastic philosophy, which has been passé for hundreds of years."

O'Connor said, "But surely, Stephen, you don't mean to say that Saint Thomas Aquinas and all those other great philosophers discovered only falsehoods ——"

"Oh no, not falsehoods. It was simply that their vision of the world became superseded by other visions of men equally great. But your doctrine of the Real Presence took no account of these."

O'Connor frowned, not because he had doubts but to find that his unobtrusive devotions had made him a stranger among his brother dog-sledgers.

"But please," Leeming went on, sensing the breach they had made by breaking the rule, common to officers' messes, that religion and politics should not be discussed. "I would like very much to believe what you believe."

And Lloyd wisely further soothed O'Connor. "To a simple man like me, it wouldn't make any difference what philosophy it was in."

"As a matter of fact," said Leeming, "besides the pallid Anglican ones, I have only one sacrament and that's an expensive one."

177

Lloyd smiled secretively, Ramsey saw, as if suspecting that Leeming was speaking of his wife.

"Antarctica is a timeless sacrament, unlike the ones we receive in churches," said Leeming. "It confers on me a sense of the absolute."

It was O'Connor's turn to pick holes. He smiled. "You must pardon me now, but it sounds a little like 'One is nearer God's heart in a garden than anywhere else on earth.'"

Leeming laughed in agreement. "One is nearer God's heart in Antarctica. . . . But no. Gardens, like rituals, are man-made. We humanize landscapes with gardens and humanize the unknown with rituals. But Antarctica can't be humanized, except in little ways—by a tent we pitch here or there, by the hot nonsense of our talk, which soon condenses on the tent wall. So Antarctica is a sacrament of the absolute, the same as all deserts are. It's a place for prophets, Arthur." He winked at Lloyd.

"Could have fooled me," said Lloyd.

O'Connor teased the leader. "If you're trying to tell us that Antarctica is a religion to you, then of course we'd never have guessed."

All four chuckled. Leeming contended, "Of course, Australia is a country in the prophetic mould too, but we have done such a stale old European job of humanizing it."

Lloyd said something about how he would have liked to be in stale old European Elizabeth Bay looking north-east across the harbour at the ships edging into Sydney for our stale old European wool.

In the light of this memory, Ramsey asked the widow not to remove Leeming's remains and not to give their care over to Denis Leeming. The poet whispered urgently, "Tell her I support you." Ramsey told her.

He heard Belle sniff, and could imagine the well-bred

head tossing, like a horse's. "Two days ago, Alec, you tell me in a stricken voice that I must decide on my own what to do, that you can't help me. So I make the decisions I think I should, only to find that now you're full of all kinds of anecdotes that are meant to be symbolic or something. I suppose that last one was intended to imply that dear Leeming would have preferred to stay in the ice?"

But the story of Leeming and O'Connor had rankled with Belle and, sniffing hope, Ramsey chose to stay moderate. "You say that at seventy-nine you're beyond making the arrangements needed. I was rash to argue with you. But in handing matters over to Denis you're condemning Leeming to an Australian burial that you yourself might find painful."

She repeated all her pleas, notably that of health. But Ramsey kept detecting an edge of dismay in her voice, testimonial enough to the validity of his story. Still she avoided the ultimate signs of bad faith, such as giving too many reasons.

One she had to give concerned Denis. "He's capable and has considerable respect for his uncle's memory. I know you'll think immediately of last night's performance. . . ."

Ramsey nearly asked which one.

". . . the fact is that in such serious dealings as these he's a different person. This is precisely the sort of responsibility he needs to shake off the effects of that appalling doctorate affair."

Ramsey made, in the poet's direction, eyes of disbelief. What he did not know was that while he spoke his mouth was set in lines of animal petulance that made the poet pity him.

He said what he had merely thought once before in debate. "I think, and I think you know, that it makes pretty indecent mechanics to balance the recent loss of a doctorate with the mummified weight of an old doctor."

"If you're quite finished, Alec. . . ." she said, but of course did not hang up with the insult unresolved.

Waiting, calm now, Ramsey shook his head again at the poet and saw the small penny-pinching mouth bunched in genuine discomfort at Ramsey's fears, or Belle's, or his own. Again Ramsey wondered in how profound a sense the man was interested in preventing Leeming's desecration. Perhaps he was given to transient moral enthusiasms, espoused loudly but with no hope of outdistancing Belle's rugged intentions. All that he knew about the poet's sense of rightness was that it seemed peculiarly sensitive in an area where his did not seem to so much as operate. It expiated a garrulous drunkenness with days off, six hundred miles of travel, two days' attendance on what passed for Ramsey's conscience. While Ramsey's own reaction in those circumstances would be to avoid that place, those people, that brand of liquor, for ever more.

"It's *my* husband you're talking about."

"My God it is! You were a grand sort of consort once. You tried to refine his pride in an almost outlandish way. You can't sign him over now, merely on the grounds that forty years have passed."

"Alec, do you actually think I'm in bad faith?"

"You haven't sounded like yourself, that's all. Not the old Belle. More like some old hen whose soul is troubled by a pulled thread in the Axminster."

"Indeed," she told him, regaining some of her balance, "I *have* come to value my carpets more as time goes by."

He said, "I'm not above begging you, Belle. Don't do it."

"Keep out of it," said Belle. "Keep out of it, Alec."

In the fellowship flat a door banged. "Denis has just come in, so I can't go on arguing about him. I mightn't see you again, Alec. But how dare you presume you're the only one who's disqualified from touching the corpse?"

On this rising question the line went dead so instantaneously that Ramsey suspected the gardening staff of carelessness with a spade. But he depressed the receiver-rest and heard a healthy dial tone.

To the poet Ramsey seemed full of brittle hope, feverish. "Belle doesn't care. If that Denis could be prevented. . . ."

He shook his head and slumped. The fast machinations needed to prevent Denis—to call on Chimpy perhaps, to call on Professor Sanders, the broaching of the question, the defining of his motives in terms they would under-. stand, the onus of professional bonhomie under which such calls would be made—all these prospects left him drained.

It was the poet who said that they must do what they could. It was the poet who telephoned and asked to be allowed to see Sir Chimpy straightaway.

"Well," said the vice-chancellor, "say in twenty minutes. I'm just finishing my speech for this afternoon."

"He'll be full of the euphoria of having prepared a good solid rant for his brother-man," the poet promised Ramsey.

Yet it seemed to Alec fantastic that they should approach the vice-chancellor: the indecency of young Leeming's intentions could not be shown by argument.

"I don't know if we should even try," Ramsey confessed. His stomach secreted apathy; he wanted to rest somewhere with drawn blinds. It was so complex, the cure he was undertaking; he wished he could go back to the tainted intimacy of his unresolved illness, his safe illness that no one tried to excoriate in a rush, that people pretended not to see, or wrote off as ulcers or overwork. Even at sixty-two one could *grow out* of one's ruinous preoccupations rather than be concussed. "In the world where Chimpy lives," he claimed, envious of Chimpy, "this matter is purely the Leemings' affair. And rightly so."

Yet the poet rubbed his hands, with some appetite for the confrontation. Sir Byron was an institutional man, he said, and could be made afraid of follies young Leeming might commit in the south: of tantrums, of frenzied likes and dislikes he might take to the American scientists, all to this university's disgrace.

"Dislikes, yes," said Ramsey. "And likes." He remembered the sexual revulsion Ella had brought home with her last night.

They were three minutes early at the vice-chancellor's rooms, and the girl in the outer office told them that, if they didn't mind waiting, Mr Leeming had promised to be no more than a few minutes. They sat feeling forestalled. But no more than a minute passed before they heard equable voices raised in good-byes, perhaps in pledges. Leeming came out, the long Leeming mouth held taut, a line of tough complacency above eyes bent to the task of closing the door as if in token regard for Sir Chimpy's good sense.

Ramsey wondered what it meant. Had Leeming been given permission to wear the university crest on his windproofs? Or to plant a copy of the vice-chancellor's *Fabian Socialism in Australian Politics* at the South Pole?

The young man recoiled before the blank eyes of the newcomers, but muttered something conventional and went off in good heart. An instant later Sir Chimpy negatived all his careful work with the door handle by sweeping the office door open and asking Ramsey and the poet in.

The poet pushed the argument based on decency and on the nephew's imbalance as preventing him from identifying what was fitting. He amplified it, counterpointed it far more strenuously than Ramsey would have dared. His passion if not his reasoning made Sir Byron sober. But slowly the vice-chancellor's face was forced into a gibbonous leer, the face of a man straitened by petitioners.

"I ought to tell you that young Leeming was here just now to appeal against the head of his school. Professor Sanders has gone so far as to refuse leave-of-absence."

"Ah then!" the poet said, seeming familiar with university protocol. "That settles it."

Sir Byron made further, if moderate, faces of lemurine anguish. "Yet it seems in some ways an unfortunate refusal. Certainly Leeming is in charge of the departmental programme and he was something like three months late home from sabbatical leave. The case you gentlemen put is impressive. But I have to be honest. To an outsider it all seems one—what you want, what Denis Leeming wants. Isn't it Mrs Leeming's affair? And as for his behaviour . . . well, we all of us seem to be having behavioural problems lately."

Alec grunted furiously in affirmation. Sir Chimpy heard it as protest.

"For God's sake, Alec, when I say all of us I mean all of us." He narrowed his eyes at them from beneath scrubby eyebrows, a gnarled figure of wisdom of the type usually found to have spent their lives in the saddle between Victoria Downs and the Channel country. "I intend to make these points to Sanders at the first opportunity, but since that may not be until this afternoon, I'd be grateful if you said nothing of it to him beforehand."

Yet Sir Byron was given his chance within seconds. Sanders was, at fifty, a pleasant man, his square jaws only just beginning to fall away into jowls that still bespoke a straight talker and a man of rapid decision. Over the past few seconds his rapid decision had been to pretend not to have heard the secretary say that Sir Byron was engaged, to knock tentatively like a secretary, to be bidden in and freeze in mid-entrance.

"I'm sorry, Byron," he said. "I thought I heard the girl say ——"

Sir Byron asked him could he wait.

But Sanders stood pat. His eyes glinted with what

183

seemed an excess of brotherhood but was probably anger. So he had to fire some of his ammunition off.

"It's simply the question of Leeming. He says he's been to see you and received certain assurances. Now I know he often overstates, but I thought I should make it clear that there are reasons why Leeming shouldn't go that I didn't, for peace' sake, reveal to him. The other reasons are adequate of course. He overstayed his sabbatical by three months, he was supposed to be preparing a timetable which, like his return, is still overdue. We're understaffed, and lectures begin in a few days' time. I don't apologize for refusing him leave on these grounds alone. But there's a better one, and that is that if he takes time off it should be to obtain medical treatment, that the man is bloody-well deranged; and the godlike stunt of resurrecting a snap-frozen corpse in front of the world's cine-cameras is going to do nothing to cure that."

Sir Chimpy let his irregular mouth be seen to waver on the edge of ordering Sanders out. But air was inhaled like wisdom, and savoir faire prevailed, or, once again, was seen to.

"But I'm intruding," Sanders mumbled. "Forgive me, Byron, Alec."

He left; and before long, so did Ramsey and the poet. Ramsey drooped; he wanted to find a room with a couch and blinds and old issues of *Time*, somewhere to spend four slack, secret hours and let his apprehensions sink to a sediment that could be seen and measured. He had had such a retreat planned for that afternoon, graduation afternoon, promising himself that his tarnished M.A. (Sydney) colours would not be missed on the platform. Yet, perhaps in reprisal for the minor impasse over Leeming, Chimpy had called after him, "I shall, of course, be seeing you this afternoon, Alec."

On the way down the path he wished for some convincing badge of illness, something that suppurated before the beholder's eyes, something that gave him permanent defence against formal occasions. Yet an after-taste of success kept rising in his throat. "Sanders won't give in. Perhaps Leeming might resign, but Sanders won't give in. And with young Leeming blocked. . . ."

He did not spoil the chances by voicing them; yet surely they would compel Belle to take on and discharge her responsibilities with a wave of her healthy hand. Which left dear Leeming where Alec suspected he should be. And so, for some reason, did the poet.

Then, at midday, the town's random transistors and the one that Ella and Ramsey tuned in with a false off-handedness announced the romantic news that nephew would resurrect uncle. Alec, fearing that the story's transmission made it fact, felt again the customary and amorphous sense of peril. Dressing for the afternoon's occasion, he was morose.

Ella tried to shake this state by asking him about the facts he had said he could remember now and utter. He was a conciliatory man by nature; yet her probing proved in no way curative, and simply maddened. He told her to stop bloody-well hovering.

Later he begged her pardon; but she was still full of hurt. It was a good pretext for her to tell him that she had gone to see Belle that morning.

"Why?" It was clear he was tantalized, not angry. He had squandered anger on a minor grievance and so put himself on a penitential footing, with less cause to protest at a secret meeting over which he had a right to protest.

Again he asked her gently why she had gone.

Ella was aggressive enough to tell the truth. "I wanted to see what she thought of her husband."

"Ah, yes."

"And let me tell you," she said as one giving him real grounds for fear, "she wouldn't mind if they exhibited old Leeming at agricultural shows."

"I can't understand it." He had become accustomed to this particular bafflement, but in his rush to make peace again with Ella he begged now for her interpretations of Belle.

Ella was thereby made bolder still. "I wanted to tell her, too, that it would be an excellent turning-point for us the day Leeming was buried by a minister of the ——"

"Anglican Church," Ramsey supplied. "And you should leave it to me to decide what the turning-points will be."

". . . Anglican Church in some place like Botany cemetery, within spitting distance of gasometers and the jail, and only a short drive from South Sydney Leagues Club."

"Except that we'd have to attend. Or compose lies. And I can't compose one that anyone's likely to believe for this afternoon, least of all for a burial like that."

"Anyhow, Belle tells me Leeming's old school has offered to have him buried, at their expense, under the floor of its chapel."

"God!" He clouted the back of an armchair. "Do you enjoy passing on these absurdities?"

"Are they absurdities?"

"What *is* she at?"

"You know her better than I do."

"She's playing around, the old freak. I wouldn't be surprised, only bloody appalled, if she made him an eternal schoolboy in that way. The idea of college chaplains invoking him in appeals against masturbation!"

"Perhaps Belle thinks his name could very properly be invoked for that."

There was no argument for him to win, just as there was no room with shutters. He asked her for time; but her anger was absolute again, and extended no credit. It damned her to be a thorny partner all afternoon.

In sharp daylight and mocked by bush flies, the colours of numberless degrees floated to the platform on the backs of dignitaries. Four rows of seats below the dais were similarly splashed and Benjamin-coated with doctorates and masters' degrees. Ramsey himself sat on high, squinting, with the high sun splashing into the corners of his eyes, trapped beyond all failures of bladder and nerve between the professors of agricultural science and geography. The big flies, gorged on a summer's sheep droppings, thudded against all these scholarly heads as abruptly as flung gravel.

Sir Byron spoke of the newly formed National Council of Student Health, of which he was a member, and fretted over the high incidence of problem drinking within this very university. The Dean and Lady Desideria, the knighted graziers on the senate, Sanders and all the heads of department, drowsed in antiseptic approval as if they were not passion's slaves or had never split wide with ripeness.

A sherry party followed on the lawns outside the administration block. New staff lined up to present their wives to Chimpy, whose doctoral cap rode quaintly that face seamed as a fisherman's. Yet it frowned, too, and took glances over its shoulder, perhaps not satisfied with the fall of the doctoral gown.

"Alec," Chimpy called as Ella and Ramsey went by. "Excuse me," he said to a new lecturer in English, and took Ramsey by the shoulder. "Look, Alec, Sadie's fifty yards away chatting with some old biddy from a cow stud." Ramsey spotted Lady Mews, seeing her to be indeed mindlessly gossiping with some breeder's wife. "She knows she should be here to speak to all these people." For a man of distinction he seemed lost; manners maketh the man, and

Sadie had always been one of his best manners. "Just ask her can I see her."

While they both closed in on Lady Sadie, Ella was mumbling. "He asked us because he knows we're too unhappy to gossip."

Showing a grand coldness, Lady Sadie considered her husband's summons for an odd time. The grazier's wife became engrossed in Sadie's failure to obey. When Lady Mews at last decided to go, seeming falsely youthful because of the grudges she bore, Alec knew that Sir Byron had not yet had his last surprise.

Professor Sanders beckoned to the footloose Ramseys, who were forced to join him. In intractable mood, Ella allowed herself to be steered by the elbow, like a convalescent forced to take fresh air.

Ramsey both liked and mistrusted liking Sanders, who was one of those men who at fifty looked thirty from a distance. The face, beaten about by the good life and somehow vacant with institutional loneliness, masked a discernible younger face. He looked like a young man done up for an old part, his smile a smear of cynicism over a raw innocence.

Innocence, or at any rate frankness. You suspected he found Ella desirable; that he had an eye for penetrating the dowdiness of academic gowns. But first he had his anger to tend.

"Did you hear the heart-warming midday news?"

"Yes." Alec, who had no appetite for revelations, said warily, "What will happen?"

"Chimpy was furious enough to begin with. Either he backs up the news report or he doesn't. If he doesn't, the dailies will find out the monstrous fact that Leeming's been refused leave. If he does, he has to persuade me. And persuaded is what I won't be." He seemed something of an ancient mariner, ready to give his story to any wedding guest who might be willing to stay and listen. "It's principle with me. I can't afford to sell out my principles as cheaply as Chimpy does, because my reputation has suffered enough as it is."

Both Ramseys were reminded of the girl last night who had been told much the same.

"But surely young Leeming won't be easily forgiven?"

"Won't he? When Chimpy called him in he came sloe-eyed with terror and dragging on auntie's hand. The old lady was contrite as hell and said she'd released the news thinking her nephew had definitely been given leave. So Chimpy's pacified now, and trying to swing me."

"Why not?" Ella muttered. Sanders did not bother to answer; Ramsey saw the question as a flexing of the bitter sinews of Ella's tongue. He felt afraid.

"Chimpy's trouble," Sanders ground on, "is that he doesn't understand how mad Leeming is in the strict sense. He thinks Leeming's objectives are just a nice little bit of nepotic carry-on. He sees me as the one who stands in the way of a reasonable settlement. He'll be one physics professor short if he keeps at it."

To check on the vice-chancellor's intentions, Alec glanced away to the fig-tree where Sir Byron had been holding court. Lady Sadie was in dutiful place, speaking with a newcomer while Chimpy managed the wife. On Chimpy's side of the tree the Kables, Belle, and Denis Leeming all waited as if for a massed audience.

Ella said, "What prevents you from a reasonable settlement?"

Sanders blinked, finding her intensity exhilarating, a thing of promise.

"Alec's deranged on the topic," Ella fought on, "and your pride is at stake. How can you dare to presume that Leeming isn't acting out of an honest understanding of what's fitting?"

Ramsey was hurt, but allowed himself to laugh. "After your recent experience of Leeming's honest understanding of what's fitting—an apt word, by the way—I thought you might be willing ——"

"Don't appeal to my prejudices, Alec. I try to rise above them."

Which Alec thought too fantastic a claim to dare reply to. "Does Chimpy know your feelings?" he asked Sanders.

"He does. And he won't be able to let his decision hang, either. I don't know when Leeming would have to leave for New Zealand if he's to go to Antarctica. . . ."

"As a matter of fact Mrs Leeming told me it should be this very afternoon," Ella told them. "So you see, you may have already won out over what Alec has the cheek to call Leeming's hysteria."

Here the debate was aborted by a new member of Sanders' staff who came up to bore them with his recent grain research. "It might occur to you to wonder," said the brilliant young drone on whom depended the wheat plains of tomorrow, "to wonder why someone interested in wheat-growing in low-rainfall areas would want to re-search the question in Wales. . . ."

But Sanders' face had fallen blank of the passions of low-rainfall grain and was aimed sadly at Ella. Ramsey swayed on his feet, agreeing at drowsy intervals that Wales was just the place and nothing matched the claims of Aberystwyth. The summer's afternoon had entered his mind, the fair translucent day and all its kin of bright days that transcended all this scholarly braying. Such were the days he would inherit or be initiated into by the settling of the question of Leeming's wronged body. His senses, in the meantime, felt strangely bound, as if his seeing was not value-for-money seeing, his hearing and touch marred, his experience of love synthetic. He was, entire, a slave to the event.

He looked again to see how, in its more banal ramifications, the event was shaping with Chimpy. Now the Kables had the vice-chancellor's ear, but Ramsey wondered at Lady Sadie's absence and was answered straightaway by her voice on his right.

"Might I speak with you a moment, Alec, if Ella doesn't mind?"

She was suppliant and old beneath the peachy falsity of make-up. She had only just passed into venerability from an era when she had always looked forty-five and what young scholars called an experienced-looking lay. Now she was young-old. On that account Alec reacted to her with an extra zeal. This reaction saddened him on reflection; Sadie had always unassailably connoted girlishness.

He was nevertheless perversely happy to join her now in her age and leave Ella to Sanders.

Chewing at her bottom lip, Sadie led him briskly towards the back of the administration building. Here, and in a sort of deference to her pallor, he took off his M.A. gown and slung it over his shoulder. A caterer's truck was parked at the back entrance, and a swarthy boy ran upstairs carrying two trays of canapes.

"Tomorrow's bitter women," said Lady Sadie, nodding at big-thighed girl undergraduates who were lobbing a ball about the courts below. She shuddered. "Not only did I have to get away from him, but I had to find someone reliable to talk to as well. You're eminently a person one can talk to, Alec. No doubt that's why you haven't gone as far in the world as he has."

"There are other reasons," Alec assured her, "not so creditable as that."

Lady Sadie uttered a small yelp of bitterness. "Do you think his brain is going? He stands there listening to pleas from the Kables about young Leeming. He listens on the grounds that Kable's father was connected with the expedition somehow and they feel there's no hope of an apotheosis for the great explorer unless young Leeming is let loose on him. Byron pretends to see their point, but all the time she stands there the old buffer's hopes are rising. Blatantly. He drags his eyes away from her to listen to solemn denunciations from Eric Kable." She said in a thin prayerful voice, "God help us. He's been down to Milton once a week since that awful night the poet was at our place. On the flimsiest pretexts." She began to splutter. "She's just not the right kind of adventure for a vice-chancellor. I'm simply more elegant than she is. It doesn't matter. The year will come when he'll bury me without a thought."

Ramsey did his best to explain the handicaps of the male mind when faced with something so immediately savoury but ultimately poisonous as Valerie Kable. Lady Sadie said politely that male cant did not convince her. "It's not anything positive like hot blood that makes him behave the way he does. It's the vacancy of men, the lack of a gift for personal relationships. One always forgives their extramural ardours for the sake of what little sap there is in the marriage one has." With surgical care, her sharp-tied shoe calmly divided a heap of gravel. "There's nothing I fear so much as the marriage I've had."

Ramsey said that it would bewilder and possibly kill Chimpy if she left him. "Do you think Chimpy regards you as outweighed by that baroque compilation of hips and breasts?"

Suddenly Lady Mews was angry. "We all have to sacrifice one thing for another. But you think men are allowed to prefer one thing to another and indulge a list of whims in order of preference."

Her hand gave up fury, though, and lay on her knee like something stray, to be lifted and petted. He tried to do such things, but may have had too much the air of the worldly-wise male quashing silly feminine fears; for she would not allow this mercy.

"Look, Sadie, you have him worried. Perhaps you've always been too reliable. You haven't taught him subtle female ways." Perhaps that was why he fell to unsubtle Mrs Kable. "Believe me, your new qualities engross the poor old man, one way and another."

She shook off Ramsey's casuistry. To win on these terms would never again satisfy honest Sadie Mews. "It's the lack of dignity. The vice-chancellor is agog. While that slut stands in front of him pleading for a lover more recent, or perhaps just more regular." The rare spite with which she spat out the last word suggested that she may have been let down by Sir Chimpy's dwindling vital powers.

Ramsey soothed her to the extent of telling her there was reliable evidence that young Leeming was not Valerie's lover but Eric's.

A great part of Sadie's anger was drained by the scandal-power of his news. "I'm too simple-minded," she marvelled. "There's a funny loyalty there, between the Kables, and an amazing compatibility."

"They're held in balance by the tensions of their own mutual queerness," Alec glibly diagnosed before seeing through himself and confessing, "It's better than nothing."

"Well, I intend to rout them. Will you come with me, Alec?"

His status as confidant had Alec almost elated and almost wise. "My position is difficult," he said. "I don't want Chimpy to think I've primed you for the act. We're allies, Sadie, you and I. As you don't want to be humbled in public, I don't want to have Leeming the elder dug up and vulgarly exposed by his nephew." Who was he to be Nemesis to a vice-chancellor? "I've already spoken to Chimpy, you see, precisely on this point. Also, he's confided in me. About the change in your attitude, I mean."

"He hasn't seen half of it," Sadie told him. She kissed his cheek and strode off in her firmest gait.

It was surprising that once Ramsey had gone the young grain-buff sensed the submerged furies of Mrs Ramsey matched by Sanders' dreaminess; in fact, a joint hostility to grain research. So he left.

Sanders, too, felt that he was standing near a dynamo whose bearings ran hot, though not in any sense favourable to him. He said with proper male humility, "You people are very wrapped up in this Leeming business."

"If you knew. . . ." Ella said.

One of the things he didn't know was that as indemnity against Ramsey she had begun to savour his own pleasant masculine looks. He would have been pleased to be admired even on such negative grounds.

"If you knew," she was saying, "you'd let that boy go and take his uncle's carrion out of what is, after all, a fairly accessible pit in Antarctica."

"I don't understand."

She explained in acid syllables that made a counterpoint to her sampling of his face. "As far as Alec sees it, that man in the ice is a power to be propitiated. He preoccupies himself with the myth he has made of Leeming. What he fears most of all, though, is that the myth might be taken away. Young Leeming will reduce old Leeming to the level of mere man. In my eyes, that's a pretty valuable service. To my husband, it's desecration."

There was a bitter, bruised look about Ella's eyes that Sanders judged as pure neurosis. He had a roué's narrow-mindedness about what intense women wed to old men needed. Ella's ardent demand that ice-bound Leeming be demythologized seemed to him a conceit, something too intensely asserted for the sake of covering more primal needs.

194

Though he knew in his bones that he had never aggrandized any woman by unselfishly attending to her primal needs, perhaps he thought that, with Ella's dark, farm-bred body before him, the thinking man who could not manage a little mental lie would be wanting.

"You'd like me to go to Chimpy and give in?"

Ella stared straight ahead, shaking her head. No visible blandishments. He could in fact see the makings of middle age in her and was humbled by pity; but waited for the sexual illusion to reinstate itself.

"I can see you wouldn't easily do that," she told him.

"No. I don't know what stories you may have heard of me, Mrs Ramsey. But the very existence of such stories makes it necessary for me to be a man of principle. One of my principles, though, isn't pride. It isn't mere pride that stops me giving in."

"Stout lad!" Ella mocked.

"I know I must sound like a town clerk defending the location of a new sullage works," he admitted.

Ella sniffed and looked away up the garden through which a few early leave-takers were filtering to the gate. "Never mind. But what is the good clean fun of principles to you is death to me."

For the vagrant excitement of it, she might accept coffee in his nearby flat when he offered it. If he did offer it; if she hadn't frightened him too thoroughly.

While she was faced away, Sanders took the chance to check her for hints of dewlaps or fallen gullet. No signs. He said, "I know, I know." With his reputation, he had to say the next lines with gusto. So played, they sounded reliable, humane, too obvious to involve danger. "I'm sick of this hubbub. So must you be. What if we were to talk this whole question out in my flat? We could have tea and some fruit-cake. . . ."

That would have to do, she decided. At least Ramsey would *presume* worse things than fruit-cake.

There was something endearing about Sanders' flat in college. They were a dreary few rooms for a man old enough for grandparenthood to call his home. Yet, bravely as a young bachelor, he had made them home. Ella thumbed through the humanism Sanders had nurtured all down one wall of his library: Patrick White and Iris Murdoch, A. J. P. Taylor and Robert Frost. She wondered why humanists themselves failed to be as tolerant of science.

"Ah, that's better," said the professor, returning from the kitchen with tea and finding her browsing.

"I was thinking that you rarely find a big science section in the bookshelves of all those humanists who rave about the barbarity of technocrats."

"That's very flattering." He growled with pleasure at her compliment. "Let's sit."

Through a few inches of opened bedroom door Ella could see the notorious Sanders bed looking lumpy and superannuated with the sun across it. But the easterly view of hills and forests growing into the sempiternal easterly afternoon fitted the spirit of dalliance well. Ella was losing bitterness, and wanted to be pleasant and even appetizing. She sat with her knees and ankles locked. Mrs Kable sat that way—to some effect, apparently.

Ramsey and Leeming the elder were their conversation; and, in case he had any doubts on the question, she repeated how she had a sense that it was important for Ramsey that Dr Leeming should undergo the bankrupt rituals of modern burial on the Australian continent.

"And you say your husband has a conviction to the contrary?" Sanders asked her. "You're a very symbolic pair."

"I know it sounds extreme," she challenged him.

"No, I can see it."

Her fever of belief, aimed through eyes that tended to become stark, somehow made her more desirable. He hoped that he might be allowed to dabble scot-free behind the ramparts of her massive obsession.

"And you think that if I unleash young Leeming. . . . Mrs Ramsey, don't be offended please, but do you think Alec should see a doctor?"

Ella's legs came unstuck, and frank annoyance made her seem very young. "Drugs can't put a gloss over this sort of thing. Anyhow, doctors merely tell you to play golf."

"They do, don't they."

By means of their shared secrets they were brother and sister; he put a hand fraternally on her shoulder. "Look, I really do need young Leeming. I've refused leave to men with better claims than he has." Rising to take her empty cup he more or less took its place on her right hand, and ventured a slack, asexual hand right round her shoulders. "To be frank, Ella, the relationship between yourself and your husband seems to me like a first-class furniture-exhibition room into which no light has been let for a long time. All the furniture of your backgrounds become shadows and the shadows become demons. You know, perhaps he *should* play golf, that husband of yours. But I put it badly."

He had. Yet she had listened to the shape of the words and not their poor imagery, and Sanders, given her engrossed air, thought that it had all made some impact. For the healthy always believe that their figures of speech are some succour to the ailing.

He said, tightening his arm at each stressed syllable, "And I *have* to *stand* by *what* I've *said*."

To emphasize the point even more deeply, he drew her against his chest. Ella came limply, admiring the indefinable musk of his maleness. And the innocence! Or its illusion anyhow, for her sad head leant from a decent distance and only tipped the suited pad of fat that was his left chest.

"So I don't think your salvation lies along the lines you suggest," he affirmed softly and brushed his lips across the chemical stiffness of her made-up hair.

"I know you say that in good faith," she said, at pains not to be breathless. "But I know what my troubles are. I've felt their sharp edges. I've had seven years' leisure to define them."

Such a long speech made her sound off-handed. Under cover of her inadvertence, his mouth made a quick *pro forma* raid down one side of her cheek. Ella sat up straight in surprise at its wholesomeness—he had been chewing chlorophyll gums in the kitchen. She actually felt flattered. This was his greatest success so far; yet he misread her surprise.

"I'm sorry," he said. "They shouldn't let women over forty look so attractive."

With the right shade of cynicism, Ella told him to be more careful in future.

He murmured, "I think that if I had any suspicion that I could contribute to your peace of mind, I'd give in. I can see—any fool could—that there's a genuine agony there, behind your insistence. If I could do anything for that agony. . . ."

He made quietly to reach for her cheeks with both hands and, as if from the very humanity of his feelings towards her, let the near hand slide away down her right breast.

Ella, one of those women who think that, come the crisis, their very organs would remain devoutly monogamous, was shocked at how much she, or her right breast anyhow, relished his hand. Flurried, she almost decided that Alec Ramsey deserved betrayal. She lolled side-on to Sanders' big chest and let his hand again and again take that one breast and leave it. His bear-fisted brand of

198

tenderness, like his furnishings, endeared. Yet she was frightened to see, down the ham of his left leg, that the male mysteries were at work. Alec could be easily dissuaded at any point in the growth of desire, but Sanders might not be so reasonable.

She was reassured by the fussy way he began the unbuttoning of her suit. He loosened two cleats, and began to sigh for the impersonal teguments of her foundation.

An abstract frown held the lady's face; she sat as still as the victim in a clinic and murmured, "But what about the Leeming business?"

She felt she had only just enough contrariety left to manage the question.

"Oh Christ," he said tenderly but far gone. "We'll have to see about that, won't we?"

"So it isn't as much a matter of principle as you thought?"

"You didn't come here just to show me up as shallow, did you?"

"Well," she said, "no. I simply mention it."

He would have been pleased to know that her stomach had actually begun on the positive business of distilling affection for a large professor of physics rather than mere bile against Ramsey. As long as she kept her eyes away from Sanders' large square face and grimacing mouth, the passion was manageable. But how or when, short of adultery, you ended the interview she could not guess.

"But you could let Leeming go then?"

Sanders still worked on fasteners; she didn't dare to verify which ones. In acknowledgment of selling himself, he began breathing desperately. She wanted to reassure him that she was no monomaniac but was only making conversation. "Yes, yes, Ella," he said. "It's not *that* important. I don't know why people like me stand on their dignity when any second they're likely to find themselves in the delicious . . . *grotesque* state . . . we'll find ourselves in very soon. Or so I hope."

Ella found herself seconding the wish by taking a long draw at his lips, making that oral vacuum-lock so popular with lovers. Then her shoulders were exposed and Sanders chewed at them.

"I suppose you've got those bloody step-in things on."

They were some defence, hard for anyone but the wearer to take down. Ella could very nearly have taken them down in a half-conscious flurry of lust, and even seemed to herself to wait for one to sweep over her. When it failed to, "Very big step-ins," she panted defensively.

"Bloody undergraduates don't do themselves up in all that stuff."

"The undergraduate backside isn't as big as mine," she said, and jumped as his hand reached up under the elastic device and notched its fingers into the base of her left buttock.

"Christ," Sanders whispered. "Like cushioned ivory."

Both Sanders and Ella herself believed she was more tenderized than she truly was. When his hand passed under her crutch she found the desecration jarring. Instantly the occasion became inhuman; he worked frenziedly, though the corselet scarcely budged to his sudden, big-fisted blatancy.

She said, "Heavens!" above his grizzled head lowered to her breasts with what seemed cannibal intent.

"There!" she said, discovering she was upright.

He had been forcing her against pillows and she had merely stood in a south-westerly direction. There she was, gazing down past the frou-frou of pawed clothing to the big knees that had plagued her since girlhood.

Half-standing himself, Sanders had the sense to know how absurd he might look upright. "Ella, darling," he said like the saddest of compulsive lovers, and she was amazed to register that despite the cataleptic streakiness of his face and the way he sat as if assailed by physical pain, it might not take many "Ella, darlings" to make her slip her buckram defences and go to him naked.

He kept calling on her. She covered her ears.

"I should tell you, Professor," she said, "I have cancer of the womb."

Tears came easily as a substitute for the orgasm that would have done her so much harm, would have perilously confused the centripetal forces of love and resentment that buffeted while they united herself and Ramsey.

"I hope you can forgive me."

Sanders nodded, looking idiotic, paled by the horrendous news, stung close to petulance by his braked passion.

"Please forgive me."

He mightn't have if it hadn't been for that magic lethal word.

"There's no question of forgiveness," he said. "Sit down there."

Ramsey sat a long time watching the big-beamed girls at their tennis. Then he lifted himself with an old man's groan and went searching for Ella.

She could not be found, so he looked then for Sanders. Sanders could not be found. "Ah-hah," he formulated to himself in self-mockery, "seduction!" He sauntered towards the car-park, and had time even to talk to the professor of English about a new study of Housman. Then, at the gate, he realized that Ella, his wife, was actually embittered; and embittered ladies were a prime mark for the lecher. He thought, as Ella had, of punitive adultery. He felt sick with pity for her, and then a sense of dispossession such as he'd rarely felt since, during two estrangements before they were married, he'd seen her in the company of men of her own age.

He began to shamble across-country then, towards

Gamma block of Morton College where Sanders had his flat. And, fearing himself cuckolded, he grieved for himself in an objective way: international footballer, man-hauling hulk, dilettante, bookman, educator, at the end of all his promise, stumbling in a parody of his Antarctic self, an equivocal and brittle gent. At last he was ambling uphill through the staked shrubs of Gamma block's garden. Sweat made him peevish, and he swore not to come panting into Sanders' rooms. But this conceit cost him a long half-minute. If that thirty seconds gave her time to perfect the act she was welcome to it.

Upstairs, even before knocking, he could hear Sanders talking soberly inside—in a voice far from bated with unlawful ardour. He answered Ramsey's knock almost immediately. There was an unwilled cringe of the eyes for a mere second, but then an easy movement of welcome with the free hand. Ella, all in order, sat in a large armchair, powdering the line of her jaw in a languorous, intimate way that implied that this foreign room had become part of her history. He suspected that she had begun to behave this way only a second before the door opened, and so was mutely telling him, "Don't dare predict that come what may I'll never take lovers." Alec knew that, in the book of her nature, the difference between adultery and her present behaviour was merely a matter of degree.

Sanders said, "I saw you running up the slope from the bridge, Alec. I hope you weren't worried. The truth is I should have left a message, but Mrs Ramsey seemed so tired—with good reason, I can tell, since she's confided in me. Her condition."

"Condition."

Behind Sanders' back, Ella made gestures of urgency, winks, wry faces.

"Yes. I do hope the treatment does the trick."

Ramsey was both annoyed at Ella's foolery yet grateful

for being asked to partner her in drollery.

"What do you mean by treatment?" he asked Sanders. Ella again made antic faces of pleading. "Oh, I see. No, it shouldn't cause much trouble."

"Well, you both seem very brave about it. I detest the very word *cancer*. . . ."

"Cancer? Of the womb, you mean?" Alec asked him in a staccato, unsettling way.

Sanders nodded.

"Oh, that," Ramsey said dismissively.

"She thinks I should let Leeming have leave."

"Oh, yes. But don't let her affliction influence you."

Ella giggled silently while continuing to ply the Helena Rubinstein into the sides of her nose.

"How about sitting down after that hard run you've had. Would you like a beer, or some tea?" Sanders was disturbed by Ramsey's sparse and ambiguous intonations.

"Now I've found Ella, professor, I'd prefer to take her home."

"Yes, I had better get," Ella admitted. She packed up her cosmetics like the enamelled lady both men knew her not to be.

Sanders was leaning forward to open the door for them when it knocked. He opened it to the tall girl whom last night he had lectured on questions of principle. She was hot and sick from, Ramsey supposed, the same walk he had done.

At the sight of her Ella stiffened, for the girl was ashamed and apologetic and, Ella judged, misused, one of the sisterhood. Somehow her arrival so soon after Ella's own near-miss infidelity underlined Sanders' culpability and shallowness for her, even though he didn't seem pleased at the young lady's coming.

Her name was Miss Bourke, and she was a research assistant in Sanders' department.

"Well, you do have busy afternoons," Ella told Sanders.

"The Ramseys were just going, Sally," Sanders said.

Yet, shown out and locked out, Ella would not leave the top landing.

"I came close to losing my virtue to that man," she told Ramsey. "I want to know what he's doing to that girl. Besides, she works with young Leeming."

"For Christ's sake, he'll be at his window to see that we really do go away."

"Rot. He gets paralytic with desire."

He became furious at her knowledge of Sanders' processes and went away and sat on the bottom step. Even there he could occasionally hear Sanders' voice raised, though not in anger. Perhaps on principle. Without warning, he wanted to tell Ella about Leeming. One of his visible reasons was that she had wronged him today herself and had some small knowledge of the lineaments of betrayal. But this was merely a reasonable cause invoked after the decision had taken him by the throat.

"Ella, for God's sake come down here. I want to tell you about Leeming," he called.

Ella hushed him. He came close to weeping.

After ten minutes she came downstairs rampant, distracted by Miss Bourke's trouble. Hustling Alec downhill, she kept telling him, "But first let me tell you. . . . *That swine.* . . ." Her pallor was as unwholesome as Miss Bourke's, though not, it seemed, for the same reason. For Miss Bourke was pregnant to Sanders. She had met a student who wanted to marry her and raise the child as his own, but who had no means. Miss Bourke's income was small. She wanted Sanders to make some settlement on account of the unborn. "I think she said three thousand dollars, nothing massive, enough to last them until the stepfather graduates and starts work. She obviously feels degraded to have to struggle with Sanders like this."

"Pity she didn't feel degraded when he propositioned her."

"Well, *you* know well how it is with the young."

"For God's sake, Ella."

He was amazed that the things that had been unspeakable for forty years were about to slip out in the middle of banter; the banter itself emerging in the middle of rage, Ella's rage against Sanders, and pique, his pique at Ella.

Ella hissed on. "He says he'll pay for an abortion but he won't pay for a child who may not even be his. *He says that's a matter of principle.*"

Ella waited for the now familiar words to settle. "She won't have an abortion because she's Catholic and holds the old-fashioned and *unprincipled* view that it's murder." Which old-fashioned and unprincipled view Ella shared. "But our friend says that her beliefs forbid fornication too. If she fornicated she should be willing to murder. Although he uses a nicer word than murder." Continually she punished her own thigh with her weighty handbag. It was a movement that fitted her self-disgust. "He can't see the difference between a random lapse and a plotted course of evil."

"Yes," said wan Ramsey.

"I hope she reports him."

"She wouldn't do that."

"Perhaps Leeming would if he knew. I hope he knows."

"Oh, don't wish that on anyone, Ella."

"The girl hadn't graduated at the time; she was still an honours student. *It is required of a steward that he be found faithful. . . .*"

Ramsey said, "Ella, listen. You know Arthur Lloyd, recently deceased? Well, Lloyd and I—no, I shouldn't put it that way, as if the guilt were mainly Lloyd's—I and Lloyd left Leeming while he was still alive."

He studied the stones at his feet. He heard Ella titter.

"I've found myself, strictly speaking, incapable of saying that," he muttered, and raised his eyes. "You're the only one I've ever told."

Incredibly, Ella gave a sort of unpretentious shrug. "Is that what has you by the throat?" She went on quickly, as if to clear away a minor point for the sake of a quick return to the subject of Sanders and his girl. "You may not believe me, but I've read Leeming's instructions to his sledging parties. You obeyed him. As he deserved to be obeyed."

"You're an absolutist, Ella, and you know a conscience isn't bound or excused by sledging instructions. He would never have obeyed them himself. No one can realize how indecent it is to leave a living thing there."

Ella declaimed, "The priesthood of Antarcticans! You mean to tell me this is the core—the thing that's taken half a lifetime to get said?"

"Well, since Lloyd died, anyhow. I had somehow forgotten it until then. I was very hazed at the time of Leeming's dea . . . well, of Leeming's final illness. Everything I felt about it was undefined, hazed, you know. Until when Lloyd was dying, he mentioned it—that Leeming had been left like that. He mentioned it to say that it had been the right thing and that I wasn't to let it distress me as it seemed to have done in the past. The moment he spoke I knew I'd always known; the fact crystallized. Look, Ella, I'm running out of breath." They waited for breath in a groin between the hills. There was a low summer creek brewing scums and withered thorn bushes. "It was like having your illness diagnosed by an expert and when he tells you what's wrong you realize he's exactly right and you say, 'Yes, that's the thing I've been dying of all along.'"

"I don't believe it," Ella told him.

Alec persisted. "It happened, we left him."

"I don't give a damn if you did. That's reasonable enough. I don't believe that all this frenzy stems from something so simply said and excusable. But it's more than excusable. It's right and sensible. Now isn't it?"

"You think your enemies are beyond all moral consideration. And Leeming's your enemy."

She sneered. "I must apologize for that. You see, he's been falsely represented to me."

"For Christ's sake keep the thing quiet, Ella. The Morton College students will be coming down here. . . ."

"What was Leeming's opinion of being left?"

"He had none. He was sleeping."

"In a coma?"

"I'm not a medical man."

"Ah, that's a point."

"You win, Ella. He was in a coma and ——"

"In a death coma."

"Who could say that? I'm afraid, Ella. Terrified."

"Lloyd pronounced him dead?"

"Yes."

"Well, *you* couldn't, could you? Lloyd was the doctor."

"Legalism cures nothing. I left him."

"I left him," Ella mocked. "Honestly, you talk as if you were his lover."

"That should be the least of your fears. And while we're talking about fear, yours about this Leeming business . . . that I was withdrawing from you and all the rest of it . . . surely you can't believe that any more?"

Ella stamped away a few yards, another excessive rage in what had been an afternoon of excess. "You mean I should believe you when you say that what has always plagued you is as simple as Leeming being five-sixths or nineteen-twentieths dead when you called it a day on the mere pretext that you were both starving? And you mean to say you didn't even know about it in those terms until I was in hospital failing to bring forth anything. . . ."

"Until Lloyd was dying," Ramsey amended.

"It's easier to believe you hate me as a wife."

"With your gift for hysteria ——"

"Don't talk to me about hysteria."

They began to walk again. There was no one to be seen. Uphill, the trees of Administration formed a barrier beyond which dons and graduates made pretence of civilized enthusiasms. Ramsey clenched both fists. He was eager to be judged; his thirst for judgment surprised him.

"What sort of moral monster are you?" He was too frantic to see the contradictory nature of the question: *What sort of moral monster are you not to see that I'm a moral monster?* He felt insulted, like a criminal who comes into a police station to confess to unsolved murders and finds that everyone is too busy tracing stolen handbags to take down his confession. "You understand what I'm telling you?"

"It's a bore," she said, to insult his sense of having sinned prodigiously.

"I swear to you, Ella, I'm not deluded. Please, Ella. I'm amazed myself at how . . . well . . . unmomentous, comparatively speaking, it all sounds. But it's very hard to bring out the importance, the quality of these things, in so many words."

"Quieten down," she told him. A straggle of undergraduates wearing or carrying gowns with the distinguishing stripes of Morton College had appeared round the flank of the hill on a course that would take them within ten yards of the Ramseys. Ella would not look at them but ambled forward bent, inspecting the track. Their passage downhill for some reason left her disturbed, chastened. Meanwhile, Ramsey became happy in a surface way that the mystery had been said; yet he knew in the blood that he was deceived. There was a new urgency in him to speak it right. For this purpose the limits of words would have to be broken.

He found Ella was calling on the objective evidence. "It sounds like a case of suggestion to me. I mean, Lloyd was old and under drugs. You didn't know *in so many words* until Lloyd told you. *Under* drugs ——"

"No, he was lucid, clear-headed. . . ."

"Perhaps it was a story that just answered your neurosis. You seized it as the cause for certain feelings you had. Perhaps all you've done is lay old Belle—which doesn't seem to have harmed the lady at all. . . ."

She could see, because he was glowering at the track now, that her contempt for his crime had hurt him. She said gently, "Anyhow, nobody will blame you for it. No one."

For Ramsey, it somehow stood as proof of the insanity of their relationship when, later that evening, Ella took the car and came home, after an hour and a half, with Sally Bourke. To her credit the girl looked wary. It was possible that Ella had said things so contrary to Sanders' suggestions of abortion that Miss Bourke felt, as never before, irrevocably with child. The Ella who tramped ahead of the girl was flushed and appeased, and distracted utterly from Ramsey's crisis.

"I've asked Sally could she stay with us a while," she told him. "We have all this space. . . ."

"Mrs Ramsey was so insistent," Sally Bourke told him in extenuation.

"She shouldn't be paying rent, with the child coming on."

Sally Bourke blushed, and Ella had the grace to rein herself in. "Alec knows. Please don't feel uneasy. Alec and I, we've made our sexual mistakes at our appointed seasons."

Alec blinked and wondered when Ella's seasons had fallen.

"Come through here and I'll show you your room." She made a jerky, dominant guide; with such a dowager as well as the Catholic mysteries all riding vigilante over her motherhood, Sally Bourke might as well acquiesce in layettes.

Ten minutes they were gone, while Alec tramped and gestured to himself, finding it hard to believe that there was not malice and contempt behind this dragging of new issues into a house drum-tight with old ones.

Ella came back alone. "Toilet," she whispered at Alec, as if their silence would assist Sally.

He said the girl couldn't stay: they were crowded in a sense that made the number of rooms they had available an irrelevance.

"That's the trouble," she said, remembering Sanders' figures of speech. "We never let in any of the light of other people's preoccupations."

He fabricated arguments. "Have you noticed that she's very beautiful and that her preoccupation doesn't show yet? When it does, people will think I'm responsible."

Ella, flushed with do-gooding, laughed off the opinions of others. "That's a reputation you could be very proud of."

A ringing telephone stopped him from giving her a chance to be compassionate towards him. She scooped up the receiver after a short robust walk of the type seen among successful corsetieres. But the frown she gave upon listening went down to the bone, was not staged.

"Oh, professor," she said.

He saw the authentic frown (signifying, on top of all her landlady-like skittishness, that she had developed concerns of her own) as reason for leaving her. He was hundreds of yards away on a walk meant to last for hours and to impair health—for which reason he was busy-minded recording what pains there were in the right side of his belly and what indigestive, perhaps cardiac, stabs rankled under his left armpit—when he remembered she had said, "Oh, professor," and wondered if it had been Sanders and why.

In fact Sanders was telling her that he loved and needed her, that her mature sense of irony was combined with a vestal quality, innate and precious to her, that girls lacked these days. Surely, too, she had needs . . . but no, he wouldn't mention her needs: he needed *her* stability, he would not presume needs in a woman so impressive as she.

She told him her needs were being met as well as she could humanly expect.

Yet he seemed to believe that the tensions in her voice were those of a lady, a *vestal* lady, under unexpected siege. He said that suddenly his criterion of behaviour was *her*. If she felt there was some benefit for her in Leeming's funeral arrangements, then he would have to give in in front of Chimpy.

She said tightly, "You have to do whatever your principles dictate."

In spite of the arguable nature of his hopes, Sanders, no liar, next rang Sir Byron. The vice-chancellor himself answered the call.

Sanders told him, "Look, Byron, I've been rethinking this whole Leeming situation. . . ."

He could tell Chimpy was distracted by a gay female voice within the lodge that Sanders could hear on the line —speaking at Chimpy.

"Brian," Chimpy said, "I have Sadie here, and she's not too well." Sadie could even be heard, arguing that she'd never been better. "Wait a second and I'll speak to you on the extension in my study."

Sanders began to sweat. Here was the same taut wariness towards his large gesture which he had already met with in Ella. In the humming vacancy of the telephone wires the woman's voice ground on remotely. Then, hollowly, Sir Byron's rose.

"Yes, Brian?"

"As I said, I've been rethinking. . . . As a matter of fact, I've been talking with Ella Ramsey."

"Oh, yes?"

Sanders would have liked to lay a fist on Chimpy, who had been stung, probably by Sadie, to overtones.

"Well, all this is very close to the bone with the Ramseys, and Ella thinks it's important for her husband that I should permit Leeming senior to be exposed to Leeming junior. I must apologize for messing you about, but if I'd known that decent people like the Ramseys were involved, I'd have given in on the issue long ago."

The vice-chancellor's voice sprang out at him. "Well, it's a bit too late for you to become magnanimous, Brian, just on the grounds that you've scored with Ella."

"Listen, Byron, if I score with anyone I'll let you know. In the meantime, Ella Ramsey is a rare creature in this age. She's a woman of virtue."

"Oh, my God!" Chimpy intoned. "As I was saying, it's a bit late to be magnanimous. I've already arranged that things should stay the way you decided. The Leemings have agreed to square things with the press. Besides, young Leeming's distracted by a letter that came this afternoon from an American publisher who wants to publish his failed doctoral thesis. So you see, he's going to get his spurs another way than by digging up his uncle. Of course, it's your department," Chimpy added after a silence.

"Perhaps we'd better let things stand then," Sanders

admitted, feeling foolish, and therefore at least starting to sicken of vestal Ella.

"One other thing, though," Chimpy said. "We've had a complaint from a research assistant of the female variety who says you offered her four hundred dollars to have a pregnancy aborted. Hullo! Are you still there? I was saying. . . ."

Sanders said, "All right then. But she was put up to it by someone. Someone she works with, I mean. Leeming, for example."

"You know that's not the truth. He would have threatened you with it first, before bringing the girl to me."

"He knew that isn't the sort of pressure I give in to."

"That's heroic of you. Listen, I'm going to try to prevent this girl's story from getting out."

"That's merciful of *you*."

"But if it can be reasonably demonstrated that you *are* the father ——"

"No need to demonstrate it," Sanders said, established again on his old tack of moral bravery. "Unless her undergraduate's been at her, it's likely that I'm the father. But it's almost equally likely that her boyfriend's had a bash." He could tell that Sir Byron, as a man who had strenuously tended his own career, was chastened, or at least amazed, by this frantic honesty. He said in grand derision, "The girl's religion, so the papers tell us, frowns on contraception."

Chimpy was rendered fraternal. "Brian, I'd recommend a settlement. Could I suggest that. . . ."

The female voice intervened again, and a grating noise as of shifted furniture.

The vice-chancellor said, "Do you mind if I phone you back, Brian? Sadie seems to be going away for a few months' rest. Of course, at my suggestion." Still, he

213

sounded patently bemused. "It's thrown the household out a lot, though."

He wisely cut the querulous background noises by hanging up on Sanders.

The night, Ramsey found, was uncongenial to deaths; mild and bright under a northerly rush of air with just a little of the breath of summits in it. For mortal man of sixty-two he made good time, though most of his way was uphill towards the university and ultimately into it. Here the union store was working late and doing trade in what Ramsey's mother called "forget-ables": thread and toothpaste and shaving-cream.

For the sanguine student thirsts of the year's beginning, the cafeteria was serving coffee, and pineapple juice from Queensland in garish cans. It was more than half-full of boys and girls practising, in lumpy clothing, the air of unexcitement currently favoured by the young.

Among them, drinking a pot of tea at an exposed table, sat Belle. Her eyebrows were arched; she looked wistful, and while Ramsey stood outside watching her, she poured out her last half-cup from the pot in a manner almost ritual. If rite it was, the import of it redounded against Belle herself. Perhaps it was easier simply to decide that she appeared rarely pitiable, shaking the pot slightly, considering complaining or ordering more, deciding with her eternal equability that there was no increase for her in tea. He went in to her table.

"Oh, Alec," she muttered. She saw clearly that there was no increase for her in Ramsey either.

"Good night, Belle. Out for a stroll?"

"The Kables are at the flat this evening. They're all eating some terrible indigestible meal bought in cartons in the town. It's a celebration. Denis's book . . . did you hear the news? Yes, uplifting news for him. He has his pride back."

"So damn uncle now?"

"Oh no. Sir Byron won't intervene anyhow. His wife came to his office this afternoon—he'd had undergraduates out looking for her—and we were having a drink there—the vice-chancellor, the Kables, Denis and myself. She was visibly angry. She said she was sorry to force an issue in front of the Kables. They were dangerous, she said. For a little while pity for me played merry hell with her rebellion. But she came back strongly and said she wouldn't tolerate Sir Byron forcing the issue with this Sanders man, since his motives in the matter couldn't be proper. She finished up like a *real* woman. She told him she'd dropped the prescription for his *veins* in to the chemist, but he would have to collect it himself." She laughed, fully and without ambiguity. The confrontation by Lady Sadie had been good give-and-take fun. Then she sobered. "I don't know about those Kables, though—whether they're good for Denis. Eric Kable's a pleasant enough man, but I'm sure Missus doesn't like me. We're both made of shark's skin." She laughed, but falsely now. It was as if she was both parodying the part of a meddling aunt and expecting Alec to see through the parody.

"You don't even care for that boy, do you Belle?"

"He's not a relative by blood," she conceded, whatever the concession meant.

He kept silence while a boy tanned from a summer on beaches steered his girl through the ruck of tables. As they passed Belle and himself, he heard the boy whisper, "God! Advanced-age scholarships. . . ."

"Belle," Ramsey said in the wake of the unwelcoming youth, "Lloyd and I—I and Lloyd—left your husband before he was dead."

She was annoyed by his emotionalism, and waved this

talk aside with a mottled hand. "Yes, yes. I always knew there must be some such thing."

"Belle, he was still breathing. I knew it; on some level or other I distinctly knew it. That was why I didn't go near the body. Near Leeming, I mean."

"Lloyd was in charge," the widow hissed in a dismissive way. "Lloyd was the doctor."

"We left your husband when he was merely sleeping."

Belle's eyes were down; she was furious over Ramsey's messy behaviour. She pushed her words through closed teeth. "I suppose that by 'merely sleeping' you mean unconscious and dying. And if unconscious and dying, how were you to know he wasn't dead? Anyhow, you know what his sledging instructions were."

Ramsey groaned.

"Ramsey," she muttered, presuming a lively interest in old scandal on the part of the undergraduates, "I won't have you confessing this nonsense to people. You presume the whole affair turns on you. You presume it's your circus."

"At some stages I've felt that I'm the only one who keeps his anniversaries. Your behaviour seems to have justified this impression."

"Alec, control yourself. And don't bother with my behaviour. It's beyond your interpreting."

He found it incredible that, as with Ella, a momentous confession was being leached down to backchat. He said again, slowly, as if deafness was a problem, that it was *her husband* who had been left.

"Stop trying to impress me, Alec," Belle warned him through her teeth, secretive and nearly as urgent as Ramsey, yet urgent it seemed merely on the grounds of good taste and the balance necessary for continued health.

"The fact is—isn't it?—that you don't care enough about Leeming to judge me?"

216

"Oh God, do you want so badly to be judged? Have I *pretended* to be heartily involved in the business? Haven't I confessed my indifference?"

"You pretended an interest in the nephew."

"I confess my insincerity then. And to my insincerity in wanting a funeral here, on so-called native soil. I confess to exploiting Denis's silliness. Anything, Alec, anything to make you behave."

Ramsey fell silent and hung his head. He saw Belle's hand on his arm. "You want me to judge you, do you, and say what a pariah you are? There's always been a big slice of Calvinism in you, Alec, and behold you've made a way of life for yourself, a whole religion, simply on the basis that one afternoon I took you to bed with me. I don't know whether to be flattered or not that the old sin still rattles round inside you."

Ramsey shook his head, but gave no clues, having none himself.

"Let me tell you about adultery," Belle continued. "There was no such crime between Leeming and myself. You may remember that I had mystical theories about self-possession, a theology you could say that I've since dropped in case I come to believe it myself in my old age. It was necessary to my vanity to believe that what was hormonal in me chastened Leeming in the bowels of Christ—you remember we both favoured, Leeming and myself, an outré streak of theology? It was necessary to Leeming's self-esteem to believe that he was being chastened, that my affairs humbled him, refined him. So I fulfilled the convention of sinning in his absence. I think, though, that basically he would have been willing to let men in by the front door, tell them a depression was moving in from the Bight and go back to his study. We just didn't suit each other."

Ramsey said, "To admit your indifference doesn't excuse you." Nor did he mean that she was not excused her adulteries but rather the traditional obligations of cherishing and mourning, and of damning the man responsible for the death. Belle misunderstood his meaning.

"Listen, Alec. That husband of mine would have been a Cistercian monk in earlier times. The world and the flesh bemused him, so off he packed to a place where the world was a series of climatic clichés. And as for the flesh, your body doesn't smell, May's shirt is still clean in August, your excreta down in the permafrost offends no one. While with Leeming—equator or pole—the devil can be trusted to look after himself."

Ramsey snorted. On top of his other urgencies, he found that it was important to him that there had been a bond and not a vacancy between Belle and Leeming.

"You undervalue your husband," he said, hoping to provoke her. "Just because there seems to be little connection between his brand of genius and the frequency of his erections."

"You painfully virtuous people always consider you have the right to speak crudely to those who don't keep your codes."

"And you people always demand tolerance of your vices but deny the same tolerance to the old-fashioned virtues of men like Leeming. Just the same, it wouldn't surprise me to find that you married Leeming precisely because you knew he'd be faithful to you."

For a second Belle's eyes galvanized; yet there was no telling whether it was the unlikeliness or the closeness to the bone of Ramsey's claim that made her consider it for a little. But she delayed her answer, and their furies dwindled to embarrassment at having swapped so many insults. Ramsey wanted to go, was under a physical demand to stamp back and forth among the hills.

He excused himself, but was warned before going that there were to be no confessions from him on Antarctic themes. The remains, if found (she said), would be disposed and coffined in a sturdy casket and returned to the earth with the blessing of the Episcopalian pastor from McMurdo Sound. "So the Americans can be gratified—they've been very decent and mustn't be given a false impression of the antipodean widow. And on my side, it's more respectable than telling the Department of External Affairs not to pester me."

"But," Alec told her, "you ran the risk of having to dabble in the swamp yourself if Denis's schemes had matured."

Belle shrugged. "I think I would simply have stayed home." A shy smile took her mouth, forced and appearing to be, like so much else that Belle had said tonight, an offered clue. "At my age a person can get out of nearly everything."

In an instant Ramsey understood, and was horrified by the way her old eyes crinkled with a look of irony usually found in the eyes of parrots. In a way more or less offhand, she had been willing to subject Leeming to an ornate burial at which his grotesque nephew would be chief mourner. It was a tableau she had worked to set up, worked perhaps with more than random energy based on a more than random jealousy of Dr Leeming's Antarctic distractions. And now her authoritative eyes were willing to say so.

"In fact, you don't even have Denis in your old age," he surmised.

She laughed, secure in another ten years of profitable widowhood, of water views and visitings with other blooming widows along that sweet, moneyed shore from Elizabeth Bay to Vaucluse.

At length, and much earlier than he had expected, Ramsey went home to sleep. At a given hour during his rest the watch changed for those excavating what could be called Leeming's ice-pit. Two sailors were lowered to dig, three to shore up the diggings. They took a risk, those five, in the (however slowly) moving ice.

Dormant and a hundred yards from the pit stood a small Swiss excavating machine, powerful for the task but indelicate enough to eat the hero whole and spit him out minced.

Another day. Ramsey kept long office hours, and drugged with work his inchoate sense of something remaining to be said: the truth that evaded mere facts and the indifference of women.

At home Ella and Miss Bourke grazed on plans for the coming child, and seemed to feel consecrated in their course after an evening visit from Dr Sanders.

Sanders had on arrival been invited to sit but would not. "I thought I knew you better," he said to Sally, "than to expect you'd be used by Leeming to take a private matter to a public authority."

Miss Bourke said she had made a complaint on her own behalf because Professor Sanders had not known her well enough to believe that when she said he was the child's father he was the child's father.

He gave her an envelope. "I hope that covers things. It's a little bit over what you asked for."

When the girl would not handle the money Ella took it in her place.

"Now then, Dr Sanders," she said. "Don't try to capitalize on what's simply a matter of paying your debt."

"You'll get it all back," the girl muttered towards the carpet.

Sanders warded off her proud intentions with his two meaty hands. "It's got nothing to do with the money," he said.

Ella suggested, "I suppose it's the principle? Then of course you'll readily understand how principle forced me to take Sally's cause to Sir Byron."

There were monosyllables and anger, and Sanders quickly left.

Insomniac Ramsey had to cough in the night to cover the noise of the radio as he tuned in the hourly news. Not that a breathless world hung on tidings of the bizarre endeavour proceeding at seventy-five degrees south; there were rare reports that nothing had been found, and during the third night, of a blizzard of one hundred and ten miles, whipping south-west from the Pole down the back of the Victoria Land mountains and the contours of coastal glaciers. Although it was not now expected that the body would be found, digging would continue if weather and the declining summer allowed.

At an hour of the early morning when sleeplessness becomes a form of whimsical intoxication, Ramsey began to reproach himself for having thought of God as an artist. Things remaining as they were might not be skilful irony in a dramatic sense, but in the real world it could be the ultimate divine comment. With this insight came an understanding of his own arrogance in that he had believed that a crucible would be provided, a zone, a time-lock of intensity; that he would be made new through fire.

He slept, and woke with his belly feeling sore in a muscular way, as if his dream of sledges had been real.

Before him Ella stood smiling warily from above a prepared tray, offered with the warranty of her curdled love. He could not manage to be grateful as she fussed him into an upright position and ramified him with pillows. His lack of gratitude did wonders: she was somehow in the mood for expiation.

It was apparent, too, that she had secretly informed herself by transistor. She told him about the recommencement of digging; he pretended he hadn't heard.

"You told me blizzards lasted twelve days." The statement sounded like a polite concession to one of his random interests.

"No. I wasn't thinking. There was one we had that lasted twelve days. They may last only twelve hours. Or thirty-six, say. This one lasted long enough." He accused her. "I thought you wanted the thing settled, too? I thought you wanted him buried at Botany or somewhere?" *Somewhere*, in his mind, had to do with a dreadful schizoid-Gothic railway station among graves on the edge of Sydney, and summer cortèges honouring uncles of his, fifty-five years dead.

"We presumed he'd be found. That corpse is a god to us. But this blizzard settles it. It shows you can fail to find his remains, just as you can fail to find any man's."

And, matronly since Miss Bourke had entered the house, she did not allow herself to be disabused, but tried to jolly him up with health small-talk and blind-raising and too much pillow-patting.

Pelham was in the office early to ask him questions of high seriousness, and Barbara harried him. He told Pelham, "God help Barbara's child if she ever has one. She'll keep its story-books in a filing-cabinet under *H for Hansel*, see also *G for Grimm*."

And when Pelham laughed, he whispered, "This morning I write my resignation, Morris."

The Englishman nodded, a nod of condolence. "I'll never work under Kable," he muttered. There was no telling whether he meant this as an axiom of loyalty to Ramsey's memory or as a commonsense reminder to Alec to plant his name before the eyes of those who would choose successors.

An hour later Ramsey delivered the letter to Sir Byron's personal secretary and caught a ride into town with a lecturer from his own department. Business was poor in the town's travel agency, where he saw posters for Patagonia and for a cruise of Antarctic waters—the Ross Ice Shelf, McMurdo Sound, the Bay of Whales. They were letting anyone into the club he didn't care to belong to. He wondered if some squatter from that rich countryside had chased Adelie penguins over the shelf-ice.

"I want to go to New Zealand," he told the girl. "To Christchurch."

The girl said it could be done, direct from Melbourne.

"Can you arrange the entire thing from here?"

"Yes."

"That's marvellous," he said. "No wonder you have people going as far as Antarctica." He nodded to the poster and she blushed as if its hanging might have been a little too fanciful of the management.

"When would you like to go, sir?"

How often did the Americans fly south from Christchurch? he wondered. Daily? Weekly? Had they given up for the summer? He would be patient in Christchurch if he had to be.

"Tomorrow," he said. "I know it's a rush."

The manager, called in, thought it possible. Ramsey promised to call back at three for a verdict.

Outside, he found the eternal Kables pottering around their car, Valerie loading a string-bag of oranges for their return to Milton. Ramsey considered screening himself behind three sauntering townswomen, but knew he had been seen and cringed from the risk of Mrs Kable's yelp of discovery. Staunch in the end, he walked straight up to them.

Valerie put on a toothy grimace that pretended to have caught him in some truancy. "Away from the office *again*, Alec? I wish Eric could organize himself as well as you do."

Eric Kable was doing something adept with the engine and, to compound the villainy, not getting much grease on his hands. "And being fitted for seven-league boots?" He smiled.

"I have a friend arriving from New Zealand this afternoon," Ramsey told them. "I was checking the time of arrival."

But if he had had a friend coming from New Zealand he would not have found it necessary to explain. He hoped the Kables were not perceptive enough to realize this.

"Well, Valerie," Kable called above the crunch of the lowered bonnet, "no more of the wrong light coming on." He muttered crisply to Alec, "Generator wires crossed." It was a brutal reality and not for a lady's ears.

"I see," Ramsey whispered, able to keep a secret.

Valerie marched up the footpath flank of the station wagon. "Well, Alec, it's been a delight. I suppose you're already hard at work arranging next year's schools for us culturally bankrupt seekers."

"Yes," Ramsey lied. "I've got even more radical plans for next year's."

"Goodness, this one was adventurous enough for an old countrywoman."

"You found it that way?"

Their cheap guise of simplicity again compelled them to swallow his cheap irony. It was all too mean for anyone to emerge the winner.

He visited the bank, and then sent the following telegram:

DIRECTOR

ANTARCTIC DIVISION

DEPT OF EXTERNAL AFFAIRS

CANBERRA

FOR REASONS APPRECIATE YOU UNDERSTAND WISH TO PRO-
CEED MCMURDO FASTEST EARLIEST STOP TRAVELLING CHRIST-
CHURCH TOMORROW STOP APPRECIATE EXPEDITING WITH U.S.
AUTHORITIES STOP RAMSEY LEEMING SURVIVOR

Back at the office, Barbara was pop-eyed from the size of
that day's mail.

"And the vice-chancellor wants you to lunch with him
at twelve-thirty."

But before he could go to lunch and acquaint Chimpy
with his Antarcticide, the telephone on his desk pealed. It
was Ella, wanting to know what was this about a friend
arriving from New Zealand; Valerie and Eric Kable had
visited her to say good-bye and to explain that they mustn't
keep her since they knew she was having a visitor.

"You don't approve of my telling fantastic lies to the
Kables?"

But he felt endangered by the persistence of that Kable
woman, who knew how to send lies home to roost.

Ella had only mild reproaches. "Perhaps we should decide what lies we're telling beforehand, so that we're at
least consistent."

"We've got better things to do than that."

"Have we, Alec?"

He heard her voice go watery in the earpiece. She was
like the Ella of the time before Sally Bourke blessed their
house with her maternity.

"So there it is," he told Sir Byron. "Never trust me on a
glacier, Chimpy."

For no reason he could understand he dropped the bread

roll he had been splitting. As his stomach jumped once within him like a snake on the move, he began sobbing.

Chimpy let the spasm go its full length, and said nothing until it was time to mutter huskily, "Now you'll feel better."

No wonder Lady Mews had left home, Ramsey wanted to say.

"Thank God I'm finished now." He meant, as a man with a career.

Poor Sir Byron was not easy. He handed a butter pat to Alec as something that should be considered prior to rash decisions. "I want you to stay, Alec."

Ramsey waited for the "But if you really feel you must go. . . ."

"I don't expect people to resign because they aren't well. If you're feeling the strain, why don't you delegate some of your authority?"

It was as if the man, a solid institutional man at that, accustomed to outright judgments, had not heard the part about Leeming. Ramsey wanted to remind him; but this delegation-of-authority business was absurd enough in its own right to call out for reply.

"If I delegated any more. . . . You see, that's what I mean. You haven't bothered to learn anything about my department because there's a sentimental tie with me based on eighty minutes of football played against Welshmen in 1922. But even if I could manage efficiently, there'd be this other question. If I was disloyal to Leeming, who was a prodigious man, how much more . . . ? You finish the sentence, Chimpy."

Chimpy kept his eyes on Alec and took from a drawer a book marked with hieroglyphics of the library. Ramsey hysterically recognized the book as one that everybody he spoke to seemed to have read.

"As a matter of fact, Alec, I happened to be reading the

relevant section only last evening." And he began to read aloud Leeming's instructions on what would be expected of those who could no longer travel. "And no doubt," he ended, "you'll cite the lie about Leeming's death, the lie given in this book. But what is a record like this, anyhow? A sort of report to the investors. I understand that. Other people would too. There are things you simply don't put in a report to the investors, things they don't even want to hear. Anyhow, this Lloyd, he was the medical man, wasn't he?"

It seemed to Ramsey to be characteristic of Chimpy that he then put a finicking smear of butter on the rind of his bread roll: a declaration that neither the senate nor thrombosis would catch him with his pants down, his books out of order, his luxuries (generally speaking) inordinate. Such a man made it difficult for others to act out whatever extreme rituals their sanity demanded. Ramsey saw with terror that such a man might make it hard also for him to retire: the department's work was proceeding under someone's (Morris Pelham's) impetus if not under Ramsey's, and Chimpy would make all manner of appeals to sense and convenience and the proper forms and the need of six months' notice so that the position could be advertised; and about all these appeals a palpable light of sanity would flicker. Like Lady Sadie, Ramsey panicked at the thought of being argued back into the old ways.

Barbara had taken a telegram for him. It read: ARRANGED REPORT TRANSIT OFFICER DEEP FREEZE CHRISTCHURCH GOOD LUCK TYRRELL DIRECTOR.

It took an effort of belief to accept that he was in fact going back. Yet the idea of facing the dimensions of the real Antarctica scarcely disturbed him. It was the highly caricatured continent of his dreams that he feared; and he was all afternoon comforted in disproportionate ways by

227

facts he had got hold of from reading old *Life* magazines—McMurdo was quite bare of snow at this time of year and barer perhaps than it had been for millennia; a school of scientists suspected the Antarctic ice-cap of shrinkage, and thaw streaked the flanks of Ross Island.

When he got home, Ella and Sally and Sally's boyfriend were all sitting in the living-room, drinking coffee. Everyone but Ella seemed uneasy. Before long he excused himself and went to the bathroom, hunting up shaving-gear for his trip. Soon Ella joined him.

"Watch out," he warned her. "You'll miss some fruitful exchange between little Miss Labour and her boyfriend."

She smiled, but it was a gamble, placed on the possibility that he was not mocking her. She said, "Chimpy rang up half an hour ago and said he'd seen you. He's anxious for you to take a holiday. And why don't we go somewhere—not just down to the coast?"

"Perth, for the wildflower festival?" he suggested mercilessly. "People seem conspired to keep you informed of my every twitch."

"Noumea's closer than Perth. Fiji's just as close. Even New Zealand."

For a second he considered whether the travel agency had exposed him. But it seemed that Ella had offered New Zealand as a bona-fide tourist alternative.

Then he told her of his separate arrangements: that he might go to Sydney, even beyond. "No *even* about it, it will be New Zealand. I should only be away a fortnight."

The luck was that she was in a contrite phase, was pale and tolerant. He could see her striving to sound like the sort of matron whose good sense keeps the diverse forces of a family together willy-nilly. "Well, I think it's a good idea for you to take a holiday on your own."

Her false sunniness called into doubt whether he could manage himself in public places without her, and included somehow the riling sense of certainty that she'd be going in the end in any case.

He disillusioned her. A separate person even *she* was, and she should demonstrate it by developing a passion for Professor Sanders while he was away.

After he had inveighed against fuss, taken care of his own packing and deliberately left out the nasal spray, he heard Ella drive away.

"Yes, drive to cause an accident," he muttered aloud, "or get yourself raped behind the Imperial Hotel. Make the old bastard really feel sorry."

Twenty minutes later she came back, tat-tat-tatting at the bedroom door.

She didn't want to interfere, she called, but she'd brought him some of his favourite Havanas. Knowing he should tell her to smoke them herself, he opened the door, imagining himself haughty but fair. Instantly she was in his arms, shuddering, wanting to be cherished.

"Yes," he kept saying, "yes, yes, yes. But I won't let you come, I won't let you pack."

It was a waking dream. The diggers found no corpse but a vacancy, and stood back, their faces all what he would call classic Antarctic faces, the type that squint out of their incommunicable suffering through the glossy skin of a coffee-table book on exploration. Of such an order was their foreignness; they would rather not have worked in the polar dusk to resurrect this blankness. Ramsey himself, dreambound on the first floor of a hotel in Christchurch, went limp at seeing the hands they had risked with digging. One of his knees slid towards the carpet. Warnings of lost balance bounced in his ears; his eyes flew open, out of their doze.

His tiredness had stopped him walking and leant him against the wall. Perhaps the dim, mothering noises of the air-conditioning had untimely lulled him. Whatever, he was still squatting when a man with chef's hat and tunic, apron, neckerchief and starchy little gut, came from the manager's office. Ramsey yawned and pretended to have trouble with a shoelace. He was content, until the chef had passed, with the characteristic Anglo-Saxon joy of having avoided being made a fool of. Then he saw that his journey was insane and that insane gestures, once done, mightily conduced to internal and genuine, bottled-in-bond insanity. And that was why he had suffered his threatening vision.

He went on down into the lounge for a whisky.

It had been drizzling all evening in Christchurch, and at the Deep Freeze installation the stylized cigar-shape of a transport plane stood out in the wet, looking finally immobilized. The scene had all the comfortlessness of a fairground closed for the winter, and the national blitheness of the young Americans who brought him illogically good weather reports from McMurdo Sound and Cape Hallett irked Ramsey. An officer made him sign a form absolving the United States of any liability for his death, told him that another Australian, representing National Press of America, was going south with him, and cast him up full of lassitude and self-doubt in the plush hotel across from the airfield.

It was fashionably built for tourists; in its downstairs bar you heard mainly senior American accents. Their strangeness made it easier than ever for him to presume that the gaiety of the Clipper Bar was conspiratorial, that he was the butt of the conspiracy. Such a presumption lasted only a manic second; yet he was grateful to hear New Zealanders talking loudly from a knot of tables in one corner. Here the conspiracy was patent; from the blazers and boasting of the men he could identify a pre-season meeting of a Rugby club. All that was being ineptly plotted was a football premiership.

He sought a lone table. There was a precedent for loneness. In a corner at a table of his own sat a thin, tanned man of about thirty-five, chewing on a savoury omelette and being served coffee and liqueur. The panting kinship of the Rugbyesque men and women and the tourists' zealous talk of travel left this young man unabashed. He seemed at ease eating alone in public places.

Ramsey suspected him for his worldliness of being a

journalist and for his sunburnt look of being Australian; the southbound NPA man.

Ramsey sat down and ordered a drink, and when the waiter had gone for it there was the younger man standing at Ramsey's elbow.

"You'd be Mr Alexander Ramsey."

"Yes."

"This is an honour, sir. I'm David Hammond. I'm going south for NPA. They were actually sending a staff man, but he's in hospital here with a perforated ulcer." He added with what he no doubt thought was the correct solemnity, "I hope we're both in time. It's marvellous that you can be there. Would you like to join me?"

It was easiest to do that, to shamble across to Hammond's table and get through the weary business of assuring him you didn't want a Spanish omelette, even at NPA's expense. Hammond was a freelance journalist from Sydney; interviews with great artists seemed to be his penchant, and reviews of the more important cultural events; but he was always willing to travel for the larger newsagencies.

Not that he told all this in a gush; he answered with a crisp sort of respect Alec's dutiful questions, rising bluntly and artificially from the older man's silences. By the time Hammond began to ask questions for himself, they had drunk three whiskies.

Hammond wanted to know whether Ramsey had ever been back before.

Ramsey told him no, and noticed that Hammond's eyebrows registered this, though not blatantly. "Take notes if you want to," he told the journalist, to shame the man.

"I ask out of personal interest," said Hammond, and fell away defensively into anecdotes about interviewing Marlene Dietrich. Ramsey laughed precisely; he was even a little grateful for the company, being still disturbed by the phantasmagoria on the stairs and being also tired beyond sleep. Nor had the boy made any demands on him—but would, you could be sure.

To block such demands, Alec began to speak of aeroplane flights, for here was a travelling man who, like freelancers as a race, must have had a crop of stories about propeller failure, fuel-blockage, diverted flight, and stuck landing-gear. Certainly Hammond told a few such, making much of his fear. Ramsey stubbornly refused to be won over by such admissions.

But later on, in Hammond's room, steadfastly drinking Hammond's liquor, he went to excess in praising photographs of Hammond's pleasant-looking wife and children. He found himself, too, making dissociated trips to the window to squint out onto the road that ran towards the centre of the city.

"It looks damper than it really is," Hammond told him.

Ramsey kept forgetting in any case that for him, for this journey, there were no weather portents in that street. Turning back to Hammond, he began to think how good it was to have a friend. The intimacy of the thought made him recoil when he found, for the second time that evening, Hammond at his elbow. This time the journalist had the inevitable book in his hand, the book with which the poet, Ella, Belle, and Chimpy had shown a quoting familiarity.

"It's a remarkable story, Alec, and if you could inscribe it. . . ."

Alec, in a mood of black humour, wrote "Don't believe everything you read" on the fly-leaf.

Hammond laughed at it, and his eyes gave promise that he would often produce the official history at the ends of evenings of Antarctic films, for a movie-camera lay casually on his bed, and what must have been hundreds of feet of film, done up in fifties, spilt over the counterpane from an insulated container. The frankness of the small domestic camera alarmed Alec, reminded of the perilous off-hand

233

interest that made men buy newspapers and feed without shame on secrets of lust and weakness in prelates and cabinet ministers. Such an interest, he felt, might well provoke him to a new and ultimate statement of the truth of Leeming in relation to himself, something that might take him by surprise as much as it would Hammond.

He stood up. "I must go. You'll want to ask questions, reasonably enough, I suppose. That won't prevent me unreasonably resenting it. Perhaps tomorrow. . . ."

But he felt a vacancy in his midriff, not knowing how, other than by drinking Hammond's whisky, he would manage to sleep.

"It's all right," Hammond smiled, and picked up the bottle and made gestures of good faith with it, as if its amber transparency was the measure of his intentions. "Let's talk politics and religion. Or even culture." He laughed. Ramsey laughed too, and sat down to take his nightcap.

Sailors woke him early, knocking on his door to take care of the luggage he would leave behind in Christchurch. They left him with his thick whiskified head, his own underwear, and swathes of U.S. polar issue. Watching a full morning sun light up the night's rain on the roofs of the naval base, he felt genial about the journey. For eight hours he would ride dormant, the navigational bias of his eyes and ears and instincts all cancelled by a mesh of electronics in the snub nose of their transport plane. Yet his elation was not simply that of the played-out business-man jet-bound between selling-stops. For the aircraft across the road promised not only to move you a given number of miles but to land you in what your illusions and elusive experience told you was not simply a polar village but a distinct state of being—the state of being *homo Antarcticans*.

234

Early breakfasters downstairs, looking twice at his lined jacket and baggy pants and white thermal boots, seemed possessed by no such metaphysical excitement; nor, already sipping coffee, did Hammond, who was engrossed in a headache. Nor were the sixteen Navy personnel, already seated when Ramsey and Hammond quit the translucent morning and climbed into the dim forward of the plane. Ramsey knew, seeing their calm inexpectant faces above crisp shirt-collars, that the sailors were right. It was for the sake of dulling last night's dream and of his fear of being forced close to an essential statement of truth that he went on nurturing his sense of being about to be taken somewhat further than mere mileage.

In the airport building he had caught fleeting sight of an inappropriate old man being fussed over by a lieutenant-commander in dress uniform. The soft, unlikely face, already wrapped in a fur-lined hood, was yet one that Ramsey felt he should be able to name; perhaps a face well-aired by the media.

Now the old man was helped into the aircraft, and to a seat, by the same officer. The hood was still in place about a face that, although free of greasepaint, seemed to demand it. A queen's face, yes; and it had a strange breed of decision on it. There would, at least, be no absurd flirtations when smooth-faced orderlies brought round the turkey-loaf at lunchtime. Since rows of seating ran down either wall and two more lay back-to-back down the centre of the aircraft, Ramsey, strapped in close to a starboard port-hole, found the old man sitting back-on to him. The officer spoke softly; so did the old man; but Ramsey heard the officer say, ". . . the bunk in the cockpit straight after take-off." Then a salute. And outside Ramsey's window an engine found its step after a few unwilling seconds. Survival information—how to don the orange emergency-suit, how to enter the raft, how long you would last in Antarctic

235

waters—was broadcast and demonstrated while they rolled down the morning tarmac; and inattentive Ramsey watched a commercial plane take off for the pleasure slopes of Mount Cook.

All that niggled at his makeshift peace was the old gentleman seated erect, hood now cowled back around his ears, distinguished enough to be promised the use of the cockpit bunk. Had the Christchurch command gone as far as inviting visiting choreographers or couturiers to visit its Antarctic stations?

Lulled by the petty question, he did not look for the lift of the wheels or for the slowly spinning city below. By the time he bothered to use his port the cratered harbour of Lyttelton could be seen distantly beneath the tail. Propellers butted into radiant cloud. For five and a half hours nothing would be sighted but their own colder and colder wingtips.

Hammond roused himself and went aft in need of the limited diversions of flying blind. Ramsey saw him chatting at a shout with the flight orderlies, visiting what the Navy called "the head", squinting out of rear ports, inspecting the cargo—a braced steel bean of fuel, amidships and dominant. It was clear that Hammond respected the tank, feeling its steel stays with his thermal boot, rat-tat-tatting here and there on its surface.

Meanwhile sailors read, or made beds for themselves along the harsh webbing seats, and one of the flight crew descended and helped the choreographer up a companionway and into the cockpit. "Long as he doesn't goose the pilot," Ramsey murmured aloud in the safe din of engines.

Making himself a pillow, he slept then, and woke to find Hammond composed and staring at him. Outside, chiller clouds were still shot with sun.

Hammond said, "I didn't realize it'd be so hard to be heard in here."

236

"Maybe we oughtn't to talk then," Ramsey articulated. "Feeling better?"

"Thanks. Too much whisky last night. Never like take-offs anyhow. Especially with people warning you about how easily you're going to die."

Ramsey's watch told him he had slept for half an hour only, but he judged that in that time Hammond had become newly conversational and had something like a profile interview in mind.

"I'm going back there," he told the arts-festival special-ist, and rose to edge down the flank of the fuel-bean. Yet the large time he spent in the head, languorously washing his hands, laying them against the pulsing fuselage, in-specting the *Playboy* nude pasted behind the door and wondering aloud who it thought it was fooling—all his delay failed to throw Hammond off. The man had cut off both the port and starboard escape routes by taking station squarely against the rear node of the bean. Ramsey took to a port and watched the wings saw at cloud mys-terious enough to hint at genuine metamorphoses. The newsman appeared at his elbow.

"Remarkable—being able to fly through this."

"They have instruments," called Ramsey instructionally.

Hammond allowed this information to settle the matter. Communally, they stared for some seconds at the outer mists. Then Hammond spoke again.

"I suppose even you, Alec, sometimes wonder where the strength came from. The strength to survive, I mean. I've merely read of such things, but there seems to me to be a time when a man is delirious and apparently beyond voli-tion, at which an automatic and fixed will to survive—or die, but after all you survived—you know, this automatic and fixed will comes into operation and operates the man like little more than machinery." He shrugged then in apology. "There, I sound as if I'm taking all the merit out of your performance."

"I'm not jealous on the question," Ramsey reassured him without tone.

"Yes, but what do you say . . . about this . . . well, let's call it an *automaton* theory?"

Ramsey begrudged thinking about it, but had uncertain ambitions about putting the press in its place.

"Man isn't as simple as all that. How I behaved in crisis was governed by how I behaved at earlier times when my control over what I did seemed very self-aware. But even what I did then was governed by follies that were written into me, into my guts. So earlier on I had no choice but thought I did, and in the crisis I had no choice but hardly knew either way. I was acting out the patterns of irony that were involved in the sort of person I was and what was my historic setting. I was acting out the patterns with all the cunning of a shit-house rat, believing myself in control."

The journalist breathed in. He hadn't bargained on metaphysics, on determinism shouted above the hubbub of engines. "If I had done what you've done, I'd be very proud."

"Pride is forbidden because it's irrelevant and doesn't meet the facts."

On a limited scale, Ramsey was enjoying himself, thinking, that's telling the bastard. He did wonder, though, that if pride was irrelevant, why wasn't shame?

Hammond said lamely, "I think you're the one who's underestimating your achievement now."

"I don't underestimate the fact of my survival, though. My survival was of importance, so that I could be shown up fully later. And that's of importance to someone—God or my wife, or both of them."

"You believe in the immortality of the soul, then?"

238

Hammond said, almost automatic about it, as if he were nearing the miscellany section of his interview with Dietrich or Malcolm Muggeridge.

Ramsey shrugged and issued a challenge. "Come on then. What are the things you really want to ask me?"

Hammond shrugged in return, and implied rash judgment in Ramsey.

"Come on," Ramsey baited him. "Anything you think your readers might like to know."

The journalist seemed mildly hurt. "There are a lot of things my readers might like to know that I've never told them. It isn't one of my ultimate criteria."

"I'm sorry. Still, feel free. . . ."

"There are matters that interest me as an individual, though I suppose I have to admit that my years of journalistic wheedling have made them easier for me to ask."

"Go on."

"Before I met you last night I would have presumed this was a sentimental journey. Is it, though? Is it just a journey to attend the funeral of an old friend?"

"Would it sound artificial if I said I came on an impulse?"

"Not if that's the way it was."

"I came on an impulse."

"We're both very late getting to the scene, you know. In my case the delay's due to NPA's staff man's ulcer, of course. Why did you leave it so late?"

"I've told you. The impulse wasn't there earlier."

"Tell me if this question offends you. I have seen the supposedly incorruptible limbs of Italian saints." Hammond visibly considered saying that he had been repelled and thought that type of incorruptibility not worth the having, but desisted, on the uncertainty as to whether Alec was casual mourner, or pilgrim, or one bereaved. "How is Leeming likely to look? Physically, I mean?"

There had been a time when Alec had been vulnerable to such a question; now he simply resented it for its crudity. He had settled himself to answer without emotion when his imagination froze. It was even more unexpected than a coronary, which in any case he believed this to be; for he seemed powerfully prevented from breathing and Hammond's agog face wavered before him, acknowledging that he, Ramsey, was undergoing some bodily derangement. And all it was was the baulking, the first and only petrifaction of his imagination.

The result being that there was an echo of his dream suffered the evening before in the hotel, the dream of a criminal vacancy in the glacier dug up by diggers. The echo did not profit his breathing, which continued stricken. But all this smotheration had, he again suspected, to do with finding a new utterance: he had the inane image in his mind of a tremulous old pierside machine whose mechanics try in loud travail to produce a card marked, *Though you do not make friends easily, you are normally respected. . . .*

So now, too, he felt the new and adequate truth to be deposited in the pit of his belly, an organ which, to speak it fair, had always been more acutely interested in the truth of Ramsey than in his food. Next he found to his surprise that there was no physical hindrance to his breathing.

"Is it heart, Alec?" Hammond insisted on knowing, and urged Ramsey to lie down on the slatted cargo bay slanting upwards behind them towards the tail.

"Blame the poor bloody brute organs."

"I beg your pardon?"

"I said, blame the brute organs, pick on poor bloody dumb things, when all the time there are bastards like you about, causing pain."

"I must apologize, Alec, but is it . . . ?"

Imperilled towards shouting the outré truth—the message on the weighing-machine tab—in Hammond's face, Alec rushed away, trembling, down the port side of the tank and concentrated on the port-side murk beyond the windows. He felt reproachful on technical grounds rather than because of Hammond. Hadn't this journey been meant to be painless, a subliminal experience? His grievance was that of the patient for whom the anaesthetic fails. Meanwhile the words he had come close to shouting at Hammond recurred to him in waves, turned his panic on and off. He knew that if this had been a train he would have pulled the emergency cord and gone sprinting away down the rails.

All he could do was move forward to the passenger area. A sailor slept before him, a cold nimbus of light framing the face. A zealous orderly smiled sideways at Ramsey and took off earphones to say, "The captain tells me, sir, that yourself and the other gentlemen are welcome to visit the cockpit."

Alec nodded, eager as any foreigner in a strange city, certain that the broader view of the miasma he would have from the flight deck would soothe him.

"Just up the stairs there."

Ramsey climbed as indicated. The width of cold light before the plane dazzled him, showing up on his retina the aftershadow of the muffled shapes he had seen downstairs. Hands in laps, both pilots sat back in high seats. The controls quivered ever so delicately; two airmen read steady needles on the starboard side. Behind Ramsey was a small sleeping-bay, and turning to inspect it, he tripped over the thermal boots of the man who sat there, staring levelly ahead.

"I beg your pardon," he stated, and found his balance as fast as he could. For he knew it must be the evocative old man whose face could now be closely viewed, even if no introduction resulted. The hair was worn arty-long, he noticed first. Like Robert Graves's. For an instant he watched the eyes glance up wryly from beneath long brows. Ramsey's stomach bounded like an animal. It was Belle Leeming there in possession of the sleeping-bay.

He shouted her name. Even above the engines, the flight engineer and navigator both heard it, and turned their heads an indolent fraction. Her presence brought to Ramsey again the certainty that he was butt to some wide-ranging joke. The poisonous farcicality of it brought sweats of anger out of him—Alec Ramsey encapsulated above the southern ocean and caught between Hammond in the tail and the widow in the cockpit!

He bent to her ear. "Why wasn't I told?"

"I asked them not to."

"April fool, eh?"

"Not at all."

Ramsey shook his head resentfully and put his fingers to his ears full of the thud of engines.

"Sit down then, Alec, and be calm."

He obeyed out of the hopelessness of his fury. He knew it gave his mouth a constricted look that he thought of as odiously Presbyterian. He wanted vainly to be able to hide his fuming and let it jump at her from hiding.

He and his old love bent to hear each other.

"I didn't know why you wanted to go, Alec, but I felt it was for your good, worth the risk of the odd behaviour you seem to think you have a right to. I didn't want you to put it off just for the artificial reason that I was going too."

Ramsey said nothing. Now, growing out of anger, he felt a suspect need to redefine Belle's moral status.

"Besides," the lady went on, "I didn't want to be delivered up to the journalist they tell me is on this plane. Not yet, anyway."

"I think you'd get on marvellously, you two."

"By which you mean he's a swine." She patted his hand. "Never mind. I really am so pleased I came. They respect poor dear Leeming so much; it isn't a front. You know I'm the oldest woman ever to visit the continent? But not the oldest person. The extraordinary thing is they took an eighty-three-year-old survivor of Scott's expedition. Only last year. So I have to be satisfied with being the oldest woman."

Openly Ramsey sneered at this late taste for record-breaking.

"Oh, I don't enjoy the fact for its own sake, but I think it's an indication of their esteem for Leeming. They're so much more gracious than Australians, too."

"Especially when they're dropping napalm on people," Ramsey perversely growled.

"Don't be political. What I mean is that they remind me of cavalry officers out of an old film, something with Leslie Howard in it. The crew has given up their toilet to me, and this berth. And I found out, listening to some of the sailors at the airport, that this is their only plane that has a walk-in toilet down the back. Usually they simply have a trough that men urinate in."

It proved hard for him to keep his anger intact, Belle being so genuinely touched by the amendments these sailors had made to their coarse male world for her sake and Leeming's. Not that he was not irked on that account, suspecting her right to be simple in heart.

"If I had only known you wanted to take this journey," he lied, "I wouldn't have complicated matters by coming myself."

For a few seconds Belle laid her eyes lightly on him, correctly reading in him that his present rancour rose from this new challenge to his pride, his pride in being at least Leeming's one true mourner.

Meanwhile the pilot had turned in his seat to motion his flight engineer to the controls and had risen and moved back with inquiries about Belle's health. Ramsey was introduced; the long and barren debate Ramsey desired had now to wait for a polite Major to cease briefing his two guests.

". . . so even though we're flying well over the height of the mountains, we'll be making a dogleg round Cape Adare. That's somewhat safer."

In a sight-seeing fervour, Belle grasped Ramsey's arm, distracting him from the officer. She pointed past the navigator's back through the floor-level pane of glass to her right front. Two miles below, through lazy cloud almost transparent in the sun of early afternoon, a distinct berg, big as an atoll, spined and contoured to make two peaks, was passed or seemed deliberately to pass them by. Both its mountains cut the thick and, to Ramsey's mind, transmogrifying fog, exposing it as a merely climatic state, exposing Ramsey as the same flat man, unendowed with new substance.

"In another fifty minutes or so," the lieutenant-commander told them, "we'll actually cross the circle."

To compound this lack of transformation, McMurdo Sound brightened before them all afternoon, and the Erebus volcano stood up, engaging as a ski-resort, when they banked across its slopes at five o'clock. Ramsey squinted at the broad normal sky, like bright winter skies over sheep towns he had taught in when young. The world, he told himself, was growing less and less diverse, more and more pointlessly uniform.

A brusque landing was made on steel skis. The forward door opened, white glare and the cold swept in. Belle, already stationed for her Antarctic entrance and encouraged at the elbow by a boy orderly, stepped out first; then, threatened by the light and fumbling for sun-glasses, Ramsey. His eyesight adapting, he saw Belle being helped down the steps, setting dazed feet on the ice-shelf, making wading movements with her arms, clearly doubting that her senses and her lungs could get the measure of the foreign air. A massed welcoming party seemed to be assuring her, but she continued dubious. Capable of all the pomp of judgment, Ramsey followed on, enjoying the apt stumble of those soft traducing feet.

And as if her discomfort were a judgment on her, he felt justified in his rudeness to her earlier that afternoon when, after a talk with Hammond, Belle had come and sat beside him. At the time, Ramsey had been looking west through the lifting vapour at the wan mountains of Victoria Land; an impressionist sun lay painted in four complex strokes of saffron on an ice-floe beneath him.

"Alec, did they tell you that there are cameramen and three journalists at McMurdo Sound?"

"I knew there were a few pressmen. I didn't know the exact numbers."

"Yes, well they're the numbers. Actually three, and Hammond makes four."

He did not resent her any the less, and had thought of asking her whether four sufficed.

"A regular task force," she had said, "ready to document our every quirk. So you have to allow me to say it, Alec; I beg you and I demand that there'll be no quirks. Really, I won't stand for them."

He knew he needed warning in this authoritative way. But he must never allow himself to accept her moral authority. "All right," he had agreed. "Since you have Hammond charmed, it *would* be a shame if the conquest wasn't extended to the entire press-hut."

On the ice three cameramen were evident. One, a sailor by the chevrons on his peaked hat, filmed equably; but working for networks had given the others an indigestive energy. They played with the calibrated rims of lenses, and grunted like lovers or sea lions. At something that was part

245

their request and part command, Alec and Belle repeated their advance to the tangerine vehicle readied to race them away across the ice-shelf, towards tangerine helicopters. In this way the widow and Ramsey were mated by view-finder, and Ramsey became on film what he had once daydreamed of—the friend doing service for the widow.

Indoors at McMurdo Station, in heavy warmth made from the piped exhaust of electric motors, they faced their press conference. Alec, still dazed, sat by expecting, despite himself, the same radical change he had looked for earlier in the day. He found it hard to attend to the sharp voices of the journalists; his ears seemed drawn to insulated sounds, the murmur of off-duty officers in the wardroom next door. He flatly answered the few questions aimed at him and, in his state of contrived numbness, could see that he would not easily be able to do himself harm: one of the few communicable images that could easily be fitted to him by pressmen was that of awed ex-comrade.

He was taken by surprise when Belle, not distracted by suspicions of some coming explosion in the cortex of the brain, announced what would be done with her husband's corpse. If Leeming could not be found, the pit would be reverently closed and prayed over. If Leeming could be found, he would be buried on the hill above the base, on Observation Hill, just beyond the crest, facing west.

"This site," she said, "was kindly suggested by the admiral." She threw a hand in the putative direction of New Zealand. "Admittedly this little town looks rather industrialized, but they tell me it's only a small feature in what can be seen from up there."

That he had been with her all day, and failed to ask her for such facts, made him anxious now for his sanity.

At dinner the base commander told them that digging could not go on beyond the next few days; most of the summer personnel had already left for Christchurch or North America. He would permit Mrs Leeming, he said with a sly Irish smile, to visit the pit site in the morning only if she got a full night's sleep, no big-eye, no waiting up for the midnight sun.

At three the next morning Ramsey woke in the same buffered state of alarm as he had fallen asleep in. He went walking through the streets of the settlement. Bare earth which he bent to touch was frozen. The sun stood at a narrow angle over the scarps of Victoria Land. Whenever the town came close to earning Belle's judgment, "industrialized", its streets led you to a sight of Scott's first hut, a stroll away, brown and like a failed grazier's homestead. Turn, and he saw Observation Hill, where Leeming would be, to his honour, buried in rock or permafrost. The trouble of making a hole up there, on that freezing slope!

There was already a cross on the hill, he could see, Scott's cross humped there over two days by bereaved men in an age of murderous innocence and fatal sentimentality.

Inside, he found himself fevered and neuralgic.

Belle seemed grey, and possibly had not slept. Even so heavily wrapped, she showed aspects of her age that Ramsey had never noticed before. She seemed brisk enough, no health risk on the long helicopter haul she now faced. Hammond carried her duffel-bag of survival clothing, and there was this difference to her: she did not accept Hammond's concern as tribute to her, as at eighty-five she would still no doubt accept kindnesses from polite businessmen at airports. Here she needed her bag carried; the way she walked testified to that. Never had she seemed older.

Ramsey climbed into the thick warmth of the machine, and sat along the wall. His cheek that faced the cold hatch ached in its sinusitic manner; on his left the caged motor of the rear shaft made sickening heat. But as Hammond and the others boarded, cherishing private and commercial cameras, he was grateful that the motors were too raucous to allow talk.

He remained placidly anguished. The blare of the machine gave even his eyes a certain torpor and privacy. As yesterday he had not been able to conceive a time beyond his arrival, so now his imagination persisted in the message that after the pit was reached, time in its accepted meaning would not continue to deliver itself, second by second.

The machine rose at a tilt, and jerked along the ice-free coast; then out across the sound to a west glaring with white mountains. Once during the journey Belle leant to him and shouted, "Alec, be good, won't you?" For some reason transcending eardrums, Alec heard and nodded. Those of the others who were not distracted by scenery tilted an ear in false hope of a press statement.

The western side held ice in the seams of its complicated coast, last winter's ice that had not found a clear strait up the sound. And massive ice, an ice-tongue, with dim blue water to the north. Then he felt the helicopter pitch and enter the course of a glacier, a neat glacier to his eyes, a geography-teacher's dream, seamed and waved at its edges, its lines of flow enforced by streaks of moraine, its north side charred with the black emergence of mountains. To the helicopter's front bulked theatrical ice-falls and summits.

Alec twisted in his seat. They would not make him believe that that spectacular white trench was the scene of his and Lloyd's hard survival. So when they swept low once over a scatter of portable huts, and a crewman threw a smoke bomb out of the hatch to read the wind force, Ramsey found himself gazing for the result with a genuine tripper's interest. His standard anxieties, no worse in this sunny, stage-managed iceway than they had often been at home, snaked about his belly as the machine plumped down between bamboo flags. Motors fell back to a lower pitch of chugging. Conversation was possible if you screamed it forth.

What was largely fear, and the desire to verify kindred fears in others, made him speak to the widow.

"Are you afraid, Belle?"

She merely smiled, like someone with a professional care on hand, and patted his gloved hand. And though this was the supreme arrival, time went on secreting itself; there came no explosion in the cortex.

Instead, he jumped down onto firm snow, and helped the widow out. Belle had her fur hood zipped to the nose, but stood making eyes of avid gratitude at the men who ran in wincing beneath the churning props to help her to the site.

Ramsey stumbled after.

A man with lieutenant's bar on the peak of his snow-cap deployed away from Belle's elbow and faced the straggle of visitors.

"Mrs Leeming and gentlemen," he yelled, "welcome."

In a most authentic manner, the cold licked at Ramsey's cheeks like something interior to them, some hot-cold facial cancer; and the added Antarctic violence of the helicopter swept them as the machine lifted sideways and went.

"You must first come and have coffee in the mess," the lieutenant concluded. He led them to a wood-framed hut of canvas, already drifted up to chest-height by the late blizzard. Inside, a portable generator hummed, making light and a startling moist warmth. The alternations of hot and cold that his hosts had provided for him woke again Alec's face pains, his fever.

Meanwhile the party were shedding their outer clothes and draping them on chairs. Before them stood a servery, and behind the servery, a bare-headed, open-necked boy pouring coffee.

"If you would care, gentlemen, to help yourself."

The lieutenant sat Belle down and fetched her coffee. And, as if Ramsey was in need of further dazing, announced, "You'll notice that I've taken the liberty of ordering a certain medicinal additive in the coffee. I trust none of you object."

The men rumbled with approval. Belle gave a dazzling smile. With a trace of jealousy, Ramsey knew that Belle admired this brand of courtesy sitting so well on the tanned and rugged features. A man of thirty-five, a paterfamilias far from his familia. Some decades back, Belle would have eaten him without salt.

Saved by the generation gap, the man talked to them while they drank. He hoped that the visit to the summer station would not be too painful for Mrs Leeming, nor for Mr Ramsey, to whom this glacier was unhappily known. He thought that it might help if he told them in greater detail the background to the . . . the event. A team of ice physicists from Colorado were interested in a range of ice properties that could not as readily be studied by drilling an ice-core as by working on the sides of an open pit. He implied that the ice properties under examination were of a venerable if not too practical scientific nature. The radio-activity of snow contaminated with thermonuclear fallout; the regularity of strata in a glacier; dating snow by the study of its hydrogen and oxygen isotopes; stress and movement. For the sake of examining stress, the pit would be marked and covered when the ice men had finished their summer studies, and revisited the next year.

So the pit was dug to a depth of nearly sixty feet, one side terraced and provided with aluminium ladders.

"There are patterns in ice," the lieutenant said, "even in moving ice. A peculiar conformation was spotted, just above head height. The wall was probed with a pick, and a series of objects were uncovered."

Knowledge of having behaved with respect pushed down the officer's lids. In the man was apparent a certain feeling of kindred towards Leeming: wreath-laying fervour at its best. If Ramsey had not gropingly cuckolded Leeming and passively murdered him, it would have been possible for him to be touched.

"We knew about Leeming and his Australians," admitted the lieutenant. "It was pretty clear what this debris might mean. The pit was closed immediately. Another one, a little upstream, was dug for the use of the scientists."

He ended by saying that before they all visited the grave of a brave man he would like to express his pleasure at being of aid to his widow.

There recurred in Ramsey an amazement that had become familiar during the past eight days: that the concrete world—an odd pattern of ice deep down—kept verifying what, he believed in his guts, had taken place on a higher or lower or *beyond* plane of being.

He had let his coffee go tepid, and drank it with distaste. Others were already pulling on outer coats and sun-glasses, and zipping furry hoods to the nose.

"Isn't he kind?" Belle asked him loudly. She would spend her last days praising American graciousness which, by cultivating all the apt emotions, had very likely conjured up in her a wistful and not unpleasant feeling for her own widowhood.

Beyond the double door the light flared in their faces. Ramsey fumbled for his sun-glasses and blundered into hock-deep furrows made by the wind. It seemed that at contact with these crusty seams, sickening memories surged in the soles of his feet. All he could hear were boots hissing through the rind of the glacier. Glare robbed him of his sense of up and down, of ridge and hollow. But for a litter of crates, but for the black line of mountains on the left, there would have been no perspectives.

The pit was marked by a windlass and four red flags on bamboo. A small petrol-motored winch chuffed unattended. Beyond the windlass, a sailor with a hand-model radio waited for communiques from below.

"The edges are presumed to be firm," said the lieutenant. "But don't go too close."

At once the cameramen danced forward for footage of the burial pit. Hammond and his brothers stretched their necks for a view, on one side, of the blue-white terraces and, on the other, of the straight, blue-grained depth that was the wall. Ramsey and Belle edged least of all, taking quick, wary squints that sensed but did not verify a hint of fluorescence at the bottom, where the digging soundlessly went on.

The officer called across the mouth. "Anything?"

"Nothing, sir."

He came to Belle's side and within earshot of Ramsey. "We can't afford to be too hopeful. I hope you don't mind those people. . . ." He gestured obliquely at the pressmen. "I suppose it's their version of reverence. But things are being done better down below."

Belle nodded. Weak in the knees, cringing within, Ramsey still heeded how the slow, weighty nod signified grief in the fibre, grief taken in and made so intimately part of her essence that tears were beside the point.

Awed by her, the lieutenant led the press team back to the edges of the site and left both mourners huddled in remembrance. Forced thus to take his passive part in the tableau, Ramsey listened to the murmur of shutter mechanisms somewhere behind him. In the name of networks, the pious moment was recorded.

"Belle," said Ramsey, forestalled by the whirring voice of public opinion at his back from speaking as ironically as he should, "do you think, perhaps, after all this, you ought to take a rest indoors?"

"Yes." Her voice was even. "Isn't it startling the way one's glasses ice up on the insides?"

What, of course, he feared from Leeming's removal, was a change in the essence of his life, a change as absolute as death. His fear felt strangely deep, as if room was left on upper levels for a show of politeness to the press and a thin crust of sanity. Modified hope and disappointment had simultaneously risen in him, now that he had seen the ice-cap that sat on Leeming, the barrenness of the pit, the poor tools to hand.

So he answered the questions of the pressmen, all the while playing with what was a grotesquely diverse lunch to be served on a glacier—rice and meatballs, slaw and chilli, corn and peas. When they asked him what he had thought when he saw the pit he managed them without panic.

"I was numb," he murmured. "Please. . . ."

"Yeah," they agreed, understanding all and nothing. They would drain him in season. For the moment, they tried more chilli.

There were glaciologists, too, at table, men from the neighbour pit to Leeming's. Like the sailors who came in for coffee, they were going home soon, their data complete, their kudos increased, carrying stuffed penguins for their kids—made-in-New-Jersey penguins that were sold in the PX at McMurdo. The season had been looted of its best days; no presumption gripped the mess that anything more would be yielded up. The atmosphere of coming departure soothed Ramsey.

The lieutenant came round, telling his guests that their helicopter had just left McMurdo Sound.

All lumbered to the pit again. The mourning party of

Belle, Ramsey, and the officer went ahead; the witnesses followed. Deserts were suggested by the harsh afternoon light, the winch made small, dry noises, drew up a hodful of ice, and dumped it on the north side of the pit. Helped by such tired sounds, Ramsey sensed the presence of all the elements that go to make a non-event. He might not have been able to itemize them, yet they subsisted in the per-during light, in the afternoon that would not end but grow to dusk at midnight, in the unzealous mechanisms detailed for the dead's recovery, in the shuffle of sixteen inexpectant feet. There would be no apt resurrection today, at Ramsey's feet and Belle's. No flair for the appropriate resided in the corpse: perhaps Ramsey had visited the glacier simply to verify the powerlessness of those remains. If he felt let down by the fact he felt also reprieved, read-mitted to the warm nastiness of the concrete world. What especially appealed to him was that he *would* use the return page of his Melbourne-Christchurch air-ticket, that it had validity to bring him back from the zone of metamorphosis.

There was a large youth pouncing towards them at the trot who stood at last before the lieutenant. Urgent mutter-ings shuttled between the two of them. Ramsey heard the boy say, ". . . so hard they're digging round it with their hands."

The officer spoke to Belle, who gave quick, acquiescent nods as if she was one of the lieutenant's men. "I'm going down," the lieutenant then said aloud. "There seems to be something. . . . This man will take you all on to the pit."

Immediately Hammond was at Ramsey's elbow.

"Alec, what was it he said? Are there indications . . . ?"

Ramsey's legs seemed gone. He felt himself to be fettered in the viscous manner of dreams.

"He's gone down to see. Oh, ghouls rejoice!"

"They will indeed," said Hammond, presuming easily

that Ramsey was making a judgment on a national basis. Ramsey turned his back.

Before him the pit gave out thin metallic noises of haste rising to the surface with something like a fluid speed. Like a clockwork ascension. He felt some iron bubble of panic fly up from his belly and stick at the narrow gate of his throat. Yet even as the clamour reached climax he mocked his lack of reason. Was it, he asked himself, the crude possibility of an ice-harrowed Leeming rising in his sight, flat and brown as a Byzantine Christ?

It proved to be the lieutenant on the ladder. Before fully emerged he began broadcasting orders; the evening watch to be roused, recovery gear to be fetched. And a chair for Mrs Leeming. At glacier level he peered concernedly at Belle and asked her if she was wise to remain. Momentarily, Belle's face crumpled, an old page licked by flame. One tear was given off by her left eye.

"Well?" she said.

"It seems this is it."

"*Seems?*" She sounded brisk.

The officer sighed. "It's him. No doubt at all."

"How does he seem? Crushed?"

"He's completely done up in a sleeping-bag. He doesn't look big. . . ."

"He was only five foot nine," Belle explained.

"That's right," said the lieutenant. "In answer to your question, Mrs Leeming, everything seems normal."

There was silence. Once more the pit seemed to Ramsey to be supremely unproductive. His disbelief became a medicinal balance to the authentic panic in his blood, a counterweight called forth perhaps by his desire not to be judged mad. So no one judged him mad as he strolled across the glacier.

"Belle," he said into Belle's ear, "you have to stop this comedy."

"I beg your pardon?"

"You have to stop this *circus*." He used words which, he sensed, had barbs to them, knowing himself within range of hurting a widow whom, until two minutes before, he had considered invulnerable.

"Shut up," she told him. "If you ruin this, Alec. . . . Shut up!"

She sat hunched and intense as a mother cat.

"God," he complained, "you were never like this. . . ."

But, with a snort, he gave up reasoning.

Even so, he stood composed by Belle's side, though it came to him as more and more viable that he could make the officer call off the retrieval.

Sailors were lowering a stretcher with the petrol-driven winch.

"Aren't they premature?" Ramsey asked of no one.

"Please be quiet, Alec. They're the experts."

The officer came to Belle's side. "They've practically dislodged the mass. I should have told you this: my orders are not to interfere with the remains. We have a large canister here. . . ."

"The insides of those aircraft are so hot, Lieutenant," Belle said. "Have you thought of the effect of melting . . . ?"

Ramsey silently laughed at this funerary nicety.

The lieutenant murmured, "We have been instructed to pack the canister with ice."

She appeared grateful to have her husband's frozen flesh at the mercy of their capabilities, their forethought.

Again the wondrous boy made for the pit, and both cameramen placed themselves to record the descent. Ramsey stumbled at speed behind him.

"Lieutenant!"

"Sir?"

"Don't you think it's time to stop this lunacy?"

The lieutenant pulled his features into a fast frown that meant not that he hadn't heard but that he was extending to Ramsey a chance to revoke.

"Come again, sir?"

A sailor intervened. "They say do you want it held, sir?"

"Didn't I say so? Tell them I'm coming down."

"No," said Ramsey. "Listen. You can't go any further with this stunt."

The lieutenant stared diagnostically at Ramsey. Ramsey went on.

"For one thing, have you considered what he'll look like?"

He had borrowed the question from Hammond, and realized it. As well, he knew it to be dangerous, the very question that had brought on a catalepsy of the imagination in the southbound aircraft.

His belly pounded. He had never been so actively afraid.

"All the experts seem to suggest that he should be quite tolerable to look at, reminiscent of the Dr Leeming you knew. Excuse me."

As the lieutenant turned away to business, Ramsey's mind fumbled with the image the young man had provoked in him. For the second time his imagination seized, constricted like a windpipe. So that again there was, yet seemed not to be, breath; again he suffered the terror of smothering yet could speak. At the same time, he felt the new and final statement of the truth bound epileptically from his belly into his throat and chest and arms. Believing himself, then, to be strangling, and jerking like a convulsive, he was still able to reach out for the lieutenant's elbow and say, "Wait there! I think I ought to tell you. . . ."

"Yes?"

"Well, perhaps not in Mrs Leeming's hearing. . . . Could I speak to you in private?"

"You must realize, Mr Ramsey, how inopportune this is."

Belle had come up. There were remarkable signs of impotence about her. Her jaws trembled.

"I've warned you, Alec," she pleaded. "Can't you . . . ?"

"Perhaps if Mrs Leeming could go back to the mess?" Ramsey suggested.

"You can't be serious, sir. Abrams. Take Mr Ramsey back to the mess. Just relax, Mr Ramsey. Get Abrams to pour you coffee with a shot—ask the cook, Abrams. What about you, Mrs Leeming? Are you cold?"

Belle explained that she wasn't. The lieutenant smiled at her.

"It won't be long."

Large and pitted-faced beneath his furred hood, Abrams neared Ramsey and played at being solicitous.

"Let's go, Mr Ramsey sir."

Abrams' mitted hand was an offered insult. Ramsey pushed it aside. He called to the lieutenant, "You can't wait, can you, to round out the little sideshow?"

"I don't understand." The officer glanced over his shoulder, and saw that Ramsey was all fever and resistance. As a result he stood still.

"Look, you need to go in and have a rest, sir. Abrams, go on."

Abrams put giant mitts around Ramsey's arm.

"Keep your hands off me," said Ramsey. "I'm not some bloody Asian peasant to be pushed round."

"I never pushed round no Asian peasants, sir."

"You've got to pull yourself together," the officer firmly called, and still did not move.

"I keep together well enough. But I want to talk to you about Leeming."

258

"For God's sake move him, Abrams."

"Ah, the crack in the Emily Post etiquette! I warn you, I'll make trouble if you don't call him off."

When they had heard the substantial, the truest truth, they would fill in the pit.

"The truest truth!" he wanted to shout at the young man as an incentive, but what would the words mean to a capable and busy officer?

When Abrams tried to take firmer hold of him Ramsey threw a punch at the hooded face. It was one way of impressing the lieutenant that an interview was urgently sought. Abrams hugged him with both arms. Composedly enough, he became aware that the officer had snatched the radio and was calling a Slavonic name into it. Then he, too, moved close to hold the madman. Two large bodies smothered Ramsey's violence.

"God Almighty," he said crazily. "These aren't the right circumstances for talk."

Hampered by his gloves, he worked hard to dislodge Abrams' arm and Abrams' concerted good temper. But a third man came up, pondering what part of the foreigner to grab. Ramsey saw Belle standing back with a neutral face.

"Don't shoot this!" yelled the lieutenant to two cameramen who were recording the unlooked-for, intrusive event.

Ramsey found himself being carried away in a professional manner. Meanwhile the essential truth chafed in him. "Hammond," he called as they passed the huddle of journalists, people for whom he had a surprise. "Come wherever they're taking me."

Hammond made hesitant steps.

"No, come on. It's going to be worth it."

All the journalists made the beginnings of avid movements, as if they had forgotten sentiment and thought they might have one of those delicious cases of service brutality. "No," he told them. "Hammond. You!"

Though toted like a marble pedestal, he was for some reason obeyed.

"I think it's just that I'm a fellow-countryman," Hammond explained to the officer.

"How well do you know him?" the lieutenant, still burdened, grunted.

"Only the last few days, but we became pretty close."

"That's a damned lie," said Ramsey.

Hammond opened the clapboard door onto the mess porch and the further one through into the fuggy warmth of the mess itself. Ramsey was conveyed through and placed in a chair. Coffee was called for.

"Stay here, both of you," the lieutenant told Abrams and Hammond. The two men glanced at each other, ill-met jailers. "Have yourself a rest, sir."

"Listen," Ramsey insisted and closed his eyes. Four strangers, he thought, three of them foreign sailors, the fourth with nothing to recommend him. Not the audience he had dreaded in dreams in which he had made ultimate confessions. "We ate Leeming, Lloyd and I. You can't dig him up. For that reason."

Ramsey shut his eyes and listened to their four long silences, the judgment of foreigners. He let tears squeeze out through tight lids. He heard the lieutenant say, "I want to speak to Mr Ramsey. This is not to get round. If I hear any talk of this. . . ."

Ramsey did not open his eyes. "You stay, Hammond. Scoop. . . ."

"We'll see about that, Mr Hammond," said the officer. "We have a public-relations man in Christchurch."

As always, Hammond rushed to prove himself a man governed by ethics, no intransigent newshound. "I assure you, Lieutenant, it isn't the sort of news I revel in writing."

"Mr Ramsey, does the widow know?"

"You tell her if you like. But now you can't haul the poor bastard up, can you?"

Without warning he opened his eyes in order to catch them abhorring him discreetly. They seemed to stand relaxedly as he sat. They could not know his sense of release at having spoken most truthfully.

"Are you telling me you actually . . . you were forced to eat Leeming?"

"I've already said it. We ate of Leeming." But he had not meant to intrude that *of*, an echo of the drunken poet and of communion services.

"*Of* Leeming? What in the name of suffering Christ is the difference?"

"I'm sorry. We ate him." How hollow it sounded to repeat. "I won't ruin the simplicity by restating or giving details."

"Pshew!" the lieutenant softly emitted. He thought talk of ruining the simplicity of a statement quaint beside what had been done to Leeming.

"Now you'd better fill in the pit, confess Leeming unfound. You'd better."

"To save your embarrassment?"

Ramsey was delighted; the lieutenant was gloriously unsympathetic towards cannibals.

"To save yours. I've got this instinct that your people will want to be discreet. Think of the danger for Mrs Leeming, who's seventy-nine."

"And who is actually waiting out there," the lieutenant reminded himself.

"This holds things up, doesn't it?" Ramsey wanted to verify.

"Come now," said Hammond.

"Hammond, stay with Mr Ramsey. I'll leave Abrams outside."

Almost gone, the officer poked his head back round

the jamb of the inner door. "But they've found something there. You didn't eat all of him?"

"I won't descend to details," said Ramsey.

The lieutenant's revulsed brown face vanished.

For a start, Hammond sat opposite Ramsey and avoided his eyes. His responses to the confession were far more ambiguous than the lieutenant's.

Ramsey spoke first. "Thank God," he said, "that when I came to say what had to be said I wasn't among friends."

"We're your friends, Alec," Hammond muttered, to humour the patient.

"My point is that friends are mentally lazy. They're used to considering you the way they're used to considering you. They fight news such as this. They'd rather risk being robbed—or eaten—by you than make the mental adjustment necessary to believe you were a thief or . . . the other."

Again Hammond rushed to assent. Friends *were* often mentally lazy.

Then there was silence, succeeded by Hammond humming a few bars of grand opera.

"They won't bring him up now," Ramsey interjected. "I can tell by instinct. I can tell they don't want any dubious relics of the classic era." He added with irony, "To which Leeming and Lloyd and I belong."

"You'd be in a better position than I am," Hammond conceded, "to decide what they'll do."

"You're welcome to print that, incidentally. Print what I told you. Once the news is out, the width of circulation won't particularly worry me."

Puzzling it out, Hammond shook his head.

"I don't understand that. You've told the lieutenant this dreadful thing to ensure he'll fill the pit in, so that no one will know how Leeming has been . . . treated. Yet you tell me to feel free to print the facts."

"It *would* be hard for an outsider to understand," Ramsey agreed. "You see, I don't want him brought up, exposed. To those silly cameras, for example."

"But what you tell me to print exposes him."

"Does it? I don't know. I don't want him dragged up, that's all. I don't want him vulgarly displayed."

"Are you sure you're right, that they won't *vulgarly display* him in any case. They don't have to tell anyone about the actual state of what they find."

"Except it would get out. Via Sailmaker's Mate Class III Kaminsky. Or me. I'd tell even your friends outside. Didn't I make that clear to the lieutenant?"

"So if they do as you say, the safe thing, to avoid a scandal and to save the widow pain ——"

"The widow feels as much pain as a gasometer."

"—— you still want *me* to cause pain and scandal?"

"Who do you feel responsible to? The U.S. press officer in Christchurch or your vast, warm-hearted public? All I said was, you're free to." But, in exaltation, he felt how his well-being would be increased beyond measure by hearing a clinical edge of judgment in the voices of broadcasters he had never met.

Meanwhile, Hammond still seemed bent on catering to Ramsey's madness with debate.

"Alec, I consider that sort of thing professionally very odious."

"You must do what you think is right."

"I don't think it's right to say that sort of thing. Not after all this time."

Ramsey laughed. He could tease without bitterness now. He said, "I was raised on cautionary tales about the way journalists welcomed reports of depravity. Are all of them soulful like you? Or am I simply unlucky?"

"Unlucky?"

"Yes. To be landed with a rare moral newshound."

Hammond blinked and said with a disturbing dignity, "I

know as well as you do how little good is served by telling news like this to a world already glutted with the morbid and the grotesque."

"You think I told you out of philanthropy? It belongs to the class of things that have to be said."

"To us, perhaps. But not the whole damned world."

"To anyone who'll listen."

Ramsey continued placid and alleviated by means of this triumphant transference of truth from his guts to the public media. A quiet need of Ella's presence rose in him.

Telepathically, Hammond asked, "Does your wife know? She'd be badly affected if this got out."

"Not much. She's a kind of primitive. An absolutist, I'm always calling her. She'll say something like, 'So that's what's been fretting you?' You see, she thinks it's herself that has been the source of my angst. She'll be relieved, and she's built for loyalty. She'll no more question or judge me than the womb questions whether it's carrying a thief or a rapist, a monster or gallows-fruit."

He saw Hammond blink in a way that hinted how the confession had begun to spur his imagination. A wary excitement had arisen.

"Have you said this to make fools of us?"

There was suddenly toughness behind the man's finicking lack of humour. The potential newsworthiness of Ramsey's confession had made him advert to the hard facts of his trade. "It isn't my sort of material. Oh, I could get away with printing it. Even if you were certified a week later, I could still plead the public interest. But to what extent are you what is called a reliable source?" Hammond raised and laid down a hand, as if passing the hideous scoop back to Ramsey. "I've told you the sort of work I specialize in. I don't need this to make me feel professional."

Alec mauled his jaw, the tip of which still felt like a tiny capsule of polar cold. "Too many Adelaide Festivals have made a humanist out of you. NPA would give you a good swift kick for thinking the way you do."

Above clasped hands, his eyes lowered, Hammond undertook to order their intentions. "Think very seriously about this, Alec. If what you say is true, and if you still want what you say you do, write out a statement, sign and date it."

"What date would you like? Today's?"

"Any, any," Hammond told him. He seemed to feel a shamed urgency to quit the subject.

There was a long silence. Hammond read the label on a bottle of sauce. The exercise seemed to take a long time.

"I'm going back to the pit," said Ramsey in the end.

"They won't let you."

"But we're not subject to *them*." He began to pull his mitts on, and his hood about his ears.

"Alec, for God's sake. . . !"

Ramsey walked out, Hammond trailing him uncertainly along the far side of the table. Abrams had vanished from the glare outside. Perhaps his large tender hands were needed at the pit. But then, Ramsey thought, why should that be so? Unless that fool of an officer had a lifting job on hand.

He walked across the uneven ice. He could see four red pennants, apparently disembodied, flapping on a white ground. As he hurried, brown figures shook off the ice-dazzle and were visible. The winch pulsed. From the ice it drew a burden strapped to a stretcher. When clear of the pit, the load began to spin crazily, four or five turns one way, three or four the other, and then lay still, though twisting in a slow arc.

Ramsey shaded his eyes, saying, "There it is. There it actually is. On the end of a hook."

It was not a large bundle, and swung absolutely passive on a hook, a concrete, a veritable hook. Ramsey's head hissed like a hive. But all he could think of was the passivity of the corpse, the tawdry quality of its resurrection. "What did you expect, after all?" he asked himself. His mind had expected nothing more than the sad resurgence he now saw. His belly had always expected grandeur and an active rising. And with this verification of mind over belly, he received further insights. He remembered what the poet had said, some days before: that he had needed a wronged and majestic god and had made one, to his soul's balance, out of Leeming.

As the bundle eked a slow semi-circle above the heads of the people Ramsey saw how he had based his world on guilt for the quite transcendent wrongs done against Leeming. But now the ordinariness of the bundle spurred him to acknowledge the ordinariness of Leeming and the pedestrian nature of his sins against Leeming. Ramsey was so angered at the years he had wasted on shame that a demand rose in him to tear his own flesh. Because of this compulsion, he turned to Hammond.

"Help me," he said. "I think I'm going mad."

Yet he did not wait for help, but ran to the pit. He wished to be sure, at close range, of the pitiable nature of that brown burden. In its harrowed brown texture and its utter passivity lay an absolution for Ramsey.

Without warning, Abrams stepped out from behind the winch.

"Sorry Mr Ramsey, the lieutenant told me to stop you."

His fist struck Ramsey's cheek with an amazing impact. There was a roar as when a train enters a tunnel. On his back, Alec fought to keep the view he had of the stretcher clear of the blues and yellows of the blow. Before sleeping, he tried to explain how he had merely been trying to prove his mind's word to his guts, that there was nothing wrong with his mind.

He slept. Somewhere warm, he opened his eyes to a

fearful noise and shut them again. His head throbbed, and he felt an instant's acute unhappiness, as if he wondered how he would fill in the years remaining, now that he had lost his reasons for expiation.

It was such a conventional hospital he woke to that he believed himself to be back in Christchurch or perhaps never to have left it. By the door, though, sat Hammond in layered trousers and coats and stockinged feet. Ramsey winced without sound or movement, lying doggo. Waking to Hammond, he thought. Mrs Hammond did it daily, except during cultural events.

As it was, Hammond had seen the twitch of eyebrows, and moved to the bed.

"How are you, Alec?"

I am different, Ramsey told himself. The mad dynamo of his belly was still. There was nothing to worry about, and nothing to threaten. He was a bemused vacancy, as if he had existed only in relation to the *ice-bound* Leeming.

He raised his head. His skull ballooned with pain; bile rushed into his mouth. The fierce effects of Abrams' strong arm. Ramsey subsided and asked at last, "Is it night yet?"

Hammond smiled, sly in his knowledge of time gone. "Daytime-nighttime." He implied a vigil of supreme length.

"The same day, is it?"

"Oh yes, the same day. Some day you must tell me what it was all about."

"What what was all about?"

"Your claims about Leeming."

"Oh Christ! Must I? Why must I?"

"They have Leeming in a room here."

Ramsey was merely angry with Hammond for being so blunt with a sick person. Perhaps he was under orders to be blunt, a sort of home-psychiatry suggested by the Mc-Murdo surgeon.

Ramsey kept cool. He dryly thought how immune to the impact of past resurrections the bulk of humanity seemed.

"Leeming's been thawed out of his bag. He's entire. Absolutely entire. What were you trying to do?"

"Don't be such a nagging bastard," Ramsey advised the newsman.

"I have the doctor's word for it. And they're letting Belle identify him."

"That's ridiculous."

"She insists. A mighty old woman, that one! They can't very well stop her. She's his wife."

Ramsey muttered, "People should have more consistently realized that. She should have herself."

He wanted to pass water. "Where are my boots?"

"They make you take them off at the door. They won't let you wear them in here. How do you feel, anyway?"

"I feel I want my boots. Humour me. You know I'm mad. I bet they've warned you, as my fellow-national, *Keep that odd-ball quiet, queue-eye-ett!*"

"Why did you say that . . . about Dr Lloyd and yourself?"

Ramsey was off-hand with the answer. "It was symbolically true. It was *sacramentally* true. My father was a Presbyterian minister, you see, and if you grow up with someone who is religiously convinced, you come to see that symbolic truth is the highest form of truth."

He paused, R.I.P. for his father. "She ate him, too."

"In a manner of speaking?"

"Yes."

"Yes," said Hammond with some harshness. "But surely you knew the U.S. Navy *and* the newspapers are rather heavily committed to literal truth."

"I was constantly forgiven the literal truth. But the things I did to him . . . I didn't find them forgivable."

"That's no reason to act up. Why, we all ——"

"Damn what you all do. Where's the gents'?"

"I'll get you a pan."

"No. Tell your readers that Lloyd and I left him while he was still alive."

Hammond chuckled. "Good God, what am I supposed to believe? As for readers, they probably think you did leave him anyhow. Or at least they know it's what they would have done in your place. They can't be shocked, Alec, and they make a rotten tribunal. Watch out, or you'll become one of these people who confess regularly to the murder of the hour."

In came a doctor, conventionally white-coated, drill trousers on his legs. An orderly followed, bearing a tray with a glass of water and a measuring-glass full of blue capsules.

"Your nightcap, sir," the doctor told Ramsey, "and we'll have you back in Chi-Chi by dusk, day after tomorrow."

"That thought must make you very happy."

Laughing, the doctor signalled to his orderly, who came forward offering the blue capsule.

"I wonder do I need that," Ramsey asked.

"I think so, sir."

"You said I'd find my boots at the entrance, Mr Hammond?"

"I didn't say yours. I said mine."

He swung his socked feet to the floor. Immediately his stomach rose. His vision went the sepia colour of photographs of dead relatives. The faces of the three men slewed burning across his brain. But he avoided being sick.

The doctor blocked his way. "Please co-operate, sir. You'll find everything you want here. Mr Hammond has moved your kit across from your hut."

"You're all such nice boys," Ramsey said. "*Sir* and *Mr Ramsey*. I suppose, though, you'll flatten me again if I don't do as I'm asked."

"There's no question of anything like that, sir."

"Well I'm going out then, down the corridor. I'll stay in your bloody hospital or sick-bay or whatever it is. Because my head hurts. But I'm not going to take pills or be shut in."

He was allowed to go. It occurred to him that they may have been given explicit orders not to use force and that the lieutenant on the glacier might have been reprimanded for his approach. Ramsey hoped not. The good intention to write to the admiral, explaining that fists had been quite in order, withered in his hollow insides.

From the hall he had a view, through the front door, of an Antarctic dusk, the sun as low as it would go tonight, its crest above the silent mountains they had visited that day. The clock above the vacant reception desk said eleven-thirty.

Opposite the desk two sallow boys sat, comforter and comforted, their heavy clothing soiled, boots off like Hammond. They sat there in their socks, which were also not clean.

"What's the trouble?" Alec asked because they looked such waifs.

"My friend here, a drum rolled on his hand."

"Oh?"

"Been out, right out. Brought him round with hospital brandy. We got the mitt off, but we can't budge the inner glove. Except it makes him scream."

A gloved hand of black leather was held to the sufferer's chest, like a small limp animal culpably damaged.

"God, it looks swollen," Alec agreed. A strangely reminiscent brand of pity filled him, a tender feeling in the diaphragm, keeping tempo with the boy's hot and cold,

270

fading and awakening pain. It was clean male pity, far from the world of women and the feminine myth that only women are vulnerable. He would have liked to treat the boy's injury in this simplified environment. "How's the pain?" he asked.

"A lot better," the victim muttered. His eyes rolled. He was about to vomit or faint, while the orderly, tracking Ramsey, stood by with a suspect tolerance for this eccentric Limey.

"Why aren't you looking after the boy's hand?" Ramsey asked with genuine heat.

"Sorry, sir, that's not the orders I've got."

"Where's the toilet?"

"Head's straight on down the corridor, sir."

"Head my. . . . And you're not going to come in there with me, either."

He had reached the right door at the corridor's end when one halfway between him and the sufferer opened and ejected, as if she had been pushed or helped too energetically from behind, Belle. The way she stood, her head tilted back, seemed to signify the least painful way of bearing the weight of her brain. Because she was still and at a distance he was able to take stock of how much hair she had had shorn off for the sake of this journey. It would not quickly grow again, back in Elizabeth Bay, where such a cut was worn only by the very young.

The officer Ramsey had met at table the evening before followed Belle, and then an orderly. The men took station, one at each elbow, presuming the old lady's collapse.

The widow impressed Ramsey in the same way as the sailor had. "Belle," he said, but was not heard. Belle staggered off between her satellites.

"Belle," he called again through the heavy dusk of the hallway.

271

"Oh, Alec," she muttered over her shoulder, recollecting him and his paranoic whims and for the moment finding them, or their possibility, too much to face. There occurred to him the surprise that perhaps she had always been capable of hurt, her reserves of strength no higher than those of any solidly ageing person.

The officer turned to keep one raised sly eye on him.

"Poor old Belle," Ramsey muttered.

As if his new insight into Belle had been immediately perceived by her, she said, "I want to talk to Mr Ramsey."

"Now, do you think that's wise?"

"You're very kind, Commander. But I want to speak to old, old friends."

But the commander did some preliminary testing on his own account.

"You feeling OK, sir?" he asked Ramsey.

"Yes, I am." He felt compelled to tell the commander that he no longer had a daemon to bait Belle, but that would mean giving a case history.

"You know, you acted up strange out there this afternoon."

"I know," said Ramsey. "I don't lack insight."

With a trace of pique, Belle announced, "If it's going to cause so much trouble ——"

"No, no, no. You can use Lieutenant Christie's office. I'll wait for you. If you want anything. . . ."

The office was in shadow, and so small that the presence of chairs forced you to sit. Alec reached for her old, limp hand.

"It's him, Belle?"

"Yes. He's startlingly recognizable. Not fully thawed yet. The face shut up with pain. The points of the cheeks in a mess. He looks very old."

He nodded. He had contributed to Leeming's finite agony, and finitely paid for it.

For a minute Belle wept, tears in full flood. They cut off without warning.

"Alec," she said, "couldn't you have done more for the poor fool?"

"I don't know, Belle. Perhaps if I hadn't cuckolded him and worried about it. . . . But no one could have saved him."

She wept again, like deeply suppressed laughter.

"What was he doing there with Lloyd and you? If ever there was a man who wanted to be vulnerable! I've been dreading to look at him—an old woman looking down on a man of forty-two. But what was the worst shock was to see how he'd aged along with me . . . more than me. The journey, or the strokes, or even the ice. . . . They've made him look very old."

In his sense of vacancy towards Leeming he found Belle's intensity disquieting, especially when it centred on an agony forty years gone. It would do her good to meet the boy outside, to feel the immediacy of his pain.

"The three of us suffered," he said.

They were silent. Ramsey examined, on the lieutenant's desk, a photograph of a homely girl. She wore a summer dress and stood before a shady stoop. Framed cameo-fashion, she promised a wealth of mothering, simple goodness on tap in some rural county ten thousand miles north. That's the sort of girl to marry, he told himself. Not the ones who infest the blood and occupy the grain, not the contrary and complex ones, the ones who hated you the more they loved, whose intentions were a mystery, mainly to themselves.

How strange it was to think of the widow and Ella as kin.

Belle freely began to talk.

The trouble had been Leeming's impotence. Not that he

wasn't capable of begetting children, of some sexual result. But it was not, in a lover's terms, a result at all. Leeming fretted, prayed, saw doctors, achieved insight but not orgasm. He declared Belle purer than he, for it took the pure to enjoy unreservedly their sexual nature. Conventionally, she had taken him at his word and become mistress to a stockbroker. When Leeming's reaction to her confessed adultery had been similarly conventional, in the midst of the standard recriminations between cuckold and bad wife, she had been forced to an ultimate cliché. "Physical solace is necessary to me. Who are you to judge me for it?" She was not sure, she told Ramsey, but she believed she could remember feeling cheated, baffled that the truism shot home. She had wanted him to beat her, to possess her by chastisement; she was willing that a climax of blows should serve for defective climaxes elsewhere. He said she was of course right, and he could accept that she needed physical pleasure, though perhaps not as much as she thought. But he knew by an instinct that she would need to work her way through her sexual needs to attain more thoroughly human relationships—something the conventionally pure could not always achieve. He wanted her always to think of him in a kindly way.

"Kindly," she said, shaking her head in Lieutenant Christie's office. "God in heaven—kindly!"

His response, Leeming had gone on to say, had been the possessive one, the middle-class one, one that required chastening. But she must not deceive him.

She had not deceived him. She had provided him with names—he had accepted them. *The thorn in his flesh*. All the time she hoped, perhaps without knowing it as fully as she did now at four-score-minus-one, for fury, his judgment, some mad statement of his sovereignty. She continued with her diverse loves in the vacuum of his forbearance.

Ramsey sat silent and startled. She was Ella, wanting to be devoured, gnashed with the teeth—the eucharist of woman.

No system of thought formed the base for her adulteries. It was as Alec had often said, that one part animal pride and one part appetite were her only metaphysics.

So she was sensual, yes, but there were more nuns than those in convents, and stranger vows of chastity; she could have been faithful. She sought Alec's wrist and held it in an avian way. "*I was capable of fidelity*," she told him.

"Is this the first time you've grieved in front of people?" he asked at last.

"What do you mean, grieved?"

"Wept. Said passionate things."

She closed her eyes. She was still enraged with Leeming. It was obvious; it was credible, too, that she wished to tend him as much as she wished to resign him to some buffoon such as Denis Leeming. "He should have shot the two of you," she said, "and survived on your meat."

Ramsey felt light. He knew that *she* would go on, burning for Leeming all her days, a votive woman, adequate to Leeming's memory. She would never be consoled that Leeming had neglected to make them pay in primal terms, in terms of blood.

She asked him to leave her alone.

Outside, the commander still waited.

"She's finding it difficult," Ramsey told him. "She was remarkably attached to Leeming."

At dawn Leeming was mourned and buried. Later in the day Ramsey assumed Hammond's name and found a place on a flight to the Pole. Great mountains marked the way up the Beardmore Glacier, improbably large when seen from the ports of the aircraft. Within a few hours Ramsey was squinting at the boggling nullity of the polar plateau. Given this god's-eye view, he suspected all the enterprises that had touched the void below and left it unchanged. It seemed indecent that men should be eaten by the white glare ceasing a whit this side of endlessness.

To him, their motivation had become a blank.

As warned, a succulent, bitter Ella, wearing sunglasses with the same air and purpose as most other bitter, succulent women—to cover what marriage has done with eyes—waited for him at the Sydney terminal.

His buoyancy was this afternoon, however, capable of rallying her straightaway. She said, "Alec, what are you trying to do to us both?" But there was no rebuke in the way she hugged him. He felt nuptial, and patted her fine, suited hip; he felt free, a private man, his own man, and despite the black farce of his second Antarctic journey, he had never felt freedom so privately attained, privately enriching, of such a personal vintage.

He sat her on a lounge and told her he was emancipated. She need not hurry to believe it; her face told that she did not. He found it easy to weep without discomfort. For in an international terminal passers-by would look on them as a reunion; and Ella held him widely, motheringly, or like a daughter.

"Excuse me," a tiny blonde woman told them. "I'm from the press."

"Yes," he said, "yes, you've been none too tardy." He thought unkindly of Hammond, who must have alerted the newspapers.

The small woman could distinguish Anglo-Saxon resignation when she saw it. "You *are* Mr Pelliadakes and his daughter, aren't you?"

Pungently Ella said they certainly were not. He had

often enough teased her on her ability to be mistaken for an Aegean.

"God," intoned the lady, and scuttered away with a photographer to hunt the elusive Pelliadakes' sob story.

Ella said little of Leeming. She said chastely she hoped that this ended it all for him.

Other matters fretted her. "I hope the hotel is up to standard. It's only got one star in the motorist's handbook. If I'd only known what the occasion was, I could have booked something much better."

Driving there, Ramsey suggested, "I suppose the one star is a punishment for my disappearance."

Ella nodded. "And abrupt return."

It was the arid task of hanging shirts that seemed to make sleep necessary. As he drowsed he told her, "I don't propose to follow a spent trajectory to the grave. Not any more. I intend to begin to live and be very demanding of a night."

From the bedside table she made grunts of mock-anticipation. Yet why she was happy he could not fully tell; she had been promised these things before and had none of the internal evidence he had that this was finally freedom. Perhaps she had made a purely temporary millennium, as she had in the past, out of his return.

"We have to learn a new sanity," he murmured, "within the limits of our old madnesses, because it hasn't made us desirable people when we've dwelt so fully in each other. We are not pretty, Ella, we are not nice to know. But there'll be no more of this cancer-of-the-womb business, and I won't let you look exploited, as if you and other women pay away more with their genitals than I and other men do."

"Eric Kable," she suggested as a good cross-sectional case.

"I'm serious, see!" He caressed her back, and there he

277

was touching the contours of his womb and sister and wife, provoker, flagellator, patent emasculator.

The Ramseys drowsed the rest of the day away on their one-star bed, unaware that the one afternoon sun mocking the threadiness of the carpet mocked also their unideal limbs for whose golden age they still held some hopes.

EPILOGUE

By Eastertide Sally Bourke was unarguably with child and suffered morning sickness as frequently as Ella could have desired. Helped thus from the flank, Ramsey enjoyed a necessary dominance over his wife.

Then autumn turned his park sere in its imported varieties and cast a strong frost for those stoic native trees. Autumn brought, too, a postcard from Los Angeles. It read, "I have considered for some time whether I should write to you. This souvenir of a far city is not necessarily a token of regard, neither of hostility. I simply don't know. But one day I'd like you to try to explain what it was all about. Yours, David Hammond."

Late in April the poet came again to town and visited Ramsey's office. He came spruce, and Barbara said he was perfumed, which for some reason alienated her finally from his verse. But he was, of course, a man in love and silly with toiletries.

He and Ramsey strolled down to the staff dining-room. In the chilly westerlies Alec too received the little man's nuptial savour. Which reminded him. . . .

"Weren't you and Mrs Turner to be married this month?"

"We were to have been."

"I'm sorry. I shouldn't intrude ——"

"I don't mind. The delay has proved temporary."

"That's good."

"Till Mrs Turner forgives me."

"Oh."

"Yes, for Valerie Kable."

Ramsey winced, a reaction that amazed the poet.

"I thought old dead-eye Ella had seen that. I thought that was why she gave me all that hearty lack of respect."

"Now that you mention it, I think she did make surmises." He coughed and muttered, "I had no idea."

"I ought to tell you that only once—or maybe there was a second time I can't well remember—did Valerie and I nurture our inappropriate and, I can swear to you, totally unsatisfactory flame. That was down in my part of the country last December. I was low, drinking, lonely, sapped, and so on. You'd have to be."

"I'm pleased you said that."

"And I swear too that I didn't know she was on the tableland when I came to you with news last February. I had to rebuff the lady. Anyhow, Mrs Turner got a letter from someone—I don't think Valerie; she's straighter than that, within her bounds. I think that little prick Leeming may have written it. Unless it was you," he added for laughter.

There was a second to hope that Ella had not been the betrayer, as in another treachery of which young Leeming had been suspected.

"But you have hopes still? I mean, of Mrs Turner?"

The poet winked. He looked a genuine village-pump lover.

"I've just done a retreat in a Franciscan friary, and I have a monk writing to her to say I need her precisely to save me from unhappy adventures. I've even hinted that I am halfway interested in turning R.C. I shall continue to hint it throughout our married life, especially when Mrs Poet acts up."

"You have the winning formula," said Ramsey.

The poet agreed; you could forgive him his country cocksureness. "I have the winning formula. All the prescribed paperwork has been done. We should be able to marry within a week or two."

So, knowing his duty towards bridegrooms, Ramsey bought white wine for their lunch.

"As for you," said the poet. "Didn't you say in February that you were finished?"

"I was overstating," Ramsey admitted. For which mistake Pelham had not forgiven him, and would take a post in Melbourne in July.

"I'm very pleased you were wrong."

"Well, I was wrong too about Belle Leeming."

"Yes, quite a performance—down to McMurdo Sound in a transport, up to the glacier by helicopter and the funeral service, and so forth."

"I can remember," said Ramsey, as if only now finding a new reverence for the motivation of preposterous human behaviour, "she had doubts about his burial at McMurdo Sound, because the place was too industrialized."

"I saw her in the end." The poet shrugged—one more quiet triumph. "When she came home. Alec, she tells me you actually believe you left Leeming when Leeming was still alive."

Ramsey said nothing, but made up his face in a way that showed he would welcome more discretion.

"She told me," the poet explained, "only because she knows you to be self-deceived. But you're offended."

"I have to be frank; I've grown out of considering such things."

"Yes, but I've been waiting two months or so to tell you about something that occurred to me in this very context. You placed the cooker top at Leeming's head because you didn't want to cover him. It was blowing thirty miles an hour and there was some drift. According to what everyone says, it was on a fairly even area of glacier—in fact, you were lucky in that regard; any other track down to the coast would have killed you all."

"I've heard such analyses," Ramsey admitted, sounding bored, sucking at his wine to cover a small fear for his own peace of mind.

"Well, they tell me that drift doesn't settle, except on the lee side of objects," the poet climatically brought forth, believing that the fact gave one last severing blow to Ramsey's serpentine guilt.

"I see." Ramsey came close to laughing at the poet's Maigret impersonation. The poet seemed vulnerable, and said with a minor petulance, "Drift settles on the lee side of mountains, huts, tents, sledges, and—I can't see why not—even cooker covers."

"Oh, yes," said Ramsey.

"The point is, you must have wanted his face covered if you put the cooker where you said you put it. Even dazed, you'd know that drift falls in the lee of obstacles, fair on Leeming in this case. Now, I can't imagine you compounding your supposed treachery in this way. To leave the man was not a crime in my book, but to put that cooker lid down required a malice and hypocrisy of which you aren't capable. So the answer is, you thought at the time that he'd died in the accepted bona fide fashion."

There arose the temptation to tease the poet, who sat neglecting his food and lobbing prognostications of the past at Ramsey.

Ramsey said, "I don't know. I wasn't much of a hand at lees and downwinds."

"Well, *would* drift have collected on the lee side of an obstacle such as the cooker lid?" the poet insisted.

"Perhaps." But he was not altogether lying when he said, "It sounds something like an academic point to me."